Mr. Time Waster
By: Jessica Terry

Mr. Time Waster

Jessica Terry

Published by Jessica Terry, 2023.

MR. TIME WASTER

First edition. June 26, 2023.

Copyright © 2023 Jessica Terry.

ISBN: 979-8988003625

Written by Jessica Terry.

I so appreciate my family, friends, readers, fellow authors, and anyone else who has showed support to me as I keep chugging along in this author life. Especially my son Langston, who often has to help get me out from in front of the computer and go to bed. Just one more chapter, son. :)

One – Claire

• • • •

"DID YOU JUST *hit* me??"

He looked at me like I was crazy, holding a hand to his cheek that I'm sure was already turning red. One could only hope.

I couldn't remember the last time I was so livid.

"What did you expect, after what you just told me? You're lucky all you *got* was a slap!"

"Claire, I can't believe you did that! Your parents didn't raise you that way! And I *know* they didn't!"

"You've got a lot of damn nerve, Montrel! You just *dumped* me on my *birthday* and you're trying to lecture me on being ladylike??"

"Sweetheart, come on..." He held his hands out to me, actually trying to look pitiful. "You *know* I love you. But this relationship...it's just gotten to be too much for me. I need a breather."

"A breather??"

"Yeah, just a little break. We can pick things back up in a few months or so after I-"

"After you what? Bang some more women? 'Cause I'm sure that's what this is about!"

"It's not that. Okay, not *just* that. Fine, since you want me to say it, I'll just say it..." He took a deep breath as he paced in front of me, looking like he was deep in thought. Though I bet he'd been planning this for days already. "I've been feeling very stifled. You want more out of this than I do, at least right now."

1

I gaped at him, not believing what I was hearing. "Are you kidding me with this? When we got back together this time you said that you were ready to go all in. You swore to me that you were ready to settle down and weren't going to punk out like you did last time. And now, barely two months in, you're dumping me *again*??"

"I'm sorry about the timing. I guess I could have waited until tomorrow. But when I saw you come out in that negligee..."

"It confirmed that you didn't want to be with me anymore. Nice." I folded my thin arms over my chest, trying to cover my cleavage in the pink silk nightie I had just slipped into. I wished I had a robe. "That's very nice to know."

"That's not what I was saying."

"Might as well be."

Tears were running down my face, and I hated it. Hated that I was crying in front of him like that. If I had been able to wait until he left, at least I could have maintained a little bit of dignity. But that was shot to hell now.

He just stood there and sighed, as if *he* was tired of *me*. "Claire...."

"Just go, Montrel," I snapped, swiping at my tears and stuffing my hands under my armpits. My eyes were on the floor. "Just...get out."

"We can still be friends, right?"

I wanted to slap him again. With an iron skillet.

"No, we can*not* be friends, you insensitive, callous asshole! I don't want anything else to do with you!"

"Now Claire, you know you don't mean that..."

"I do so mean it!"

"You don't. You always say that and then once you come down off your tantrum-"

"Tantrum??" I stomped my foot and looked around for something to throw. "Get out!!"

"Fine," Montrel conceded with another sigh, holding his hands up. "I'll call you in a few days, after you've had a chance to cool down."

"Don't bother!"

"Okay." He actually looked amused, as if this whole thing was a damn joke to him. "Happy birthday, Claire."

He walked out.

I stood there, incredulous, staring at the door as if I was waiting on him to come back in and tell me it was a really bad (and really cruel) prank. But that didn't happen. Montrel had done this to me again, and this time, on my thirtieth birthday.

This had happened before, as much as I hated to admit it. We'd done this break-up-to-make-up routine a few times. We initially got together almost two years before after a chance meeting at the grocery store. After hitting it off immediately, we dove head-first into dating and things moved rather quickly. We even declared our feelings after our second date, and I thought I had found the one.

But it didn't take long for the new-relationship love fog to clear for him, and he started getting restless and broke up with me. But I took him back.

Then he dumped me again a few months later...then I took him back.

And then after about six or seven months...well, you get the picture.

I admit, there was something about Montrel that I just couldn't let go of. Part of me kept holding on to the belief that one of these times he came back to me, it would stick.

After it was clear he wasn't coming back, I plopped onto the couch in my wasted new nightie, still crying. I couldn't believe this was how my thirtieth birthday turned out.

When my phone chimed, I dove for it, hoping it was Montrel. What can I say? I was in love with the asshole. Maybe he had realized how wrong he'd done me and changed his mind. I would have been willing to forget the whole episode with a heartfelt apology. And a foot rub.

But nope, it was my best friend Chichi, probably wanting to get an update on how my birthday was going. She never did have a lot of patience. What if Montrel and I had been having a great evening? Yet here she was, blowing my phone up.

I ignored it. She would be able to tell something wasn't right and it was a little too embarrassing to admit that I'd just been dumped on my birthday. Especially since I had declined her offer to throw me a party so I could spend the evening with Montrel. I wanted a romantic evening with my man more than I wanted to make the rounds in a room full of people. Now I wish I had taken her up on her offer. Boy, she was never gonna let me hear the end of this.

And there was no *way* I would've been able to tell her that I already wanted Montrel back. She'd certainly cuss me out.

Two – Claire

• • • •

THE DAY AFTER MY MAJOR fail of a birthday, I headed to my parents'. Not because I wanted to; I'd much rather have spent the day curled up on my couch eating peanut butter toast and lattes and getting the most out of my Disney+ subscription.

But they wanted me to pick up my gift that I was too busy running around getting ready for my date with Montrel to get the day before.

And no, Montrel still hadn't called.

I tried to put it out of my mind and secure a neutral expression on my face. I didn't want my parents to know about my being dumped any more than I wanted Chichi to know. They were never big fans of Montrel's, even though, unlike Chichi, they generally kept their opinions of him to themselves.

"Y'all are repainting in here?" I marveled once Mama let me in. It seemed like every time I went by there, they had changed something else.

"Yeah. We've been talking about changing the color for a while now."

"Why?"

"Why not?" Mama shrugged. She pushed up her glasses and tucked her bobbed hair behind her ear. "Now that your brother is gone, we can finally experiment the way we want around here."

"Uh-huh." Ever since my little brother Benny went off to college, my parents had been doing a lot of *experimenting*.

Taking trips, making exotic recipes together, redecorating the house that had been the same as long as I could remember it. My usually mousy parents were taking full advantage of their empty nest.

And I had done a pretty good job of putting that time I heard them getting it in through the laundry room door out of my mind.

"Your gift is in here," Mama informed, strolling to the living room. She retrieved a box from the coffee table and held it out to me. "Hope you like it."

"Thanks, Mama." I already knew it was another pair of pajamas. She got me pajamas every year, for my birthday and Christmas. I could open my own outlet. "I appreciate it."

"You're welcome. So, how did your birthday evening with Montrel turn out?"

Ugh, I'd been hoping she wouldn't ask about that. "It was all right."

"Just all right?"

"I mean...nothing really to tell. It's not like he proposed or anything." I chuckled nervously.

Mama was looking at me suspiciously, as if she knew there was more to it than I was saying. And she probably did. I wasn't exactly known for my poker face.

"Well, I know how smitten you are with Montrel, dear. But there *is* someone your father and I would like for you to meet."

I immediately shook my head. "No thanks."

"Why are you being so dismissive?"

"I'm not being dismissive; I'm just not interested in meeting anyone else."

"I wish you'd reconsider. His name is Warner Branson and he's a very nice young man. And, in my unbiased opinion, *very* easy on the eyes. If nothing else, you two could become friends."

"I'm sure he doesn't want to be friends with me."

"Why would you say something like that?"

There was no need in getting into my reasons for that statement. My parents probably already thought I was pitiful enough for continuing to deal with Montrel after everything he'd done. I had no desire to give them more ammo with my skinny girl self-esteem issues.

"Just a feeling," I finally answered.

"Well, you're wrong. Warner isn't like a lot of men out here. And he thought you were adorable when I showed him your picture."

I gaped. "You showed him my picture??"

"It's not like it was a secret picture, Claire. I got it off of your Instagram page thing."

The highs and lows of social media. "Well, that's nice and everything, but I'd rather not waste anybody's time when I'm hung up on someone else."

"If you say so," Mama shrugged. "He said he was going to follow you or send you a friend request, or whatever you all do on there. I hope you at least respond if he reaches out to you. Like I said, he's a nice young man; don't be rude to him."

"I wouldn't do that. As long as he doesn't try to overstep any boundaries, we're good."

"Right."

Since Daddy wasn't there, I left a few minutes later. I was thankful to get out of there without having to admit that Montrel had dumped me again. Even though my mother probably would've just focused on comforting me rather than bashing Montrel, I still didn't want her to know about it since I had every intention of getting Montrel back.

I'm really not pathetic. My wanting Montrel was something that I knew didn't make much sense to anyone else, but it made sense to me. For whatever reason, I had it in my head that he was the one I was supposed to end up with and if I just stayed diligent and patient, he would realize that, too.

I'd told myself I wasn't going to call him. It hadn't even been a full twenty-four hours since he gave me the boot; he hadn't even had time to miss me yet.

But I was already missing him, and I managed to talk myself into calling. Figured it couldn't hurt.

Plus, my curling iron was at his place. I needed that.

As soon as I got home, I parked it on the couch and took several deep breaths, trying to work out what I was going to say. Should I act like this was a random causal call and not mention what happened last night, or jump right into how much what he did hurt and insist we talk about it? Should I give an ultimatum? Invite him over to talk? Ask that he bring me my curling iron?

Too impatient to make a decision, I decided to just wing it. My leg bounced furiously as I dialed and listened to the repeated rings. It occurred to me that he might not even answer. I quickly tried to decide what I'd say on his voicemail when I finally heard his voice.

"Now really isn't a good time, Claire."

That stumped me a little bit. "Why? Are you at the nursing home?"

"No." Just then, I heard a moan in the background. A woman's moan. It was clear as day and probably done on purpose. "I'm not there but I *am* busy."

"You mean *getting* busy," I retorted accusingly.

"Claire..." He sighed. "What do you want?"

I felt like an idiot. Here I was willing to forget what he did and try again, and he was already banging somebody else. I hadn't felt this ridiculous since yesterday. My mind questioned for the hundredth time why I would possibly want this man back.

"You know what? Never mind, Montrel. Just...forget I called." I hung up, face red and feeling stupid, wishing I could erase the last two minutes.

Three – Montrel

• • • •

"WHO WAS THAT?"

I glanced over at Venus after I hung up the phone. Her microbraids were falling all around her face, making her look sexy as hell. "Just my ex."

"Mmm." She snuggled closer, licking my chest and throwing her leg over mine. "She want you back or something?"

"Probably."

"Well, she can have you after I'm done with you." Venus climbed on top of me, kissing me hard and grinding on my dick. We had just finished sexing when Claire called, and she was already ready to go again. She never could seem to get enough, which was one of the things I loved about her.

I rolled her onto her back and got inside of her, not bothering to get a condom. Venus and I had been getting down off-and-on for so long that we didn't bother with them anymore. She was my go-to; my five-foot-nine walking stress relief. I kept this girl on speed dial.

"Harder," she instructed, wrapping those legs around my waist. "I want it harder, Montrel...I *know* that's not all you got...you can fuck me better than that."

I frowned and began pounding into her like my hips had a motor. She knew I didn't like it when she said stuff like that. Just tell me how much you like what I'm doing; don't try to challenge me. This wasn't a pickup game. Not that I played basketball.

Really, sex was the only time I didn't mind getting sweaty. I preferred to stay crisp and clean most of the time.

Once I showed her just how hard I could give it to her, I rolled off of her and ran a hand down my face. I didn't want to say anything about how tired I was. Venus had already dropped hints in the past about how I needed to work out more. Thankfully I had my mother's good genes that kept my physique intact without much effort.

Speaking of my mother, I remembered I still needed to pick up the flowers to give her when I visited her later, after I met up with my boy Forrest.

"You know I have an Etsy shop, right?" Venus asked as she rolled to her side and lit up a joint. I eyed the jaguar tattoo that covered her entire left hip and thigh. Some days I thought that tattoo was ridiculously sexy; other days I just thought it was ridiculous. How was that going to look when she was ninety?

"No, I didn't know that."

"It's true. I make my own soaps and body butters."

"That's...that's nice."

"You want some samples? I have a few extras that I decided not to put on the site."

"No, thanks. I have rather sensitive skin so I'm very careful about what I use on my body."

"You definitely need my stuff, then. It's all natural."

"That's all right."

"Well, damn. Just gonna shut me down like that, huh?" Venus sucked her teeth before taking another drag from her joint. She held it out to me but I shook my head; she knew better. I was already holding my tongue about her not waiting until I left to start smoking that mess. "I thought we were better than that, Montrel."

"It's nothing for you to take personally. I'm sure you're going to do very well in your business. I'd just rather not have any homemade body products."

"Too good for that, huh? I get it." She eyed me as she took another drag and blew smoke through her slightly darkened lips. I was gonna have to take a shower before I went to my mother's.

"That's not what I said."

"But that's what you meant. Since you're so concerned about personal hygiene, maybe you oughta start manscaping that jungle down there. I'm always picking hair out of my teeth for days after you come over here."

My face tightened. It was officially time to go.

"Thanks for the advice," I mumbled, grabbing my clothes from the chair in her room. "I'd better get going."

"I didn't hurt your feelings, did I?" Venus sat up on her elbow, looking at me as I headed towards her bathroom. That looked like a smirk on her face. "It was just a suggestion."

"Yeah, I know. You're certainly entitled to your opinion. I have some things I need to do, is all." I stepped over her clothes that she had tossed onto the floor when she was getting naked for me. Like it would have been too much more trouble for her to put them on the chair with mine.

"If you say so." She plopped onto her back.

I quickly got dressed, wishing I could wash up but noting that she had nothing but her bootleg homemade soap in her bathroom. And I didn't have my toiletry kit with me. It would just have to wait until I got home.

Not interested in engaging in any more conversation with Venus after that, I just stuck my head in her bedroom when I was finished getting dressed to let her know I was leaving. I got in my car, slamming the door to my BMW M8 Coupe a little too hard. Venus really had a lot of nerve commenting on my grooming. For her information, I trimmed down there regularly. Any more and I'd be bald.

And anyway, as long as we'd been fooling around, she knew good and well I didn't allow anything to be amiss on my body. I spent good money on self-maintenance. Venus was just trying to tick me off because I didn't want any of her raggedy soap.

After shooting over to my place to take a quick shower, I headed to Forrest's. Forrest had been my boy for years, since college. I knew he was going to ask me about Claire – that is if his wife Giselle hadn't already filled him in, since she and Claire were friends - and then he was going to bite my head off about breaking up with her.

I wasn't wrong. He wasted no time getting on my case.

"You mean to tell me that you actually dumped that woman on her birthday?"

"Man...don't start, all right?"

"Don't tell me you don't see how fucked up that is."

"I did her a favor."

"What?"

"We don't want the same things right now. No need in wasting her time."

"And you couldn't find a better time to tell her that than on her birthday? When you're the one who asked her out?"

"I acknowledge that it wasn't gracious timing..."

"Why do you keep doing her like that? Claire is a good woman."

"So is Giselle but you're halfway out the door on her."

He frowned. Guess he didn't like it when the tables got turned on him.

"That's different, man," he retorted, practically growling at me. "Giselle is my wife and we're going through a rough time right now."

"A rough time? You're mad at her because she can't get pregnant."

"I'm not mad at *her*; I'm just mad. We've been trying for months. It's frustrating trying to do something that's supposed to be natural and that fuckin' teenagers can do without even trying to."

"Well, it's not her fault."

"Did I say it was her fault?"

"You act like it. Especially since you went and got your sperm tested, *without her*, and found out there's nothing wrong with you."

"Shut up, man."

"Why wouldn't you tell her about that, Forrest? Does she know that you don't blame her? Or that you're not going to leave her if she can't give you a child? Or that the main reason you married her in the first place is because she's mixed and could make pretty-haired babies?"

"Man, I was kidding when I said that. You can't tell when I'm joking after all these years?"

"You sounded pretty serious to me."

"Whatever. You're just trying to change the subject off of how wrong you did Claire."

"Claire will be all right," I said dismissively. "When I'm ready to settle down, I'll take her back. You didn't have patients today?" He was a successful pediatrician and absolutely loved kids, which was part of the reason for his angst that he and his wife hadn't been able to conceive yet.

"You know good and well it's Sunday. Quit trying to change the subject. You think Claire is just gonna be sitting around waiting on you, huh?" Forrest shook his head, going back to his couch and grabbing the laptop from his coffee table. The white t-shirt he was wearing looked stark against his dark skin. Ever since Giselle told him he looked sexy in those, he wore them damn near all the time. "Are you really that arrogant?"

"It has nothing to do with arrogance. It's just facts. Claire wants the world from me right now and I'm just not ready for that."

"So why don't you just leave her alone, then? Let her find somebody who's ready for what she wants."

"It's not like I don't love her. She's going to make a great wife one day. When we're together and things start getting deep, it's like a vice grip tightening around my neck. That has to be a sign, right?"

"Yeah, sure. And when you get her wedding invitation to another man, I hope you remember all this."

"I could say the same about you and Giselle. Though instead of a wedding invitation, it'll be divorce papers."

Forrest looked at me with those droopy eyes of his shooting daggers. "You got jokes, huh? You don't know a damn thing about what it's like to be married to somebody, man. It takes a commitment and diligence you can't even imagine. Your mama got you thinking you're the king of the world and nothing can touch you."

"Why are you bringing my mother into this?"

"Because she spoiled you after your dad died. Got you thinking you can do no wrong. So naturally, you think you're totally justified in jerking Claire around like a bad dance partner. I'm telling you, man, you're gonna regret it."

I waved him off. So my mother did a little extra doting on me after my dad died; that's to be expected. I was ten years old. It didn't mean I was spoiled. Forrest didn't know what he was talking about.

When I was ready for forever, I'd go back to Claire. In the meantime, she was perfectly free to do as she pleased. Though I had a feeling she wouldn't.

Four – Claire

• • • •

"OKAY, SO WHAT HAPPENED with you and Montrel?"

I suddenly became intensely focused on my latte. "What makes you think something happened with Montrel?"

"Bitch, don't try to play me. You and I both know you try to get all scarce when y'all are going through some drama. What, y'all broke up again?"

"No!" At Chichi's knowing arched brow, I sighed. "Yeah."

"What bullshit excuse did he give you this time?"

"Said he was feeling stifled. Said I wanted more out of the relationship than he did. Or something like that."

As if I didn't remember exactly what Montrel said. I'd replayed it in my head more times than I cared to admit.

"And when did this happen?"

I hesitated. I really didn't want to talk about this but Chichi dragging the details out of me was inevitable. "On my birthday."

"Damn! So the bastard dumped you on your birthday this time, huh? Let me guess, it was right after sex?"

How did she always manage to ask the very questions that would make these conversations more embarrassing than they already were? "No...we, um, we hadn't gotten to that yet."

"What, you busted out a new negligee or something and then he dropped the hammer?"

"What are you, psychic? Or did you put some cameras in my house when I wasn't looking?"

"I read a lot. So *please* tell me that him dumping you on your birthday without even bothering to get any first is enough to make you leave him alone for good this time?"

"I don't know *what* I'm gonna do, Chichi. I'm still kinda stinging from all that."

"I bet. That had to be pretty humiliating. Just don't make it worse by calling him."

I wished my skin was darker because I felt my face automatically flush. And I so, so wished I was better at lying.

She recognized the guilty look on my face and plunked down her coffee cup so hard I actually jumped. "You called him??"

"I had to!"

"Why did you *have* to?"

"He...has my curling iron."

Sucking her teeth, Chichi crossed her arms over her ample bosom. "You can do better than that."

"I really can't."

"You tried to get him to take you back after that? Do you not have *any* pride about yourself?"

Frowning, I set my own cup on the table. "I resent that, Chichi. You make it sound like I'm some pitiful, desperate-"

"What would *you* call it? I love you, girl, but you seem to lose all your good sense when it comes to Montrel. He just dogs you over and over and you go crawling back for more every time. It makes no sense at all. I could see if the man was fine but you can't even blame *that*."

"Hey! Montrel is very handsome!"

"He's all right. A little scrawny for my tastes. But even if he was the second coming of Method Man, he still ain't worth all this."

"Chichi, I love him, okay? I don't know how else to explain it."

"That's it?"

I sighed. It wasn't like I was unaware of how foolish I sounded. And Chichi wasn't wrong when she said I lost my good sense when it came to Montrel. He just had a hold on me that I couldn't explain or make myself try to break free of. Part of me felt like when it was all said and done, he'd appreciate the fact that I wouldn't give up on him and us.

Seeing my anguish, Chichi thankfully decided to back off. She got up from her kitchen table to head over to the pantry, her long purple braids bound in a ponytail hanging down her back.

"I thought I had some Fig Newtons in here," she muttered, hands on her hips. "Those damn kids of mine eat up everything."

"It's okay; I don't want any Fig Newtons."

"Hell, *I* did!" She slammed the pantry door shut. "This is exactly why I hide my snacks. Take my advice and do *not* have triplets, I'm telling you."

"I don't think that's much of a possibility right now, anyway."

"I didn't think it was for me, either. Triplets don't run in my family. But now me and Gerard have three knuckleheaded boys with one pop."

"Well, at least you have a good man to help you with everything. Gerard isn't going anywhere."

I sounded more somber than I meant to, and Chichi noticed. She came back to sit at the table, looking at me intently. I prepared myself for some gentle admonishment.

"I wish you thought as much of yourself as you do of that man," she finally said. "He keeps doing this stuff 'cause you let him. Love or not, you deserve better."

Maybe I did. But I couldn't help wanting what I wanted.

She eyed me, noting my silence. "What did he say when you called him?"

There went my face flushing again. "It wasn't a long conversation."

"Why? He was busy or something?"

"You could say that." I sipped my lukewarm latte, avoiding her eyes.

Chichi cursed under her breath. "He was with another woman, wasn't he?"

I didn't want to admit it out loud, but I was humiliated enough as it was, so might as well. "Yes."

"Claire. Why in the world would you want to be with a man who would get with another woman not even a day after dumping you? On your birthday? What is he gonna do next; bring a date to your parents' house? To your job? I wouldn't put it past him."

"He wouldn't do that."

"Why wouldn't he? You've already established he can pretty much do whatever he wants and you'll take him back, regardless. He has no respect for you, girl. Why do you like being disrespected?"

Something about that question jarred me. Amazingly, I never considered Montrel's treatment of me as disrespectful;

I'd managed to frame it as him just running from his feelings for me. And I'd made myself believe that he would inevitably realize that and stop running, so I just had to be patient.

But Chichi's question struck a nerve. My mind automatically replayed everything Montrel had taken me through, and I felt myself getting angry.

I really *was* an idiot for wanting that bastard.

After I got home later, I flopped across my bed, staring up at the ceiling. My mind was all over the place. Part of me was still reeling from Chichi's question; part of me wished I could somehow expunge all memories of Montrel from my mind, and still part of me (a tiny part) wondered what he was doing and who he was with right then.

I reached for my phone and perused my messages. Of course, none from Montrel. I don't know why I expected anything different.

This was stupid. *I* was stupid.

A new notification popped up, letting me know I had a new follower on Instagram. I wasn't huge on social media but I liked to peruse every now and then, doing more looking than posting. My page wasn't anything all that fascinating so it always surprised me when someone found me interesting enough to follow.

When I saw the name Warner Branson, I frowned slightly, trying to remember where I'd heard that name. Then I remembered Mama telling me she showed some guy my picture and that he was going to follow me on there. I might not have been trying to hear it at the time but I was intrigued now.

I went to his profile and my brow arched in surprise. Okay, so the brother was cute. Low-cut black wavy hair. Thick eyebrows. Skin so smooth it was unfair. Body looked nice, from what I could tell.

"Not bad, Mama," I muttered.

I started to follow him back but stopped myself. What if he took that as an invitation? I still didn't know if I wanted to actually meet this man. I had never been one that was able to jump from one man to another. My head was still jacked up over Montrel and I knew that; there wasn't anything this Warner guy could do for me.

Dropping the phone, I buried my face in my hands before rolling onto my back. I had no idea how I'd gotten to be such a mess. All I wanted was a relationship that didn't make me want to pull my hair out. Where I wasn't always wondering when the other shoe was going to drop. And with someone who would make love to my little petite body as much as I wanted him to.

That last thought had my hand inching down to my woman parts. I hadn't had sex in weeks, and I was feeling the withdrawal. Without even trying to, I thought back to the last time Montrel and I were together. I can't say he was the best I'd ever had, but he was serviceable.

So yeah, I pleasured myself while fantasizing about Montrel. Whispering his name and everything. And it felt awesome. But afterwards, when I opened my eyes and realized what I had just done, I immediately felt foolish. I couldn't even masturbate without including him.

"Ugh!" I screamed, hitting my fists against the bed. How was I going to make myself snap out of this trance Montrel seemed to have me in?

Retrieving my phone again, I went ahead and followed Warner back on Instagram. And before I could come up with an excuse not to, I sent him a message. Just something simple thanking him for the follow and saying he had gotten high praise from Mama. It wasn't too long before I saw he was typing a response, and I actually looked forward to what he was about to say.

Five – Montrel

• • • •

"WHERE DO YOU WANT THESE, Mother?"

"Just put them on the end table, darling. This was such a nice surprise. You know how much I love carnations."

"Only the best for you."

I moved the crystal vase of pink carnations to the polished end table as my mother, Annie, watched with an approving smile. I always liked bringing her little gifts, just as she always taught me I should.

"I'm so glad that you came by to see me today," Mother commented as she took a seat on her ecru linen couch, motioning for me to do the same. Chopin played through the hidden speakers in the walls; classical music was on practically twenty-four-seven in her house. Not exactly my preference but I'd learned to tune it out. "I wasn't sure you would."

"Why do you say that?"

"I thought maybe you would be entertaining that...*girlfriend* of yours. Cathy."

"Mother," I shook my head. "You know her name is Claire."

"Hmph."

"But it doesn't matter anyway because she and I broke up."

"Oh, again?"

"Yes, again. I just realized that I wasn't quite ready to be with her right now."

"It sounds like you're considering going back to her at some point."

"Well, sure. Eventually. When I'm ready."

"I see. Well, this is good news."

"Why, because you never liked her?"

"I never said I disliked her. I just think you can do better. You're far too handsome and have too much going for yourself to be with someone so common."

I frowned slightly at that comment. "She's not *common*, Mother."

"She's certainly not on *your* level. I mean, she's not unpleasant to look at but I wouldn't call her beautiful. She has that regular job that probably won't go anywhere. And she clearly has low self-esteem."

"What in the world makes you think she has low self-esteem?"

"She's a grown woman wearing colored contacts. If she had more confidence about herself-"

"She does not wear contacts. Her eyes are really green."

"Hmph. Well, don't get me started on her eating disorder."

My frown deepening, I turned to Mother fully. "What are you *talking* about?"

"Please. Anybody *that* thin must have something going on with them. I'd be surprised if she was over a hundred pounds soaking wet. It's just not healthy."

I didn't get upset with my mother very often, but I tended to get agitated when she started downtalking Claire. It had been that way ever since the first time I brought Claire over to meet her. Mother took one look at her and decided she wasn't good enough for me, and she never missed a chance to remind me of that.

"With all due respect, Mother, that's ridiculous."

She arched a brow. "Excuse me?"

"Claire does not have an eating disorder and never has. She can eat like a linebacker when she wants to. She's just naturally thin and doesn't gain any weight. And she's not *that* thin; you make it sound like she's skin and bones."

"And she doesn't go purge herself after-"

"Mother." I looked at her pointedly. "Please."

"Fine." She held up her hands. "I still maintain that it's a good thing you two are no longer together. I know several other women that would be way better suited for you."

"I'm sure." I stood before she could run down the list. "I'm going to go get something to drink. Would you like anything?"

She gave me a knowing look before waving a delicate hand. "No, thank you."

I wasted no time leaving the room. I'd only been at Mother's house for a half hour and already needed a break.

Ever since my father died, it had just been the two of us. And okay, yes, maybe she *did* spoil me. But I didn't see that as a bad thing; thanks to Father's life insurance and the trust he had set up for me when I was born, money was never a concern and never would be. And Mother just liked to make sure I had the best of everything, including women.

And I'll admit that Claire was a departure from the kind of women I usually brought home. She didn't come from a rich or cultured family or have some kind of high-powered career that looked good on paper. She was cute, but far from a supermodel. But none of that mattered to me; I liked her, anyway. She was sweet and caring and down-to-earth, and way more fun to be around than those mannequins Mother was always trying to set me up with.

Claire would make a wonderful wife one day (even though I was sure Mother would be anything but thrilled if I were to propose to her). I knew she wanted to be my wife. Yet every time I thought I was ready to go the distance with her, I found myself feeling restless and smothered shortly after we got back together. That's why I kept taking those little breaks from her; it wasn't because I didn't love her or want to be with her. I just didn't want to be with her *right then*. That's understandable, right?

I just needed her to be patient and let me be ready for her and us in my own time.

After taking my sweet time getting some infused water, I headed back into the living room to rejoin Mother. I hoped that she would be ready to talk about something other than my love life by then.

"So, about those other women I mentioned," she said as soon as I sat down.

Damn.

"Mother, can we not?" I droned. "I appreciate the concern, but I really don't need any help finding women."

"Of course not, sweetheart," she quickly agreed. "A man as well-dressed and handsome as you certainly can have his pick of women. You probably have them falling at your feet."

I didn't say all that but I wasn't going to correct her. "Sure."

"I'd just like to help, that's all," Mother continued. "I know of a few absolutely lovely women that would be perfect for you."

Only because I felt I had to, I asked, "Like?"

"Anita Blakewood."

As if I was supposed to know who that was. "And who is Anita Blakewood?"

"She's the daughter of one of my sorority sisters; she just passed the bar on her first try and already has a job lined up at one of the top firms in the city."

And was probably as dull as wallpaper paste. "That's nice."

"And Dorothy Meadows just got promoted to vice president of her brokerage firm."

As if I'd ever even entertain anyone named *Dorothy*. "Awesome."

"Violin Abernathy was just named Chief Resident at her hospital. *And* she does charity work."

"Violin?"

"Yes, it's a ridiculous name but she is absolutely gorgeous. I'd love to get her skincare regimen."

"Hmm. Well, I'm sure these ladies are nice and all, but-"

"Before you go dismissing anything, you should know that I've really been singing your praises recently," Mother informed me. "They were all at the Black Abundance Brunch this past weekend and I could almost *see* their ears perking up as I was describing you."

Mother was always going to brunches and luncheons and fundraisers and banquets; that, shopping, and needlessly redecorating the six bedroom, four bathroom house Father left her were her main activities, because she hadn't worked since she and Father got married not too long before I was born over thirty-two years ago. So I guess it shouldn't have surprised me that she had so much energy to act as my personal pimp.

"And of course, I showed them your picture," she continued, smoothing a hand over the side of her French roll. "I told you that getting those professional shots taken was a good idea."

"I thought you just wanted some nice pictures of me, though. Didn't know they were going to be used for matchmaking purposes."

"Both reasons are valid. And their mothers certainly agreed that you're a looker, which is no surprise. And I know they've been talking you up to their daughters. They're very intrigued."

I couldn't help but sit up a little straighter upon hearing that. If nothing else, it was flattering. "Oh, really?"

"Of course. Why wouldn't they be? These are highly educated women who know a good catch when they see it. I'm sure after some time, they'd all love to be Mrs. Montrel Burns."

"Jumping the gun a little, aren't you, Mother?"

"Not at all. These women know what they want. And they would look so good on your arm. Way better than...well, the last woman you were with."

I chose not to comment because there was no point. And anyway, if Mother didn't like Claire, she'd probably have a heart attack if she ever met Venus. She was *nothing* like the women Mother was always trying to set me up with, which was a large part of her intrigue.

Well, that, and the way she used her mouth to-

"Montrel."

My eyes snapped to Mother. "Yes?"

"Have you been listening to me?"

"Of course I have."

"So you agree that it's time to get serious about finding yourself a suitable wife? You're over thirty, you know."

"I'm aware."

"And I would like some grandchildren before I'm too old and feeble to enjoy them."

"Yes, you've mentioned that, also." It was funny how she was acting like she'd actually play with any grandchildren. Her idea of quality time would likely be enrolling them in lessons or activities that would look good on their resumes down the line.

"So you don't mind me arranging some meetings with these ladies, then?"

I started to say I absolutely minded, but then I thought better of it. Maybe Mother was right. Maybe I *did* need to up the caliber of women I chose to spend my time with. Just because the women she tried to hook me up with in the past were mind-numbingly boring didn't mean this batch would be. It couldn't hurt to at least meet them.

The more I thought about it, the more I warmed to the idea. I'd been doing this back-and-forth routine with Claire for damn near two years now. Maybe that was a sign that she wasn't the one. Surely if she was, I wouldn't want to keep breaking up with her, right? The fact that I kept needing all these breaks had to mean something.

Claire was wonderful, but it was time for me to move on from her, for good. I needed someone that wasn't so needy, and these women Mother were talking about would have more than me going on in their lives and wouldn't need to be up under me so much like Claire did. Claire had a career but it wasn't like she had many hobbies outside of it. She just liked to sit around watching the news while eating that nasty peanut butter toast. I mean, what was she, eight?

Yes, this was a good thing. I started to get excited about the prospect of a more cultured, mature woman. Claire was in my past and it was time to start thinking about my future.

As soon as I got home after leaving Mother's, I went about packing up all of Claire's things that she had left at my place; some toiletries, a pair of pajamas (she had a ton of those, seemed like), a couple of books, some kind of hair curling thing, and some snacks she liked that I refused to buy. I packed them up real nice and arranged to have them sent over to her, wanting to avoid the big scene that would surely happen if I took them myself. Surely this would send the message that I was done, no ambiguity.

It was better this way. We both needed to move on.

Six – Claire

• • • •

THIS BASTARD REALLY did that.

I'd gotten all excited when I got the delivery from Montrel, thinking he had sent me a nice gift to try to ease his way back into my good graces. But I was way off. He'd actually sent back everything I'd left at his house, even the Twinkies that I liked to keep by the bed. It was like he was trying to get rid of any trace of me and that was like a huge splash of cold water to the face.

Of course, I tried to call him. And of course, he didn't answer. He couldn't even talk to me and let me know what was going on. There wasn't even a note in the damn box. I guess I didn't deserve that kind of courtesy.

I plopped onto the couch, staring at the box as if something else was going to pop out of it. Tears were stinging my eyes but I was trying my damndest not to let them fall. I'd cried over Montrel enough. And I was tired of being stupid over this man.

I was done. Montrel's high-yellow ass could kick *all* the rocks.

My phone was still in my hand and before I lost my nerve, I went ahead and deleted Montrel's number from my contacts. If it wasn't there, then I couldn't use it. Never mind that I knew it by heart; I could only hope that I would forget it eventually. Kind of an if-you-don't-use-it-you-lose-it kind of thing.

One number that I *did* want to use, though, was Warner's. Call it a rebound thing, but I needed him to help keep my mind off Montrel. We had talked a few times since I followed him on Instagram and sent him that initial message. He was really cool, and I enjoyed our conversations. I noticed when I talked to him, I managed to put everything out of my mind for a while. That was a major plus.

Before I could give myself an excuse not to, I called him.

"Hey, Claire."

I kinda liked that he always greeted me immediately like that. "Hey. You busy?"

"Not really. What's going on?"

"Oh, nothing much." I wiped my wet eyes, looking away from the box in front of me. "I'm sorry to bug you in the middle of the day like this..."

"It's no bother."

That made me smile. It was nice to not be a bother. "Hey, listen...I know this is out of the blue but...would you want to maybe...meet up? The phone conversations have been nice but I'd like to finally officially meet the man behind the cute voice."

"Oh, you think I have a cute voice? That's good to know," Warner replied. I could tell he was smiling, which only made me smile harder. "Do you like my voice as much as I like your eyes?"

My one redeeming quality. "I don't know...maybe if I heard your voice and you saw my eyes in person, we could compare notes."

"Sounds like a plan to me. I'd love to."

I breathed a small sigh of relief. Being impulsive wasn't usually my thing (nor was asking men out) so it was nice to know I hadn't made a fool out of myself.

"Good."

We set a time and a place, and I already felt better. So much better that I went ahead and unpacked my things from the box Montrel had sent, telling myself that he'd done me a favor. No need in continuing to waste time with a man who clearly didn't want me.

• • • •

I GOT A CALL FROM GISELLE, Forrest's wife. I smiled as I answered the call, since it had been a little while since I'd talked to her.

"Hey, girl. What's going on?" I greeted.

"Claire, girl, I really hope you're not busy right now and have a few minutes to listen to my whining."

"No, I'm not busy. Something going on with you and Forrest again?"

I heard her sniff, as if she'd been crying. "He slept on the couch last night. We had another argument."

"Oh no..."

"I don't know if he slept out there because he was still mad at me or because he didn't want to bother to keep trying to make a baby. We've been trying for so long that we're both extremely on edge and at each other's throats all the time."

"Wow, is it really that bad? Is the baby thing the only issue or is there something else going on? Not trying to get too much in your business or anything..."

"No, stop that. You know I would have told you if there was something else. This is our main issue. At least, as far as I know. The fact that we both want to make a baby but can't is just causing so much tension."

"So, how 'bout if you stop focusing on it so much? Don't try so hard. Just enjoy being together and let things happen naturally."

"I thought about that...this has been consuming us for *so* long that it's really all we talk about. At least, when we're not arguing and blaming each other."

"I'm so sorry you two are going through that."

"Me, too. I don't want to lose my marriage just because we can't conceive a child. He just seems so *angry* all the time; I really feel like he thinks it's my fault that we haven't gotten pregnant yet. He hasn't said that, but the way he looks at me sometimes..."

"Y'all need to talk that out. Pointing fingers isn't doing anybody any good. Have you...seen a doctor? Like, checked to see if one of you has some fertility issues or something?"

She got quiet for a second. "I'm not proud of this but...between you and me, I *did* go get myself checked out but I haven't told Forrest. I didn't want to see the look on his face if it turned out I was the problem. Thankfully, the doctor said I'm fine."

"That's a relief, but, Giselle..."

"I know, I know. Keeping secrets is never a good thing in a relationship."

"No, it's not. I doubt you'd appreciate it if he did something like that behind *your* back. Seriously, y'all should just take the focus off baby-making, 'cause it's clearly causing a rift. It'll happen when it's supposed to happen. Sometimes Mother Nature is just on her own timetable. It's not anybody's fault."

"I guess." Giselle sighed. "At this rate, you'll be pregnant before I will."

"Ha! Girl, please."

"I know Montrel wants to have kids someday. And y'all are together..."

"I guess Forrest really hasn't been keeping you updated, 'cause I'm sure Montrel has told him how he dumped me by now."

Giselle gasped. "He what? I thought you said that last time was only temporary. Or did he dump you *again*??"

I couldn't help but wince at the question a little bit. It was just a reminder of how many times I'd been a fool for that man. I'd been *so* confident when I'd told Giselle that I'd be getting Montrel back that I felt straight stupid now. Thankfully, Giselle was too nice to rub that in my face. "Yes, he did. I *thought* this latest time would only be temporary but clearly, I was wrong. He even sent over all of my stuff that I had over at his house. Guess he didn't want to risk his new conquest seeing it."

"Oh, Claire...he got with somebody else already?? I'm *so* sorry. Forrest didn't mention anything about that to me."

"Well, whatever. I'm not over here pining over Montrel this time. I actually have a date with someone else."

"You do? Who are you going out with?"

"This guy my mama set me up with. His name is Warner."

"Well, I'm glad to hear that you're moving on and all but...are you *sure* you're okay? I know how into Montrel you were and it's totally understandable if you're not over him yet."

I sucked my teeth. "Into him or not, it doesn't do any good if he's not into *me*. And him dumping me on my birthday pretty much summed that up."

"Oh no, not on your birthday..."

"Yes, the bastard ended it on my birthday. Basically said I was smothering him and he needed space." I'd been intentionally vague when I'd told Giselle about all of this initially but figured I might as well spill all the beans now. "The very next day, he was running up in somebody else. And I admit I only know that 'cause I called him, wanting him back, like an idiot."

I didn't mind telling Giselle everything. She wouldn't cuss me out like Chichi would.

"Girl, we've all been there; doing something foolish for a man," Giselle assured me. "I shudder at some of my thirsty moments. Even with Forrest, I have to remind myself that he's my husband and I don't have to run up behind him like I did when we were dating."

"At least Forrest sticks with you through the rough patches, though. Montrel just jerks me around, being all about me when he's feeling romantic and then when the novelty wears off, he's over it. I can't keep putting myself through that."

"And you shouldn't. I love Montrel like a brother but I hate he does that to you."

"Me, too."

"I wonder how big a hand his mother had in that decision, if any," Giselle mused. "You know she tends to be a little too involved in his life sometimes."

"Girl, don't even get me *started* on that. I have no idea of her involvement but it doesn't matter. Him being such a mama's boy is just another reason I need to leave him alone. Annie doesn't like or approve of me and I can't say it's not mutual. I'm sure she's already trying to fix him up with some kind of debutante."

"Well, girl, I'm glad to hear you're handling this so well," Giselle said. "And I hope things go great on your date with Warner. I want all the details afterwards. I'm claiming it's gonna be amazing. You deserve someone that makes you happy, girl."

"I appreciate that."

"I wonder how Montrel will react when he finds out."

"I don't give a damn how he reacts. He made his choice and I'm making mine. Montrel and I are over."

Seven – Claire

• • • •

BEFORE I WAS TOTALLY ready for it, it was time for my date with Warner.

I'd been swinging between anticipation and looking for an excuse to cancel. It wasn't that I didn't want to go out with Warner; it was just the closer that it got to the date, the more anxious I became. Montrel consumed my attention for so long that I didn't think I'd know how to act around anyone else. And it was one thing to exchange texts and talk on the phone but it was going to be a whole other ball game when I was right in front of Warner.

But then I thought, that's ridiculous. I'm a grown woman. And yeah, I might be a little nervous at first, but I liked Warner for a reason, and not just to keep my mind off Montrel. He was cool and funny and seemed to really like me. And he was consistent; ever since I initially hit him up on Instagram, he had reached out to me every day, even if it was just a text to see how my day was going. It was a little thing but it meant a lot. Montrel surely never did that, even when we were going strong.

After I spent too much time agonizing over what I was going to wear and how I was going to do my chin-length hair, it was finally time to leave. It was strangely important to me to look my best on this first date with Warner, even though we were just meeting up for drinks. I just wanted to start off on the best foot possible; it was important for my bruised self-esteem.

"Wow, you're even prettier in person," Warner told me when I arrived at Fourth and Long, a local sports bar. We shared a very light hug.

I grinned so hard I thought I'd catch a cramp. "Thank you, Warner. I can definitely say the same about you. I mean, not the pretty part, but...that you're more handsome...ah hell."

"I get it," Warner assured me with a chuckle. He held my chair out for me. "And thanks for that."

"No problem." I silently told myself to get it together and quit acting like I'd never been on a date before.

"So what are you in the mood for?" he asked me once he was seated, perusing the drink menu. "I'm kinda hungry so I'm probably gonna get a couple of appetizers, too."

My stomach decided to growl at that very second. If Warner heard it, he didn't comment, thank god. "I probably will, too. I'll need a minute, though, 'cause I can be frustratingly indecisive."

"It's all good. I can be unbelievably patient."

Him saying that helped put me at ease a little bit.

We ordered our drinks and appetizers and continued with the whole getting-to-know-you part of dating someone new that usually was too exhausting for words, but it wasn't so bad with Warner. He didn't just sit there and interview me; he actually started a conversation and seemed genuinely interested in what I was saying.

That's more than I could say for Montrel. He usually steered the conversation to something pertaining to him. If he felt like talking at all.

"Is your life anything like you thought it would be at this point?" Warner asked, sipping his Stella Artois. "You know how people make a list of things they want to do by a certain age? I know I've made several drafts over the years."

"And what's the verdict? Are you living out that latest draft?"

"Ehh, for the most part. I'm healthy. Got my degree like I promised my mama I would. I'm my own boss, like I've always wanted to be. I go to plenty of baseball games. Own my own home and have a car with good mileage-"

"Really? You had it on your life wish list to have a car with good mileage?"

He hunched his shoulders, smiling. "I'm not super into cars like that. I've always just wanted something that looks nice and is reliable, and that I wouldn't have to be taking to the shop every other month. My main thing is not having a car note, which I won't have in a few months."

"I feel you on that. One less bill."

"Exactly."

"You've pretty much got everything you want, sounds like."

"Not quite."

He gave me a look that made parts of my body wake up. I knew I was probably blushing, too. I grabbed my White Russian and took a long sip.

"So what about you?" he asked me after a few moments. "Is *your* life the way you want it to be?"

I swirled my drink in my glass a few times before setting it back on the table. "I haven't thought about it in a long while but now that you mention it, I *did* have one of those lists back in the day. And some of the things I wanted have happened but not all of 'em."

"Such as?"

"Well, my job is cool but I can't say being a school counselor is my heart's desire. I've never been to Italy, which is near the top of the list. I'm still skinny, so that's a fail. I don't get pedicures every week. And I thought I'd be married with at least one child by now."

"Pedicures every week?"

"Yeah, it's my one indulgent thing. I've always loved pedicures because I love getting my feet rubbed. But sometimes the budget doesn't allow me to get them as often as I'd like."

"I understand. You know," he leaned in a little. "I happen to give damn good foot rubs."

I almost dropped the mozzarella stick I had just picked up. "Really?"

"Mm-hmm. And I wouldn't mention that unless I was willing to prove it."

This man was making me blush entirely too much. I liked it.

"I might have to take you up on that, then," I made myself say.

"I hope you do."

I stuffed half my mozzarella stick into my mouth as he proceeded to dig into his chicken nachos. The thought of Warner rubbing my feet was way more titillating than I expected it to be. I wondered if he was trying to turn me on or if he was just naturally adept at it, because it was working, either way.

More importantly, though, I appreciated him even offering. It was like pulling teeth to get Montrel to rub my feet. He always acted like they were contaminated or something, and whenever he did indulge me for a couple of minutes, he *had* to wash his hands immediately afterwards. I'm all for hygiene but that was a little insulting.

"And about the skinny thing," Warner spoke up after a few moments. "I don't see why you consider that a fail. God put you in a beautiful package, just the way He wanted you. And I can certainly appreciate the end result."

There he goes *again*. No one had *ever* complimented my body like that. I'd always hated how thin I was, especially now that thick women were all the rage. I must've tried a dozen methods to gain weight over the years but nothing really worked, so I pretty much gave up on that mission. But Warner was talking like he didn't mind my not having so much junk in the trunk.

"Wow," I marveled, smiling at him. "Thank you for saying that. I must say, that's a first."

"That's a shame. Whoever you've dated before was slacking on the job, if they didn't let you know that. Put on some weight if you want to but if nobody else tells you you're beautiful just the way you are, *I'm* telling you."

I wasn't used to all this praise. And part of me was wondering if he was laying it on thick because this was our first date or if he actually meant everything he was saying. Men were always complimentary and sweet at first, but a few months go by and all of that adulation usually fades out. Montrel certainly stopped doling out the compliments after a while.

"And in case you're wondering if I'm just blowing smoke to gas you up, I'm not," Warner continued, pretty much reading my mind. "I don't say stuff I don't mean, but I get it if you're skeptical. I can show you better than I can tell you, though."

Something in me believed him, which scared me. It was too soon for me to be believing everything he said. It was like I hadn't learned anything from my relationship with Montrel.

Then I checked myself. I needed to stop thinking about that asshole. Warner and Montrel were two different men and I didn't want to be one of those women who made the next man pay for the last man's mistakes.

But I'd be a fool *not* to remember what I'd already been through, right? Wasn't it just good sense to keep all the undesirable crap in the back of my mind so I'd recognize it if it came up again and avoid it?

But I'd drive myself crazy if I tried to keep track of *everything* Warner did and compare it to *everything* Montrel did. Warner deserved a clean slate. And I wanted to move on from Montrel. There was no way I could do that if I kept obsessing about every little thing.

"You back from your trip yet?"

I blinked and looked at Warner. "Huh? What?"

"You seemed like you were somewhere else for a minute, there."

"Oh...I'm sorry about that. I guess my mind wandered for a little bit."

"I see I need to work a little harder, then, if you're zoning out like that."

I couldn't tell if he was joking or not. "Oh no, please don't take it personally. I'm just...dealing with some stuff and it can be hard to completely put it out of my mind sometimes. But you are very, very good company and I'm sincerely enjoying myself with you."

"I'm glad to hear that. Does that mean you'd go out with me again?"

I grinned. I couldn't help it. It was a huge relief to know my awkwardness hadn't been a total turn-off.

"Of course. I've love to go out with you again."

He smiled. Gosh, he was even cuter when he did that. "I'm glad."

• • • •

MY DATE WITH WARNER was still on my mind a couple of days later when I was hanging out with Chichi and her boys, Branson, Caron, and Devlin. Chichi had refused to name them all cutesy, rhyming or alliterate names. Which I totally cosigned with.

"You know, any time you want to babysit these little jackals, you can just say the word," Chichi reminded me. As she did pretty much every other day.

"Yes, I know. As *soon* as I'm ready to have my place torn up and all my food eaten, I'll call you immediately."

"They know how to act. You know Gerard and I don't play that."

"They might not be Bebe's Kids but they still have *way* more energy than I do."

"Hell, than me too, a lot of the time," Chichi admitted, chuckling. She watched the triplets as they ran and chased each other around the playground. "They're seven years old now and seem to get more active the older they get. I actually thought it was going to be *easier* by now."

"Well...at least you don't have to worry about diapers anymore."

"True enough." She took a sip of her grape soda, then glanced at it with a regretful expression. "I know I shouldn't be drinking this. After seven years I *still* haven't gotten rid of this mommy belly."

"You don't work out."

"I hated working out even before I had these rascals. Having three kids at once is a lot. Between dealing with them and Gerard, I don't have the energy for much else. Maybe I should just get liposuction and be done with it."

"Girl..." I shook my head. "You don't need any lipo. Why don't you just get a workout in while the boys are at school? At least you have the luxury of being a stay-at-home mom and can set your own schedule, pretty much."

"You think being a stay-at-home mama is a luxury?"

"Would you rather work a job you don't enjoy?"

"Why does it have to be something I don't enjoy? Some people actually *like* what they do for a living."

"I'm just saying; you're fortunate that you don't have to worry about a job *on top of* taking care of triplets and a husband. A lot of families don't have that option."

"That's true," Chichi conceded with a small smile. A wistful look came over her round mocha brown face. "I *did* snag me a good man. Gerard takes damn good care of all of us. Can't say I have anything to complain about."

"No, you don't."

"Maybe when the boys are older, I can start looking for something to do for myself," Chichi commented, taking another sip of her soda. "It *is* nice being there when they get home from school. I was a latchkey kid since my mama worked two jobs. Being able to take care of my kids and my husband *is* a huge blessing, even if they do wear me out."

Just then, the triplets ran over to us, wanting us to join in on their game of dodge ball. Chichi groaned as she allowed Branson and Devlin to pull her up, and Caron grabbed my hands.

"Come on, Auntie Claire," he urged. "I'll try not to throw the ball too hard at you."

"I hope you don't. You know I bruise like fruit."

"You mean plums?"

"It's just an expres—never mind. Let's play some dodge ball."

The five of us played a few games, with Chichi fussing (but laughing) the whole time about how hard the boys were throwing the ball. Caron kept his promise about not hurling the ball too hard at me, but unfortunately Devlin and Branson hadn't made any such promise.

"Ow!" I screamed when Devlin nailed me right in the stomach. "Boy!"

He tried to look innocent. "That's what we're *supposed* to do, Auntie!"

"Whatever!"

Despite my total ineptitude for dodge ball (or pretty much anything sports related), I had fun playing with the boys. Watching them have so much fun with Chichi like they were, and thinking about how Chichi had a loving husband at home, it made me a little envious. Not in a bad way; I loved my girl and was super happy for her. But I'd be lying if I said I didn't want all of that for myself. I wanted a family of my own. And as much as I tried to avoid letting my thoughts veer to the pessimistic, I often wondered if I'd ever get it.

After another hour or so at the park, I went with Chichi while she took her tuckered-out triplets home, stopping at Popeye's on the way because she declared she was entirely too tired to cook. Once the boys were fed, bathed, and spending time with Gerard, who had just gotten home, Chichi and I parked it in the living room.

"Girl, I am *so* done," Chichi panted, leaning her head back on the couch. "Nothing like a game of dodge ball to remind me how out of shape I am."

"I'm kinda wiped, too. I had a good time, though. Got my steps in for the day with all that running around."

"I'm glad you could hang with us today. Though I thought you'd be spending the day with your new boo."

I lifted my head to look at her. "Who, Warner? We've only been on one date. He's not my boo."

"Could he be?"

"I don't know," I shrugged. "I don't hate the idea. He seems like a good guy, and I'm definitely attracted to him."

She eyed me. "I know there's a 'but' coming somewhere..."

I both loved and hated that she could read me so well. "I don't know; it's crazy but I couldn't stop comparing everything about him to Montrel. I wasn't trying to; it was just automatic. It's kinda hard to fully enjoy yourself when your mind keeps wandering."

"Hmm. Was Warner able to tell that your mind was somewhere else?"

"He brought it to my attention once; said I had zoned out. I didn't even realize it. Thankfully he was cool about it but I hated that I was sitting there agonizing over Montrel while I was with him."

"Yeah."

"Go ahead, let me have it," I droned, eying her. "Bite my head off for thinking about Montrel after everything he did."

Chichi chuckled. "I wasn't gonna do that. Believe it or not, I get it. You were in love with the bastard; it's not like you're gonna forget about him just like that. It'll take some time. I just hope that Warner can help speed the process up some, if you really like him."

"I really do. Part of me wonders if it's too soon for me to be trying to start something with someone new, though; I only reached out to Warner because I was in my feelings about Montrel sending my stuff back like he did. I just wonder if it's fair to Warner to get involved when I'm not completely over Montrel."

"While I get what you're saying, I think seeing Warner is exactly what you need," Chichi insisted. "Let's face it; if you don't have something—or someone—to keep you busy, you'll just sit over there in your house obsessing over Montrel, driving yourself nuts. And knowing you, you'll talk yourself into calling him or texting him, and set yourself back when he tells you yet again that he doesn't want a relationship with you, that's *if* he even answers the phone."

"Is this supposed to be a pep talk?"

"But, if you're hanging out with Warner, you won't have as much time to worry about Montrel. And as time goes by, maybe your thoughts about Montrel will decrease, especially if you're enjoying your time with Warner. That's a good thing."

"Yeah, but is that fair to Warner, though? Who wants to date someone who's still hung up on somebody else?"

"It's not like you're using the man, since you said you actually like him. But if you're worried about that, be straight up with him. Let him know that you just went through a bad breakup and you're not totally over it, but you *want* to be. I'm sure he can understand that."

"And if he tells me that he'd prefer I got over Montrel first?"

"Then, hey," Chichi threw up her hands. "Nothing you can do about that. It's understandable. All I'm saying is that he'd probably appreciate that honesty and could deal with it better if he knew where your head was. And if you're sincere about wanting to get to know him and moving on from Montrel."

"I am," I insisted quickly. Probably *too* quickly, given how Chichi cocked a brow at me. "I just don't want to hurt anybody or do Warner like Montrel did me. I know how it feels when the person you're into turns out to not be all in like you are."

"I know you do. Which is why I say again to just be honest with Warner about everything. If you're having concerns, tell him that. You can't control how he takes it but you'll at least be able to say that you didn't keep him in the dark about anything."

"That's true."

"I really hope you give this Warner a chance. I looked him up on Instagram; he seems to have a lot going for himself. And, not at all bad to look at."

"Not at *all*," I couldn't help but smile with some strange sense of pride, as if Warner was my man already. To be honest, part of me kinda wished he was.

But to say I didn't miss Montrel at all would be a lie. It was just hard to purge all of that out of my system when I was as deeply into Montrel as I was. Yes, he dogged me. Yes, I knew I needed to move on. But it was one thing to know it and another to actually make it happen. Feelings sometimes had minds of their own, unwilling to be tamed.

But at least I wasn't calling him anymore. And I got my curling iron back.

Eight – Montrel

• • • •

SOMETIMES I REALLY wished I had an assistant.

I was out running some errands, wasting my day away. Whenever possible, I had the things I needed delivered to my house. But my car needed an oil change, I had to pick up some dry cleaning, and some other mundane tasks. Things started to look up, though, when an absolutely *gorgeous* woman entered the waiting room of the dentist office I was sitting in.

I eyed her as she checked in, then took a seat near me. Her skin looked so smooth, like liquid gold. Dark thick hair that hung down her back, and if it wasn't real, it certainly looked it. Legs that went on forever. And I could already imagine myself kissing those lips of hers over and over.

Not gonna lie, my body was already reacting to her. Her fragrance was enveloping me like a sweet-smelling cloud. I officially wanted her.

Thankfully, we were the only two people in the waiting room so I wouldn't have an audience when I tried to shoot my shot. The receptionist seemed to be too engrossed in whatever was on her phone to be paying attention to anything else.

"You're exquisite."

She didn't even look up from her magazine. I cleared my throat and tried again.

"Excuse me, miss."

She looked at me. Damn, she was like a young Halle Berry.

"I said you're exquisite."

"Oh," she gave me a polite smile. "That's very sweet, thank you."

She went back to her magazine and I debated whether I should move to the seat next to hers. She clearly must have thought I was just trying to make random conversation.

"I'm Montrel," I announced a little louder. "What's your name?"

It took her a few seconds, but she looked up at me again. Her polite smile seemed tighter this time. "Jacqueline."

"Love that name. It suits you. Kinda gives an old-soul vibe; very attractive."

"Right." She went back to her magazine again.

Clearly I was going to have to be more overt. She wasn't catching what I was throwing.

"Would you mind if I moved over next to you?" I persisted, leaning forward.

With a sigh, she glanced at her watch and looked up at me again. "Um, Montrel, is it?"

"That's me."

"I don't want to be rude, I really don't. But I'm just here to get my teeth cleaned; I don't need to be macked. So, if you don't mind, you can stay where you are, I can stay where I am, and we can just each mind our own business until it's our turn to go back there. Okay?"

Without waiting on my response, she went back to her damn magazine, essentially dismissing me. I glanced over at the receptionist, who was looking at something on the computer but her lips were quivering like she was trying to keep herself from laughing. I felt my face heat up.

It always tripped me out when women acted like they were too good to be bothered when someone was just trying to get to know them. I step to her respectfully and she gives me the brush-off?

Whatever. Forget her. It's not like she was the hottest thing walking. Her hair was probably one of those wigs everybody seemed to be wearing now. And that perfume of hers smelled like dead flowers.

"Mr. Burns?"

Thank god. Now I could go see the damn dentist and not have to be around the long-legged stuck-up anymore. I walked by the receptionist, who still had that amused smirk on her face.

I managed to put that incident out of my mind and get on with my day after I left the dentist. I was feeling a little antsy and restless, and felt like burning off some energy. This is where most men would do something like go to the gym, but I wanted to burn off my frustrations another way.

My phone rang and I was a little surprised to see it was Venus calling. Her call might have seemed timely but I wasn't all that thrilled to hear from her, surprisingly.

"Yes, Venus."

"That's what I hope you'll be saying later on when I'm riding you."

This was her greeting to me. Just classless. "I beg your pardon?"

"You wanna come over later? I've been taking some ginseng and I feel like I could bounce off the walls. I hope you drunk your Gatorade."

"I don't need any Gatorade, as if I drink that, anyway. I'm not gonna be able to come over tonight, Venus."

"And why not?"

"I don't really need an explanation. I just can't come."

She paused. "Why you sound like that?"

"Why *do* I sound like what?"

"You're talking to me like I'm bothering you or something. Like you didn't used to blow up my phone trying to get over here and bang my back out."

"Do you always have to be so crass? Maybe this is part of the reason I'm declining."

"Oh, I get it," Venus surmised. "Think you too good for me now, huh?"

"No, it has nothing to do with being too good for anyone. I just want different things now, that's all. It's nothing personal."

"Uh-huh. Whatever. You've tried this shit before. We'll see how long it lasts this time. Please believe, you're not the only one I can call." She hung up.

I shrugged as I put my phone back into my pocket. Venus was all right, but she didn't hold the same appeal for me that she used to. Now she just seemed so...bottom of the barrel. Like I was settling, even though the possibility of a relationship with her was never even on the table. She was just for fun. And fun was all good but now, she just screamed *downgrade*. I deserved better than that.

And yes, I had made declarations like that with her before, but I really meant it this time.

I pulled my phone back out and scrolled through my contacts to see who I could call to spend some time with and take this edge off. But none of the women in my phone were suitable.

When I saw Claire's name, I paused with my thumb over her name. She would do.

But just as quickly, I came to my senses. She'd just try to take any invitation, no matter how casual or indifferent, as some kind of sign that I wanted to get back together. I didn't need that. She had finally stopped calling me, and the last thing I needed was to open those floodgates again. It was best that I left well enough alone.

· · · ·

I ENDED UP SPENDING the evening jacking off in my bedroom like some kind of adolescent. It pissed me off that I didn't have *any* suitable contacts I could reach out to for times like this. This was one time I missed being in a relationship.

I was musing over all this when I got a call from Forrest.

"What are you doing?"

There was no way I was going to tell him what I'd just spent the last hour doing so I just replied, "Nothing. You?"

"Just got in from the gym. Had to work off some frustration."

"You and Giselle had another fight, then, I guess."

"We had a disagreement."

"A fight."

"Were you here? You don't know."

"I know y'all. And you fight more than you do anything else, especially lately."

"We're just both on edge. We thought we had actually conceived this time and then she got her period this morning. She flipped out on me like it was *my* fault."

"It's a stressful time for her. Cut her some slack."

"Where is all this empathy for *me*? *I'm* supposed to be your boy."

"You *are* my boy. And I'm sure it's hard on you, too. I'm just saying, you two being at each other's throats isn't going to bring you a baby any faster."

He sighed. "I guess."

"Have you two thought about looking into other options? There are all kinds of things they can do with infertile couples nowadays."

"Giselle is hellbent on doing all of this naturally. She doesn't want to 'bring science into it', as she says. If you ask me, it's bullshit. There's nothing wrong with getting a little nudge from science, in my opinion. I'm a pediatrician; hell, a quarter of my patients were conceived 'unnaturally.' Maybe I should just crush up some fertility pills and put them in her waffle batter."

"Romantic."

"It will be if I serve them to her in bed."

"Stop talking."

"At least her mood gets better after she spends time on the phone gabbing with her girlfriends," Forrest said. "I know she had a *really* interesting conversation with Claire the other day."

I had been headed out of my bedroom and paused at the mention of Claire's name. I sometimes forgot she and Giselle were so close. They only knew each other because of me.

"Oh really?"

"Yep."

"I'm guessing you think I'll be interested in what they talked about, the way you prefaced that."

"Maybe. *Would* it interest you to know that Claire is dating somebody else?"

I tripped over my own foot and banged my shoulder into the wall.

"What was that?" Forrest asked.

"Uh, nothing. What do you mean, Claire is dating somebody else?"

"What do you think I mean? She met some dude and went out on a date with him."

I rubbed my shoulder, frowning. Though I wasn't sure if I was frowning because of the pain or because of what Forrest was telling me.

"Who is it?"

"I don't know all that. Somebody her mama set her up with, I think Giselle said."

Claire's mother never did like me. She was polite enough, but she was always giving me those looks like she didn't quite trust me or something.

"And Giselle didn't tell you what the guy's name was? I'm sure she did."

"Why do you care?"

Pursing my lips, I tried to gather myself. I was sure Forrest was going to try to clown me for my reaction but I couldn't help it, even to my own surprise.

"Don't go trying to read too much into my asking all this. I'm just curious, that's all."

"You don't sound curious. You sound jealous."

"Why would I need to be jealous? I dumped *her*, remember?"

"Oh, I remember."

"I just find it...interesting that she's dating already, that's all."

"Why? You thought she was going to be sitting around in her bathrobe eating chips and drinking wine and watching sappy movies while she cried her eyes out?"

"I didn't say all that."

"You didn't have to say it. You're in your feelings 'cause she's moving on from you. Just like I told you she would."

"It just seems wrong. She was always talking about how in love with me she was and here she is, already going out with somebody else..."

Forrest actually laughed at me. As if any of this was funny. "You really are something else."

"Thank you."

"That was not a compliment, dumb ass. You're really that full of yourself that you didn't expect her to get on with her life. You keep giving her the runaround, getting with her and then dumping her when you start to itch, then you ship all her stuff to her without so much as a note, and think she's gonna sit around pining over your conceited ass."

"Did Giselle tell you what they did?"

"Even if she did, I wouldn't tell you. Not when you're acting like this."

"Acting like what?"

"You know what, Montrel? I'm gonna get off the phone with you. 'Cause right now I feel like I'm talking to a child who threw away his toy and then decided he wanted it back when somebody else got it."

"Who said anything about wanting Claire back? I was just asking a few questions out of concern. And I feel like she only told Giselle 'cause she knew it would eventually get back to me."

Forrest sucked his teeth. "Childish ass. Bye."

I mindlessly hung up the phone, a slight frown on my face. I didn't care what Forrest said; there was nothing wrong with my wondering about what Claire was doing. And I fully intended to find out.

Nine – Montrel

• • • •

IT WAS THE DAY OF MY regular spa day and man, did I need it.

Ever since Forrest had told me about Claire dating someone, I hadn't been able to get it out of my mind. I can't say why; I had always maintained that she could do whatever she wanted. I left her; it was foolish to get upset about her moving on like I said she should.

Yet, there I was, unable to let it go. I'll admit there were a few times I started to reach out to her just to talk (and casually dig for details about who it was she was dating) but I always stopped myself. That would make me look silly, and I abhorred looking silly. I told myself that what Claire did and with whom she did it was simply none of my business.

Being pampered made it easier to take my mind off of it, even if just temporarily. Mother had gotten me hooked on spa days a long time ago, and I made sure to have them at least once a month. Between the facial, herbal body wrap, 90-minute massage, hand and foot treatment, and the delicious spa lunch, I had no worries for a few hours. But it only took seeing the receptionist drinking a latte to put Claire back on my mind. Claire loved lattes.

"How was everything?" the receptionist asked me.

"Everything was great, thanks."

"Would you like to go ahead and book your next spa day now, Mr. Burns?"

"Yeah, that's fine. The last Saturday in the month, if it's available. Same time as today."

"No problem." She entered some stuff on the computer while I glanced at my phone, part of me expecting to see something from Claire. I guess her doing all this new dating explained why I hadn't heard from her.

"All set, Mr. Burns," she announced a few moments later. "We look forward to seeing you again."

"Thank you."

"I know *I* am."

She had said it under her breath but it was still loud enough for me to hear it. I glanced at her, mildly surprised. "Is that right?"

She gave me a timid smile. "Maybe this is inappropriate and unprofessional but...I think you're really attractive and would love to give you my number so we can talk sometime."

"Oh, really?"

"Yes."

Well, this was flattering. She was usually working the desk when I came in and I never paid much attention to her but now that I was looking, she wasn't too hard on the eyes. I'd even call her cute. With a glance at her name tag, I saw her name was Liza.

"Well, Liza, you sure know how to flatter a brother," I commented with a smile. "Sure, I'll take your number."

She grinned and quickly wrote her number on the back of one of the spa business cards on the raised edge of the desk. I took it, slid it into my pocket, and wished her a good day before turning and walking out.

Would I actually call? Probably not. But I could always just say I lost the card she gave me.

• • • •

I MIGHT NOT HAVE CALLED Liza but I *did* call someone.

I'd been stopping myself from calling Claire for days and I was over it. I wanted an explanation for her going off and dating someone else so soon after our relationship ended. And regardless of what Forrest said and how many kinds of 'jackasses' he called me, I felt I deserved that.

But, amazingly, Claire didn't answer. It was the weekend, so I knew she wasn't working. She didn't go out much, unless she was hanging out with her loud friend Chichi. She could've been at her parents', but I doubted it. So unless she was taking a nap in the middle of the day, it didn't make sense that she wasn't available to take my call. Because I know she wasn't just ignoring me.

Unless...

Was she with this new man she was seeing? From what Forrest told me, Claire had gone on one date with whoever it was, but now I was wondering if there had been more. If it was *becoming* something else. Were they claiming each other? Had he been to her place, sitting in the same spaces I sat in? The thought didn't sit well with me at all.

I started to call Forrest and see if he had any more updates from Giselle, but I already knew how that would go. He'd just clown me even more than he already was.

After calling Claire again and again getting her voicemail, I practically threw my phone to the backseat of my car (then I quickly retrieved it to make sure it wasn't damaged; that thing was expensive). I didn't know why I was so consumed with what Claire was doing, anyway; I had broken up with her for a reason.

After going by to see Mother and enduring another round of suggested candidates to be the future Mrs. Burns, I headed home. Mother was way more concerned about my getting married than I was. Sometimes hearing her go on and on about it got a little exhausting. Not to mention frustrating. I started to tell her I'd reconciled with Claire just to get her off my back.

And once that thought was in my head, I didn't totally hate the idea.

Before I knew it, I was sitting in front of Claire's house. I couldn't even remember when I decided to go over there; I hadn't planned on it. But somehow on my way to treat myself to a new sport coat (or three), I steered my car to Claire's place instead. It was encouraging to see her car out front; at least I knew she was home.

So of course the next question was, was she in there alone and if so, why hadn't she answered my calls?

Without even meaning to, I was banging on the door like I was with the police. I stood up straighter when I heard footsteps.

"Who is it?" she called out.

"It's me, sweetheart."

"Montrel?"

Who else would it be? "Yeah. Open the door."

The door opened slowly and she peeked around, looking at me with a slight frown. My eyes darted around over her shoulder, trying to see if I could detect any traces of another man being there. A jacket, a pair of sneakers...

"What are you doing here?"

I could hear the attitude in her voice. She wasn't happy to see me, which, I'm not gonna lie, stung a little bit.

"I wanted to see you."

"Why?"

"Claire, can I just...can I come in, please?"

"Now isn't a good time, Montrel." She folded her arms, those green eyes darkening and shooting daggers at me. "And I really don't appreciate you just showing up like this."

"Well, if you would answer your damn phone..."

"I didn't want to talk to you. You can't take a hint?"

"Apparently not. Why can't you let me in? You have company or something?"

"If I did, it wouldn't be any of your business, now would it?"

"Why are you acting like this? Like you hate me or something?"

"I would be very well justified if I did, the way you dogged me. You wanted me to leave you alone and I'm gladly doing that. So, if you don't mind....hell, even if you do..." She started to close the door.

"Claire!" I blocked the door from closing with my hand, looking at her incredulously. "I've never known you to be like this."

"Yeah, well," she shrugged. "A person can only take so much, you know?"

So she was still angry about my breaking up with her. I took this as a good sign. Her being this upset meant she still had some feelings for me. She wouldn't be this emotional if she didn't give a damn.

"Okay, Claire," I conceded, holding up my hands, "I get it. Maybe it's time we get everything out on the table."

"No, thank you."

My hands fell. "Really?"

"What's the point? You'll just tell me whatever you think it is I wanna hear, get me to let my guard down, and then it'll only be a matter of time before you're feeling *smothered* and I'm right back flat on my face again. That's how it is with you every time, Montrel. And I'm over it."

She was serious. This wasn't like the other times when she'd said similar things but it didn't have any weight behind it; she'd be putting up a tough-girl front that we both knew I saw right through. But this time was different; she didn't have the same look in her eyes for me that she used to. The hint of yearning that was always there was nowhere to be found now. Maybe she really *had* had enough this time. And...I didn't feel great realizing that.

"Claire, I'm not trying to bullshit you. I swear." I looked right into her eyes, hoping to convey how sincere I was. "I can understand why you don't believe me, but...knowing me and how I am, would I *still* be standing here trying to get you to hear me out if I wasn't sincere?"

She paused, considering my words. I could tell she knew I had a point. I was usually too proud to ask for something more than once, and she knew that.

Sighing, she opened the door a little wider. "Five minutes," she announced. "And I mean it."

She went back into the living room while I stepped inside and closed the door. I had no idea what I was going to say; I was really winging it. All I knew was in that moment, it was inexplicably important to me to get Claire's forgiveness.

"All right, you're in here; what do you want?" she droned, standing across the room from me, her arms folded again.

I stood near her secondhand plaid couch that her parents had given her (and that I at one point tried to encourage her to get rid of) and hurriedly tried to figure out the right words to say. It felt strange being in the same room with Claire and not being allowed to touch her or kiss her. She used to love that. But now her eyes were warning me to keep my distance.

"I fully get that it was messed up of me to break up with you on your birthday like I did," I began, hoping bringing that up didn't upset her even more. "And-"

"What about being all up in another woman less than twenty-four hours later?"

I pursed my lips. There was no way I was going to admit how I didn't think I was necessarily wrong for that since I'd already dumped her by then. "Okay, fine, that too. I'll admit that I just...I guess you and I getting serious kind of scared me, in a way. It's not because I don't love you or want to be with you...if I'm honest with myself, it's because you've had an effect on me that no other woman has and I clearly don't always handle that very well."

She just kept looking at me. So I kept talking.

"Claire, you know I love you. I react stupidly and rashly because of it. But at the end of the day, I know I want to be with you." I took a step towards her. "I think we belong together."

"All of a sudden, huh? Just like that, you've had the epiphany that we're destined to be together?"

I wondered if she knew that I knew that she was dating someone else. In that moment, though, it didn't matter. I didn't care about that other man, whoever he was. All I wanted was for Claire to take me back. Something I didn't even think I wanted that morning but right then, it was the most important thing in the world to me.

"Yes, just like that," I replied, moving even closer to her. She eyed me, but didn't tell me to stop, so I continued my cautious approach. "I can't stand the thought of you hating me. And I can't stand the thought of you moving on with your life without me in it. I want us to be together, sweetheart. More than anything."

Her face looked like it had softened a bit, but just like that, her hardened expression was back. "And when you wake up tomorrow or a week from now and come down off whatever this high is you're on right now and decide that you're no longer in the mood for a relationship, then what? You'll kick me to the curb again? Maybe dump me in front of an audience next time?"

"I wouldn't do that."

"I believe you *would* do that. And I'm not trying to find out." She shook her head, glancing at her watch. "That's it. Your time is up."

"It hasn't been five minutes!"

"My watch is fast. And you're not saying anything I'm trying to hear, anyway."

She stomped around the couch towards the door, and I grabbed her wrist as she tried to brush past me. She pushed against my chest as I pulled her to me, holding her around her small waist. She punched my shoulders, leaning as far away from me as she could.

"Let go of me, Montrell!"

"Do you still love me, Claire?" I urged, trying to get her to look into my eyes as she struggled against my hold. "Can you honestly say you don't love me anymore?"

She was avoiding my eyes, which I took as another good sign. "So what? That doesn't mean anything."

"I think it does."

After several quiet moments, she finally stilled and looked up at me. "Yeah, I love you," she admitted. "My feelings for you are real and can't just be turned off because you hurt me, as much as I wish that was possible. But I'm finally learning that love by itself doesn't cut it."

"Who says?"

"It clearly doesn't. Because you were saying you loved me before and you still dropped me. So clearly, love only goes so far. Either that, or you have no idea what real love is."

That struck me a little bit. "I think I know what it is," I grunted, my eyes momentarily dropping to her lips before going back to her eyes. "And I haven't felt it for anyone but you. Can you give me another chance?"

Those pretty green eyes started getting a little misty, then she blinked rapidly and tried to push away from me again.

"Let me go," she ordered, her voice strong.

I reluctantly did as she asked and she immediately went over to the door, opening it.

"You talk a good game, Montrel," she spat, "But you know the one thing I *haven't* heard from you yet? *I'm sorry.*

And I'll think its bullshit if you try to say it now, so don't even bother."

My face tightened. "Claire-"

"And if you're not sorry for what you did, how do I know you won't do it again? I'm not trying to go backwards anymore. It's time for me to move on from you. So you need to go."

Pursing my lips, I quickly searched my brain for what else I could possibly say to get her to calm down and let me get my point across. Clearly, I wasn't doing a very good job, here (which was why I probably shouldn't have tried to wing it). But she meant business, and I knew words weren't going to cut it.

Going over to her, I pushed the door closed with one hand and pulled her to me with the other. Before she could react, I pressed my lips to hers, grabbing the back of her neck. Her hands pushed against my chest again, but I just backed her against the door, pressing my body to hers. I kept kissing her, taking my time, eventually easing my tongue into her mouth. Her hands slowly stopped pushing against me and began gently grabbing my shirt. Then I felt her mouth open wider, allowing me to deepen the kisses. Her tongue began stroking against mine. Before too long, we were fully making out and grinding against each other against the door, our hands all over each other.

I kissed down her neck, between her small breasts, down her stomach, and ducked my head underneath the t-shirt dress she was wearing. I heard her sharp intake of breath when I moved her panties aside and began licking her, and she grabbed my head, holding me under there. I lifted her leg over my shoulder and she started moving against my mouth, repeatedly bumping against the door as she gasped and whimpered about what I was doing to her.

Never mind that oral sex wasn't something I was usually in a hurry to administer. Claire and I had butted heads about that in the past, where she actually called me selfish for loving to receive but not give. So I had no idea what was compelling me to go down on her then; it just felt like the right thing to do in the moment. My usual mindset was totally off.

"Oh *god*," she moaned, writhing against me. Her knee buckled and it felt like she was about to collapse right on my head, so I abruptly stood, grabbed her hand, and led her to her bedroom. I didn't even take the time to properly put my clothes aside this time; I just let her toss them to the floor as I pulled her onto the bed.

"You believe I want you back now?" I panted as I moved in and out of her underneath her light pink comforter. I palmed her breasts, brushing my thumbs over her nipples, which I knew drove her crazy. "You believe me, sweetheart?"

"Yes," she whispered, her mouth widening slightly as her back arched. Her nails were dug into my back and I resisted the urge to ask her to ease up on that. "I believe you..."

"Will you take me back?"

When she took too long to answer, I began stroking harder and deeper.

"Oooh!" she exclaimed, opening her eyes to look at me. They were bright green now. I was looking right into them, a determined frown furrowing my brow. I pulled her thigh higher on my hip and changed up my stroke, pushing into her as far as I could go, making her shudder harder than I'd ever seen. "What are you trying to do to me??"

"I'm trying to show you how good we are together," I responded, breathless. Sweat dripped from my brow to her chest. "I want you, Claire. Take me back, sweetheart. It's you and me, you know that..."

She whimpered, and I wasn't sure if it was from enjoyment of what I was doing to her or because she didn't want to concede to me. Either way, I wasn't trying to stop until I got a yes.

Which I eventually got. When I sat up and pulled her onto my lap so she could ride me, which was her favorite position, she looked thoughtfully into my eyes as we moved against each other, my hands on her backside. My eyes roamed her face; I loved how flushed her pretty brown skin got during sex. Her arms tightened around my neck and she bit her lip, groaning a little in a mixture of pleasure and defeat.

"Okay," she whispered, almost where I couldn't hear her. "Let's try it again."

I slid a hand into the back of her tousled hair and pulled her to me for a deep kiss. It'd been a while since I'd been as happy and relieved as I was right then. Our pace began to increase and get more concentrated, and I flipped her back onto her back and started pounding into her like a wild man. She looked at me in mild surprise; I'd never been that aggressive with her. But something had come over me that I couldn't explain; the thought of losing Claire to someone else had me acting outside of myself.

Later, after we calmed down, she laid against my chest, lightly stroking my stomach.

"I really can't believe this is happening," she said softly. "Part of me feels like I'm about to wake up at any second."

"It's real, sweetheart," I assured, kissing the top of her head. "I'm back."

"I'm glad," she finally admitted, looking up at me with a smile. "I missed you."

"I missed you, too. And please know that I meant everything I said earlier."

"I believe you."

"Good."

We laid there in satisfied silence for a while before I reached down and gently pulled her face up to mine. It was like I couldn't get enough of her. Usually after I got mine, I was pretty much done. But I was so keyed up by Claire giving me another chance that my erection just refused to go down.

We kissed languidly, deeply, taking our time as Claire lightly held onto the wrist of the hand that was caressing her face. She was an amazing kisser. It was funny how I hadn't realized that before.

"Sweetheart?" I mumbled between kisses.

"Hmm?"

"You think it's about time to get another pedicure?"

Her eyes opened. "What?"

"I was just asking," I clarified quickly, going in for another kiss before she could say anything else. "Don't get upset."

I didn't need her getting mad at me and putting me out. I only mentioned it because I noticed she clearly hadn't had one in a while and figured since we were back together, she might want to get back on that.

She eyed me warily but let me continue to kiss her, and eventually her eyes slid closed again as she leaned into me. I wrapped her tightly in my arms, loving that she was mine again. And I wasn't about to be stupid and let her go this time.

Ten – Claire

• • • •

I WASN'T ALLOWING MYSELF to think too much about what happened. The only thing I let myself do was be happy to have my man back.

Montrel was sincere this time; I could tell. For one, he was *never* so persistent before about getting me to talk to him. Usually, he's too proud to do anything even remotely related to begging. But this time, he wouldn't leave me alone until I heard him out.

For two, he went down on me. It wasn't necessarily a first, but it certainly wasn't something he volunteered to do. He usually indulged me a couple of minutes of that only after some heavy fussing on my part, and even that didn't work every time.

And three...I could just tell, okay?

There are some people you just have a soul tie with, and Montrel and I had that. Our road to forever just had more bumps than other people's. And I loved him enough to ride those out.

But I made sure to make it clear that this was his *last* chance. If he switched things up on me again, that would be all she wrote. And I'm sure he knew I meant that.

As glad as I was to have Montrel back, there was still the little issue of Warner that I had to deal with. He and I were sort of dating, even though we weren't exclusive. I liked him. And I had no clue how to tell him I'd taken my ex back.

So...I didn't.

I avoided his calls. And I fully acknowledge how cowardly that was. But I couldn't conjure up a way to tell him I'd gotten back with Montrel that didn't make me look like a fool, especially since he knew all about how Montrel had dogged me before (I was kinda regretting telling him about that). And I couldn't act like I didn't care what he thought because I did. Warner was a good man and I had grown to care about him in our short time knowing each other; I didn't want him thinking ill of me.

So I just quit talking to him altogether and hoped he'd lose interest.

Montrel and I spent the weekend after we got back together holed up at his place, cuddling and kissing and sexing. He actually fed me grapes in bed, which was another indication that he had changed because he usually hated food of any kind in the bedroom (despite my telling him how much fun that could be).

I managed to forget about the outside world for a couple of days while we played cards, ate takeout from my favorite Italian restaurant, and snuggled up on the couch watching documentaries (he wasn't that big on movies). He seemed to be content with us just fooling around and eating and not talking about much of anything, but of course I had to dig:

"Montrel..."

"Yeah."

"Since we're back together now, I was curious as to what you wanted to do from here."

"Meaning?"

"Meaning, like, long-term. I'm not dating you just to be dating you; I'd like for us to have a future together and I'd just like to know your thoughts about that. You know, make sure we're on the same page."

His eyes barely flicked towards me from the television. "Do we have to talk about this now?"

"I'd like for us to. Especially since I know you've seen this documentary at least three times so it's not like you don't already know what's happening in it."

"Can it at least wait for a commercial break?"

"It's on Netflix, Montrel."

He sighed. "I'd just rather not get into this right now, if you don't mind."

"Oh okay, so when *will* you feel like getting into it? Since you're acting like I'm trying to start an argument instead of just discussing our future together."

"I didn't say you were trying to...look, I'm just saying I'd rather sit here with you and watch this and not talk about anything so serious. That's all. I didn't say I'd never want to talk about it in life; just not right now. We *just* got back together; we'll get to all that eventually."

I shook my head. "Whatever, Montrel."

"Is that okay?"

"I guess it's gonna have to be, won't it? It's not like I can *make* you talk."

"Don't start getting an attitude for no reason, Claire. We've been having a nice time..."

"And what, I'm ruining it?" I threw the blanket that was covering my legs aside and stood. "Wouldn't wanna do that."

"Now, see..." He lifted a hand towards me before letting it fall back to the couch. "Where are you going?"

"Well, I was *gonna* go to the bathroom and then get some juice, unless that will kill your vibe, too."

He just shook his head and turned back towards the television.

I left the room, in no hurry to get back in there with him. It didn't sit well with me that discussing our future wasn't something he was all that eager to do. And I didn't know if it was because he sincerely just didn't want to talk about it right then, or if he didn't want a future with me at all. Maybe our relationship was just something for him right now, but he had no intention of making me his wife one day. We hadn't really talked about marriage much before; anytime we started, the topic suddenly veered elsewhere. I couldn't help but see this as a not-so-good sign.

We managed to get through the rest of the evening and weekend without fussing, but we also never had the conversation I wanted to have, either. *He* certainly never brought it up, and I didn't bother because I sensed he didn't really want me to. Sure, being together in his house was nice, but I just wanted to know what I was getting back into. Because if we didn't want the same things, we were just wasting our time.

Needless to say, I wasn't that thrilled with Montrel after that weekend, especially after he also refused to tell me anything about the woman I heard in the background when I called him the day after my birthday dumping. Actually tried to say it wasn't any of my business. We didn't talk much after that, and I feared we were right back to how things were before, with everything being about him and what he wanted, with no concessions for me.

But then, Monday morning as I was getting ready for work, I got a delivery of a dozen maple bacon doughnuts and a large latte. With it was a note:

Just wanted you to know I was thinking about you. And that I *do* care about what you want.

Montrel

Okay, I melted a little bit at that. It was an incredibly sweet move and I appreciated it. Montrel wasn't exactly known for his romantic gestures, so I was touched that he thought of me enough to do that. I felt a little better about things, especially when I got home later that day and there was another package waiting for me. There were a couple of balloons taped to it, and I smiled as I carried it into the house. Two gifts in one day? Montrel must have either been really sorry for being such a dick or really trying to show me he changed. Could be both but then I'd have to start wondering if some alien had taken over his body.

After stashing my purse and kicking my shoes off, I tore into the box. There was a fluffy pink bathrobe...

"Nice," I muttered, holding the robe against my body and snuggling with it for a few seconds before putting it on the couch and turning back to the box.

Some kind of fancy spa products...

"I see he's still going to that spa. He's *so* damn metrosexual."

Some dried fruit, crackers, white wine...

"More of a Montrel thing than a Claire thing but I'll take it."

And a home pedicure kit.

"I know this bastard didn't."

He actually gave me a home pedicure kit?? He was always trying to throw little jabs at my feet, telling me I needed to get pedicures and stuff and refusing me when I asked him for a foot rub. You would think I had the nastiest feet on the planet, the way he avoided them. And he certainly never treated me to any pedicures or took me with him on any of his spa days; not once in two damn years. (Hell, he acted offended when I even dared to ask which spa it was he went to). Did he actually think I would be touched by this?? Yeah I loved pedicures, but I loved *getting* them, not *doing* them on myself!

I threw the kit on the floor and plopped onto the couch in a huff. I started to call Montrel and go off, but stopped myself. Was I really about to cuss him out because he sent me a gift? Just because I thought it was insensitive didn't mean that's how he meant it. Maybe in his deluded mind, he was doing something thoughtful. There was no reason to raise hell; I'd just throw it under my bathroom sink and try to forget about it.

And he *did* send me a bunch of delicious doughnuts earlier. At least he got *that* right.

• • • •

I HAD A FEW MISSED calls from Warner and Chichi, and I still wasn't ready to talk to either of them. I didn't know how to face Warner after taking Montrel back, and I wasn't in a hurry for Chichi to cuss me out. Of course I knew I'd have to face the music with them eventually, but I was gonna stretch that out as long as I could.

Instead of worrying about that, I chose to focus on good things. Montrel had really seemed to make a change for the better since our reconciliation. He was calling every night, sending gifts, doing the occasional check-ins during the day. That was something he didn't used to do because he didn't want to distract me at work, even though I repeatedly told him it was no big deal for him to shoot me some texts. I didn't have to check it right when he sent it, but he was ridiculously adamant about that. It was good to know he was starting to listen to me.

"There's my pretty girlfriend," he greeted one day after I'd gotten home from work. He'd called and asked if he could come over when I got off, and was at my door with flowers and takeout not ten minutes after I got home.

"Hey there," I replied. "Why are you smiling so hard?"

"Because I'm glad to see you. Now take this stuff so I can give you a kiss."

Grinning, I hurriedly removed the flowers and bags from his hands, stashing them on the coffee table before rushing back over into his arms. He immediately laid a deep kiss on me, his arms wrapping around me tightly.

"I missed you today," he murmured once the kiss tapered off, rubbing his nose against mine.

"I missed you, too. You should come visit me for lunch tomorrow; I've never gotten busy in my office before."

He leaned back with an amused expression. "You'd really do that?"

"Absolutely! My door locks."

"What time do you go to lunch?"

We shared a laugh before he went in for another kiss. Eventually we ended up on the couch with me on his lap, making out and teasing and giggling. That ended up pretty much being our evening, and I loved every second of it.

I'd never seen Montrel so light and carefree. For six blissful weeks, he was the ideal boyfriend, and I just knew in my soul that this was it; we'd gotten it right this time. He was finally ready for me and for us. Finally!

And everybody who had doubted Montrel's sincerity about me (and my common sense about him) would have to eat a vat of crow, because we were going the distance this time.

Well...

I guess I should've known it would only be a matter of time before the back-together high would start to fade.

One evening, we were out at his favorite museum, checking out the same exhibit I knew he had seen at least five times about Black inventors. As fascinating as that was, I didn't really want to be there. But I had a feeling if I didn't tag along, I wouldn't see him that night at all. He'd been rather quiet and subdued most of the time we were out, yet he kept insisting that everything was fine.

"You're *sure* there's nothing on your mind?" I asked him again, slightly trailing behind him.

"Yes, Claire," he droned. "You've asked me a dozen times."

"Well, you seem kind of withdrawn. I'm just concerned, that's all."

"I appreciate the concern. But there's nothing for you to worry about." He squeezed my hand gently. "I'd tell you if there was."

"All right," I shrugged, tired of asking anyway. "I'll take your word for it, then."

The rest of the day pretty much continued down this same crappy path. Montrel's mind just didn't seem to be all the way there; he was clearly distracted yet he kept insisting he wasn't. I was trying not to get frustrated, but it wasn't working.

Just like I was trying not to start getting a bad feeling in my gut. We were barely two months into this latest round of our relationship and he was already slipping back into old habits; the calls had slacked off slightly, he wasn't as eager to have our quality time, and the cute romantic gestures that he was doing right after I took him back had fallen off. And for a nice little cherry on top, he stood me up when we were supposed to have dinner with my parents.

"I thought Montrel was coming with you," Mama commented when I showed up to their house alone.

"Yeah, he was. Something came up," I replied as casually as I could. "He told me to tell y'all he was sorry, though, and he hopes he can get over here soon."

Total lie. He didn't say that. I don't even know why I bothered saying he did.

"Well, that's nice." Mama poured some cran-grape juice into a glass and handed it to me. She had a cute little set-up with a glass pitcher and nice glasses and a tray of cheese and crackers. They never used to do this kind of stuff. Guess Mama had been watching *Barefoot Contessa* or something.

"Maybe you can take him a plate. We made enough for four and you know your father and I don't eat that much."

"Sure, I'll take it to him." I'd take it but I'd likely end up eating it myself. Montrel could be real funny about eating people's cooking.

Just then, Dad came in, smiling when he saw me. "Hey, when did you sneak in?"

"Just a couple of minutes ago," I answered, smiling as I accepted his customary kiss to the forehead. "How are ya, Dad?"

"I'm great. Looking forward to Mexico."

"Mexico?"

"Yeah, Randy and I are going on a little vacation," Mama chimed in. "We're leaving next week for four days."

"Wow. Whenever I wanted us all to go on vacation back in the day, the best we ever got was driving down to Savannah."

"Don't exaggerate, Claire. We took you kids more places than that."

"Oh yeah. I forgot about the time we went all out and spent a whole three days at Myrtle Beach."

Dad shook his head as he joined Mama on the couch. "Nothing wrong with enjoying our retirement. Anyway. Where's Montrel?"

"He couldn't make it."

"Everything all right with you two?"

"Totally." I took a really long swig of juice. "He hated that he couldn't be here but something came up at the last minute that he couldn't avoid."

I was lying again. The truth was, I didn't know *why* Montrel had bailed on me, or where he was. He called me thirty minutes before we were supposed to be at my parents' and said he wouldn't be able to make it, and that was it. Didn't give a reason, didn't say he'd try to come after this mysterious thing that had suddenly come up, really didn't even apologize. It took me a good ten minutes to calm down enough to even be able to go my parents' house myself, 'cause I was majorly pissed.

"What is it that Montrel does for a living, again?" Mama asked, spreading some brie on one of her fancy crackers. No more cheddar and saltines up in this piece.

"Oh, uh...he doesn't have a traditional job. He mostly does charity work; you know, philanthropic-type stuff. Doing good in the hood."

"That's wonderful," Mama commented.

I was lying yet again. The closest Montrel came to charity work was giving his spare change to a homeless person.

But, to give him his credit, he *did* do some occasional volunteering. And he seemed to enjoy it. So that was something. I guess.

"He must be in a pretty good position financially if he's able to just focus on that and not have to work," Dad surmised.

"Oh, yeah...well, his dad left him a ton of money when he died. He didn't want Montrel or his mother to ever have to worry about anything."

And his mama spoiled him so much that he thought he was above working like the common man, since he didn't have to. But of course I kept that part to myself.

Thankfully, the subject changed to something else and we proceeded with our evening. To my (pleasant) surprise, Mama didn't bring up Warner at any point during the evening. After I told her that Montrel and I were back together, she was surprised and I knew she had questions because I had admitted to her once that I liked Warner more than I thought I would (had probably jumped the gun on that) but she didn't try to dig too much. One thing about my parents was they realized I was a grown woman who was going to make my own choices, and they kept their opinions to themselves, for the most part. I both appreciated that and resented it; sometimes it would have been nice to get some actual feedback instead of polite platitudes.

It occurred to me that my parents really didn't know all that much about Montrel. He only spent marginal time around them, and their rapport was pleasant but that was it. Montrel was never all that eager to visit them, and I knew my parents only invited him to be polite. And I wasn't making anything better because I didn't do anything to try to bridge the gap between them. They might not have said it out loud, but I knew my folks didn't care for Montrel all that much.

And I wasn't helping matters with all the lying. I actually cared what my parents thought, and I didn't want to give them the impression that I was repeatedly reconciling with a spoiled, selfish inconsiderate trust fund baby. Even if I kinda was.

The evening turned out pleasant enough and I tried to cheer myself up with the thought that I'd at least get to spend the night with Montrel after I left my parents'. And I figured since he had bailed on me with basically no explanation, he would be extra eager to get back on my good side.

But...no.

"Claire, can you scoot over a little?" he groused when I was trying to cuddle with him. "It's hot."

"You going through male menopause or something? It's not even sixty-five degrees in here. How is it hot?"

"I just need a little space, that's all. Don't take it personally."

"Just like I wasn't supposed to take it personally when you bailed on me earlier when we were supposed to go to my parent's house? They were expecting *both* of us."

"I told you, something came up."

"Yet you didn't tell me what that something was. Or should I say, *who* it was."

He leaned back, looking at me with a frown. "Are you really gonna try to go there? You think I'm cheating on you? That's an insult, Claire."

"Well, what else am I supposed to think, Montrel? You're acting real funny all of a sudden and you always give me the brush-off when I ask you what's up. This is just feeling a little too familiar."

"What's that supposed to mean?"

"What do you think it means? It's not like this is the first time you started withdrawing from me all of a sudden. And it was only a matter of time after that that you ended things. I'm not trying to go through that with you again."

"You're not. I keep telling you nothing's wrong. I just have some things on my mind, that's all."

"*What*, Montrel? I'm not trying to be nosy; maybe I can help."

"Look, I'm not trying to be difficult, but...I'd rather not talk about it."

"Of course you wouldn't." I threw the covers back and swung my legs off the bed. "Just leave me in the dark like you usually do. Our communication is going to crap again and I'm the only one that seems to care."

He sighed. "I think you're overreacting."

"Figures." I stood up, slipping my feet into my puffy house shoes.

"Where are you going?"

"Away from you."

"Claire," he reached for me. "Come back."

"That's all right. Wouldn't want to suffocate you with my body heat. We all know your aversion to sweating."

"Claire..."

"Unless you're gonna tell me the real deal about where you were earlier, we don't have anything to talk about right now."

He started to say something, then looked away. My face flamed to what felt like way more than sixty-five degrees.

"Fuck you, Montrel," I spat as stomped out of the room.

I was pissed but I was always worried. Montrel was acting funny again and I was starting to wonder if I'd made a mistake in taking him back. This was classic being -on-your-best-behavior-until-you-get-your-hooks-in stuff. He'd done this before, but I had convinced myself that this time would be different. This time we would really make it happen. Maybe it was foolish to take against-the-door cunnilingus as an indication of his sincerity, but I let myself believe that he was just that desperate to get me back, not that he was being manipulative.

Of course, I certainly hadn't gotten a repeat performance of that. Not against the door, in the bed, or anywhere else. And I surely asked for it.

I tried not to let myself think about how I had halted things with Warner when they were going so well. I'd had a good feeling about him that only got better the more time we spent together. He was attentive, funny, and a sweetheart who gave damn good foot rubs, just like he said he did. It really felt like we were starting to build something and I couldn't help but miss that, especially right then with Montrel acting like an asshole. I kinda wanted to call him, but knew I couldn't do that with Montrel in the house.

The rest of that night was a bust, needless to say. I eventually went back to bed, but I stayed on my side and he stayed on his. And two days later, I wasn't feeling any better about things. I wanted to talk to Chichi, but knew I'd have to pay the cost of her cussing me out in order to get her input.

I figured I might as well go ahead and get it over with. When I was leaving work, I dialed her number and braced myself.

"It's about damn time!" she answered on the second ring. Loudly. "Is there a reason you've been ghosting me, bitch?"

"I'm sorry about that. I've just been kinda busy."

"Look, I get that you like Warner and y'all are having a good time and everything, but that doesn't mean you have to shut your girl out. All you've done is send some texts that didn't really say anything, which is the only way I at least knew you were okay. Damn, Warner got your nose open like that already?"

"I actually haven't seen Warner lately," I informed her, trying to sound strong. Sounding timid like I was doing something wrong would only give her more ammunition. "I've been busy with other stuff."

"Something with work?"

"No, it's got nothing to do with work. To be honest, I've been hanging out with Montrel."

"What? What did you say?"

"I said I've been spending my time with Montrel."

"And why would you be doing that?"

"Because..." I squeezed my eyes shut, *so* glad we were having this conversation over the phone and not in person. "We're back together."

"*What??* You mean to tell me you actually took him back again? What the *fuck*??"

"Chichi, will you calm down? There's no need to yell."

"Hell yeah, there is! Your dumb ass is just never gonna learn, are you?"

I winced a little at that. "Give me a little credit. I wouldn't have gone there with him again if I didn't think it was going to be different this time."

"Isn't that the same bullshit you said when you took him back *last* time? And what did he do? The same damn thing he always does; sweet-talk you until you let your guard down and give him another chance and then he goes right back to doing the same shit he had been doing before. Taking you for granted. Making sure everything is on *his* terms. Keeping you in the dark about your future with him, which, I keep telling you, should tell you more than enough right there."

"Okay, Chichi," I sighed, already drained from the conversation. I wasn't about to acknowledge that she had a point. "Just go ahead; get it out of your system. Cuss me out, rip my head off, make my ears bleed...whatever you need to do. Let's get it over with."

"For what? It's not gonna make any difference. I did all that the last three times you took this punk-ass back and what good did it do?"

"Look, I get that it might seem like a stupid decision to take Montrel back again," I commented. "But...I can't explain it. I had it in my head that Montrel and I were over but when he came to see me out of the blue, it was different than any other time. He was contrite and sincere and persistent..."

"Whatever."

"I really wish you wouldn't be like that."

"And *I* really wish you would open your eyes to what this man is."

"And what is he, Chichi?"

"He's a Time Waster," she informed. "He leads you on to nowhere. And when you dare try to move on, he can't stand it and will do or say anything necessary to get you back, even though nothing will really change."

"So, what, he just doesn't have any feelings for me at all, huh?"

"Maybe he does. Not enough to progress to anywhere, though. He might like the *idea* of being with you, but when he's actually in it, he punks out. He doesn't want to see you with anybody else because he likes keeping you in his pocket for him to play with whenever he's in the mood for you."

"That's...that's ridiculous," I scoffed, even though she was making sense again. That *did* kind of sound like it applied to Montrel and his pattern.

But I didn't want to admit or believe that. I couldn't. My heart was locked in on believing that Montrel had the purest of intentions with me; that we were on the same page when it came to what we ultimately wanted out of a relationship with each other (despite the fact that we still hadn't *really* talked about it). If that wasn't the case, that would make me a comically big fool and Montrel would never make a fool out of me like that.

Would he?

"Claire," Chichi sighed. "I see there really isn't anything I can say to you because you're so sprung over this man that you can't see the real deal. You've got blinders on to what's as clear as day to everybody else. And unfortunately, I'm seeing that it's probably gonna take you getting big-time hurt or humiliated or both before you finally get the picture."

I'd already been humiliated plenty. It's funny how that was my mental defense instead of an eye-opening revelation. Your man wasn't *supposed* to humiliate you. But I had become quite adept at making excuses for Montrel's behavior, almost without even realizing it.

"He's gonna hurt you again," Chichi predicted. Her voice was so calm now that it was making me a little uncomfortable. "You're going to end up flat on your face, girl. I wish to high heaven that I was wrong, but I've seen this too many times; my sister went through the same thing for damn near six years. And like her, one day you're gonna look up and realize that years have passed and you and Montrel will still be doing the same dance you're doing now. That's if he doesn't go off and marry somebody else behind your back, like my sister's ex ended up doing. Only then will you realize just how much time you wasted on someone who doesn't want what you want; time that could've been spent with someone that actually appreciates and respects you. And you're gonna kick yourself for that."

"I appreciate the concern, but there *is* the possibility that you could be wrong about all this," I felt I had to say. "Sometimes it takes people longer to come around than others. It doesn't mean he's going to string me along for years and years. Montrel loves me; I sincerely believe that. He wouldn't knowingly do me like that."

Even though I'd been having concerns and doubts about my and Montrel's relationship, I still felt compelled to defend him. Defend *us*. Montrel wasn't perfect but he wasn't evil, either. And to me, anyone who would purposefully waste someone's time and love like that was evil.

Chichi didn't even bother with a rebuttal.

"Okay, girl," she sighed. "For your sake, I hope I'm wrong."

For my sake, I hoped she was, too.

Eleven - Claire

• • • •

BIG SURPRISE, I COULDN'T get Chichi's warning out of my head.

As much as I wanted to brush it off and forget about it, I couldn't. Even if I didn't admit it out loud, what she said had some merit. Montrel *did* have a pattern of being on his best behavior at first and then sliding back to sometimey, inconsistent, standoffish asshole territory.

Why the hell did I love this man, again?

Maybe it would be common sense to leave him alone; see if I could make anything happen with Warner or whoever else. Montrel had taken me through a lot and yet, there I was with him again. And why? Because he voluntarily ate me out? Even I knew that was a stupid reason.

Yet and still, I was determined to prove Chichi wrong. I didn't want her to be right about this, because that would say a lot about me. Despite everything, I loved Montrel, even if nobody else could understand why. And I believed he loved me. Yes, I knew love wasn't always enough. But it even said in the Bible that love was patient and kind. Montrel was worth my patience and (sometimes forced) kindness. It might take some time and some adjustments, but I truly believed we could make it. Not every relationship is a straight line to forever.

After I thoroughly hyped myself up with all this, I called Montrel. My energy was up and I needed to do something to get this prove-Chichi-wrong train moving.

"What's up, Claire?"

"Hey...what are you doing?"

"Doing my weekly shoe shine."

My eye roll came all on its own. Couldn't help it. "Yeah, so I was wondering if you wanted to hang out tonight. I miss you."

"Uh, tonight?"

"Yes...is that a problem?"

"It's not a *problem*. Can we do it tomorrow night, though?"

"Why? What's wrong with tonight?"

"I just have something to do, that's all."

"What?"

"Why does it matter?"

"Why can't you tell me?"

"I'm not sure what's up with all of your suspicion lately, but I can't say I'm in love with all the grilling every time I say something you don't like."

"Oh yeah? Well, I can't say *I'm* in love with how secretive you are every time I ask you for details on something. For someone who's always saying he has nothing to hide you sure do keep some tight lips. You wouldn't like it if I did that to you. And don't try to say it's none of my business; I'm not asking for your social security number. I just want to know what it is you're doing this evening. Why is that such a big damn deal?"

"Okay, fine." He sighed. "If you just *have* to know, I'm going to see Mother."

"Nice. How 'bout I just go with you?"

He hesitated. Why was he hesitating?

"Why are you hesitating??"

"Claire, you...you don't have to do that," he finally stammered. "We're just going to be sitting around drinking coffee and getting caught up. You wouldn't enjoy it."

"I don't mind. It would be nice to spend some more time with your mother."

I was stretching the truth with that. I actually didn't care for the stuck-up heffah. But she and Montrel were so close and he would surely have an issue with my not liking her, so I'd gotten really good at faking it.

"That's sweet of you, but I wouldn't want to subject you to that. Why don't you just stay in, watch one of your movies, maybe give yourself a pedicure..."

My face tightened at that statement but I chose not to address it. He was always making little digs at my feet and one day he was going to catch me at the wrong time and get told off. But I'd let it pass this time.

"I've already done that," I lied. "I'd like to go with you. Then we can spend the night together later doing various fun things in my bed."

"Yeah?" he quickly responded, sounding way more energetic than he had a minute earlier. Men were so easy. "I guess it *would* be beneficial for the two of you to spend a little time together."

"Of course it would."

"All right...I'll come get you in about an hour. Can you be ready by then?"

"I'll just meet you over there. I have a couple of things I need to do first."

Truth was, I wanted to be in my own car in case Ms. Annie said something off the wall to me like she had a tendency to do, and I could go ahead and leave. I didn't want to have to sit there and wait on Montrel, who seemed oblivious to her condescending and sometimes rude statements.

"Okay, just try not to be late," he cautioned. "You know how Mother is about punctuality."

I didn't see what the big deal was for being right on time to sit in her prissy living room; she didn't even serve dinner or anything on these visits. It was always just coffee and maybe some kind of pastry or finger food. I wondered if the woman even ate hearty stuff.

But I kept those thoughts to myself. As usual. "Yeah."

Montrel

• • • •

I DID NOT WANT CLAIRE going with me to Mother's.

Mother didn't like her. And I wasn't stupid; Claire wasn't exactly a fan of my mother's, either, though I knew she tried to be for my sake. For my own peace of mind, I just tried to avoid the two of them getting together as much as possible.

But, Claire was my lady, and she was important to me. And Mother was the most important person in my life. So I knew I couldn't keep them apart forever.

I headed over to Mother's early, hoping to get a call or text from Claire telling me that she'd changed her mind or something had come up. Or that maybe she'd decided to spend the evening with her boisterous friend Chichi, instead. It was one time I wouldn't have minded being stood up.

"Come in, dear," Mother greeted me when I arrived. She accepted my kiss on the cheek as I entered. The music of the evening this time was Beethoven, apparently. "It's good to see you."

"You, too. You look nice," I informed, admiring her silk off-white sleeveless top and pants. I couldn't remember many times at all where Mother had dressed casually. She didn't even own a pair of jeans. I held up a gift bag that contained one of her favorite perfumes. "This is for you."

She smiled, taking it from me. "Thank you, dear. That's very considerate. Come; I have lattes and pastries."

I followed her into the living room, figuring this was as good a time as any to let her know about our unplanned guest. "You know else who likes lattes? Claire."

Mother stopped and turned towards me with slightly narrowed eyes. "Okay..."

"Isn't that a fun coincidence?"

"Not really."

"I think it is."

"You're being nonsensical, dear, and you know I don't care for that."

"Okay, fine." I pasted a smile on my face. "Claire is going to be joining us this evening. Isn't that nice?"

Mother slightly rolled her eyes before taking a seat on the chaise, tucking the gift bag next to her. "You invited her?"

No. "Sure."

She cocked a brow. "Sure?"

"Well, I agreed that it would be good for my two favorite ladies to spend some time together."

"I see. You know, dear, I was a little surprised when you told me the two of you had reconciled."

"Why?"

"I just thought you had moved on, is all."

"I changed my mind."

"Again?"

"Mother..."

"I'm just saying, Montrel. You've *changed your mind* several times with this young lady. I don't understand why you're so indecisive."

"I don't think it's a matter of being indecisive...sometimes I'm just not entirely sure what I want and I jump the gun a little. But clearly she's someone I want to be with since I keep going back to her."

"*Or*, there could be something *else* behind that," Mother hedged pointedly, spreading a linen napkin over her lap.

Before I could ask her to elaborate, the doorbell rang. Mother looked at her watch.

"She's *not* late," I quickly defended as I stood to get the door. Mother just took a delicate sip of her latte.

"You're late!" I hissed at Claire as soon as I opened the door.

"Sorry; there was some accident that had the traffic backed up," Claire explained, stepping into the house. "And I'm like ten minutes late, if that."

"You know how Mother is about tardiness."

"What is the big deal? It's not like I could help it. I left in plenty of time."

"This is why I should've just picked you up."

"Montrel, why are you acting like I missed the unveiling of some kind of rare find that only a select few are privileged to see? We're sitting in her living room."

"Keep your voice down!"

"I'm not even talking loud. Oh my gosh, I hate when you get like this..."

"Like what?"

"All extra and paranoid when it comes to your mama. She has some kind of weird hold on you."

"I have no idea what you're talking about."

"Of course you don't."

"We don't have time for this." My eyes swept over her, taking in her outfit and making sure nothing was out of place. She was wearing a light sweater and jeans, and a pair of ankle boots. We looked so mismatched since I was donning a button down, sport coat, slacks and freshly-shined Prada loafers. She would look just fine if we were going to Starbucks but I wished she hadn't dressed so casually to join me and Mother. I didn't think I had to tell her that but I guess I should have.

Choosing not to comment on it, though, and start another argument, I just grabbed her hand and led her into the living room to join Mother.

When we entered the room, I saw Mother give Claire the once-over just like I did, though she wasn't as subtle about her distaste for what she saw. I felt Claire's hand tense up in mine and I prayed she didn't say anything disrespectful.

"Look who's here, Mother," I announced, smiling probably a little too hard.

"Hello, Mrs. Burns," Claire greeted politely.

"Claire." Mother nodded to her slightly. "Nice of you to join us."

"Thank you."

"I'm surprised you and Montrel didn't arrive together, seeing as how you've reunited...again."

Claire's polite smile grew tight. "I had some errands to run so I figured it would just be better to drive my own car."

"Hmm. Please, have a seat."

I held on to Claire's hand as we sat next to each other on the loveseat. I felt Claire trying to ease her hand out of mine but I held on to it, as if doing so would put on a united front or something. I had a feeling it would be necessary.

A few awkward moments passed, with Mother sipping her latte and looking elsewhere. She didn't seem to want to engage in conversation now that Claire was there, so I figured it was up to me to keep things moving. It wasn't like there was a TV I could turn on to distract us; Mother didn't like most television and rarely watched. The only television in the house was in the rarely-used den, and I bought that for her.

"Want a latte, sweetheart?" I asked Claire.

"Sure, yeah."

"What about a croissant? They're filled with lemon curd. Made fresh just this morning."

She shot me a strange look. "No, thanks. Not a huge lemon curd fan."

"Hmph," Mother scoffed, having just put a croissant on her saucer.

I glanced at Claire and chuckled as if that was some kind of joke before pouring her latte. Mother certainly wasn't going to do it. She was already acting like Claire wasn't even there.

"So..." Claire hedged after some sips of her latte and more strained moments of silence, "What were you two talking about before I got here?"

"That doesn't concern you, dear," Mother immediately responded before I could.

"You weren't missing anything, anyway," I quickly added, rubbing Claire's knee and silently begging her to stop shooting that death glare at Mother. "It was just some small talk."

"Yes, that we were quite enjoying before we were interrupted," Mother added. "I wasn't aware we were going to be having guests."

"Mother..."

"I didn't think my coming by would be such an inconvenience," Claire replied in a clipped tone. "And I thought Montrel would have mentioned that I would be coming."

"Oh, he did," Mother confirmed, dabbing her mouth with a napkin. "Right before you arrived."

"Oh?" Claire cocked a brow at me. "You waited until the last minute to-"

"I admit it slipped my mind but what does it matter?" I interjected with an uneasy chuckle. "You're here now and we're happy to have you."

"Speak for yourself, dear," Mother corrected.

"Mother!"

"I'm sorry...do you have a problem with my being here or something?" Claire asked Mother, sitting forward in her seat. She sat her barely-sipped latte on the coffee table and I immediately moved it onto a coaster before Mother could say anything about it. "Or do you just have a problem with me, in general?"

Mother put down her own saucer and looked right at Claire. "Well, now that you mention it-"

"Whoa, let's not go there!" I cut in, sitting forward in my own seat. "Mother, did you spike your latte or something? Or forget to take your *special pill*?"

She narrowed her eyes at me but I silently pleaded with her to chill out. The last thing I needed or wanted was for her and Claire to get into it. Claire's politeness was only going to go so far and I knew that; it would only be so many snide comments before she stopped caring that she was talking to my mother.

Thankfully, Mother seemed to heed my quiet pleas and picked up her saucer again. I turned to flash a smile at Claire, but she was looking anything but happy.

"It's fine," I mouthed at her, trying to assure myself of that, as well. Claire shot a wary look at me, but just gave a slight nod.

This was not going well. We sat there yet again in silence for several minutes, with Mother clearly having no interest in conversation with Claire and Claire having already run out of whatever small amount of interest she had when she got there. I didn't know what was up. Of course I knew that Mother was never a fan of Claire's, but she was always somewhat pleasant towards her. Now, she was just being rude and I didn't understand why. Even if she didn't agree with my taking Claire back, it didn't mean she had to behave like this.

"So, sweetheart," I finally said to Claire, after forcing down two croissants. This silence was driving me crazy. "How have things been going at work? I bet those kids have been keeping you on your toes at the school."

"Um, yeah," Claire responded. She seemed to be willing to forget the previous few minutes, which I appreciated. "It's actually been kind of heavy. You wouldn't believe what some of these kids have to deal with at home. It can be tough to listen to."

"But I bet they feel better after talking to you, though," I replied sincerely. I really did respect what Claire did for a living. Her being a school counselor might not have been impressive to Mother but it was to me. "They must feel some comfort level with you to confide in you, I'd imagine."

"I'd like to think so. Sometimes it can take a little work to get them to open up, though."

"That's understandable. Kids can be kinda skeptical. I doubt I would have confided in a counselor when I was that age."

"Not that you had anything to complain about," Mother chimed in, easing the last of her croissant into her mouth. "I made sure you had everything you needed, so you didn't need any counseling."

Claire's face hardened. "With all due respect, Mrs. Burns, having everything doesn't mean people don't have problems. Some of the most privileged people have the most issues."

"Nobody is ever satisfied. You can give some children the world and they'd *still* have something to whine about."

"Uh, it's not *whining* when they're feeling ignored because their parents think that buying them something is a substitute for quality time, or when they're being emotionally abused, or when they feel like a pawn that one parent is using to get back at the other."

"Everybody has problems," Mother dismissed, helping herself to another latte. "Life isn't always supposed to be easy."

"Nobody said it is. But there are some things *no* child should have to go through."

"I see. And you're the person to make that determination, I take it?"

"It's more human decency than anything."

I winced at that. That was a definite dig and I wished yet again that I had tried harder to talk Claire out of coming over there. I should have known it wouldn't go well.

Mother paused at Claire's words, then slowly turned to look at her. "Are you implying something?"

"Not at all. I'm saying it flat-out."

"Okay!" I clapped my hands. "Let's talk about something else!"

"Well, then it's only fair for me to say something *flat-out*, then," Mother replied to Claire, ignoring my desperate attempt at diversion. "Since we're being honest."

Claire shrugged. "Come with it."

"I'm not thrilled about you being with my son."

Oh no...

"Oh really?" Claire sat forward in her seat, resting her forearms on her knees and looking straight at Mother. I noticed her hands clenched into fists that I could only *hope* she wasn't planning on using. "And why is that? Don't think I'm good enough for him or something?"

"Not *or something*; I *don't* think you're good enough for him," Mother confirmed flatly, matching Claire's glare. "You two don't have anything in common, you don't come from the right kind of background-"

"The right kind of background? What, the kind where we actually have to work and earn whatever we have? I'm *so* sorry that I didn't have someone in my family die and leave me so much money that I could pretend like I'm royalty and above everybody else."

Mother's face tightened and I looked at Claire incredulously. I couldn't believe she said that. Yes, my father left us enough money when he died where we'd be set for life, but that wasn't something that needed to be tossed in our faces like it was a bad thing.

"You're beneath Montrel," Mother snapped, clearly giving up on any attempt at restraint. "I don't know what it is he sees in you that makes him keep coming back to you time and time again, but I pray for the day that he finally stops wasting time and finds someone more suitable for him. I assume the main reason he can't seem to stay away from you is to satisfy his primal physical desires."

"So I'm only good enough for sex. Is that what you're saying?"

"I'm saying that has to be the reason he's attracted to you. Even though you're certainly different physically than the nice ladies he used to date. Only he knows what the attraction is, but I'm sure it's only temporary. He'll snap out of it soon enough." She looked at me. "Right, dear?"

I felt my face flush as both Mother and Claire peered at me expectantly. I knew I was supposed to say something but for whatever reason, I couldn't make myself speak. Part of me was still so stunned that I was in this position at all. Mother and Claire had never been best friends but this was the last thing I was expecting to happen.

The more seconds that ticked by, the more heat I could feel radiating from Claire beside me. The fact that I hadn't already vehemently denied Mother's proclamation was probably just pushing me farther back into the doghouse, but I'll admit, Claire's little dig about how we got our money had kind of annoyed me. Why'd she have to go there?

"Nothing to say, Montrel?" Claire asked pointedly. Her question seemed more of a confirmation than anything else, because in the next second she stood and grabbed her purse.

"Oh, you're leaving?" Mother asked with a sarcastic smirk.

"Yes, I'm leaving," Claire confirmed. "And I sure as hell won't be coming back over here."

"Finally, some good news."

Claire opened her mouth to say something back, but I quickly grabbed her hand and looked up at her, my eyes pleading with her to let it go. She looked at me incredulously before her eyes darkened, and I knew she was pissed. Not that I didn't already know, but this was a different level. There was a flash of emptiness before she yanked her hand free, turned, and stomped out of the house, slamming the door behind her.

"So unladylike," Mother scoffed, picking up her cup.

I just dropped my head into my hands.

Twelve - Montrel

• • • •

NEEDLESS TO SAY, CLAIRE wasn't talking to me.

It had been four days since the showdown at Mother's, and despite several attempts to apologize, I was no more on Claire's good side than I was before that disastrous coffee date. She wasn't trying to hear anything I had to say.

"I don't blame her one bit," Forrest declared when I told him about all this. "I wouldn't be talking to your ass after that, either."

I sighed. "So I hesitated a little bit. I was put on the spot."

"There shouldn't have *been* any hesitation, Montrel," Giselle chimed in, bringing bowls of dip and hummus to the table Forrest and I were seated at in their dining room. "Your mother totally disrespected your girlfriend and you said nothing to defend her."

"Well, it's not like Claire was totally innocent in all this, either. I told y'all what she said about our money."

"Hell, was she lying?" Forrest asked. "Your pops *did* leave y'all enough money where you don't have to work and neither of you really do anything-"

"Hey, I resent that! I do volunteer work and stuff. And why worry about working a job I don't like when I don't have to?"

"It doesn't have to *be* something you don't like. You're in a position where you don't have to do anything you don't like. Idiot."

"Regardless, Claire didn't have to say that."

"She was defending herself. Since you clearly weren't doing it."

Giselle placed three bottles of water on the table before taking a seat next to Forrest, tucking some of her big curly hair behind her ear. "Seriously, Montrel, you can't understand why Claire is so upset with you?"

"Hey, I tried to apologize. Even though..."

Forrest looked at me. "Even though, what?"

"I don't *really* feel like I did anything wrong."

"How the hell do you figure that?"

"Okay, Mother stepped over the line. But what was I supposed to do? I can't disrespect my mother."

"But it's okay for your mother to disrespect your woman?"

"I didn't say that..."

"You basically did. I wouldn't be surprised if you agreed with the shit your mama said and you're actually relieved that you didn't have to be the one to say it."

"That's ridiculous!"

"Is it? Because if you *really* wanted to, you would have stood up for your lady and your relationship. Shouldn't nobody be able to say anything about what's going on between the two of you, regardless of what issues you have going on."

"That's true, even though I'm sure Montrel knows all about *our* issues," Giselle interjected, dipping her tortilla chip into the hummus. "There's no telling what you've told him about us."

Forrest's head swung around to her. "What does that have to do with anything?"

"So you'd be willing to tell me *everything* you've ever told Montrel about the problems we've been having getting pregnant and everything else?"

"I confided in him like you do with friends, and like I'm willing to bet you've done with Claire and all those other girlfriends you're always gabbing to. But I haven't disrespected you to anybody. And I damn sure wouldn't let anybody else disrespect you in front of me."

"Oh, really?"

"Yes, really."

"Maybe you don't say I'm beneath you or anything like Mrs. Burns said about Claire but I'm sure you've said *something*. You certainly have plenty to say when we're fighting around here."

"Can we not do this right now? We're fussing at Montrel."

"And I'm just saying you should probably think about taking your own advice."

"What the hell are you talking about? You just want to assume I've dogged you and you're taking that and running with it without any kind of proof whatsoever. I'm not trying to go back and forth with you about this shit."

"See, this is part of the problem, Forrest; you just dismiss my concerns like they're nothing. I don't appreciate that."

"And *I* don't appreciate how you're always trying to *make* something out of nothing. We were doing perfectly fine before you had to start a fucking argument."

"That's not what I'm doing!"

"The hell it's not. Sometimes I think you just like stirring stuff up so you'll have something else to tell your friends about."

Giselle gasped. "Excuse me??"

Thankfully my phone rang right then. I quickly pulled it out of my pocket and was only marginally disappointed that it was Mother calling.

I excused myself from the table, not that the feuding lovebirds noticed. They kept going back and forth with each other as I stood and eased out of the dining room.

"Hello, Mother," I answered the call after I had stepped outside.

"I have some very good news, dear."

"Yeah?" Part of me hoped to hear that she contacted Claire to apologize for the things she said, but I knew better than that. "What is it?"

"I've met the woman you're going to marry."

"Um, excuse me?"

"I met your future wife. Her name is Aurora Chadwick and she's a doll. I've already told her all about you and she can't wait for you two to get together."

"Get together?"

"Yes, Montrel," Mother confirmed, as if I was on the slow bus or something. "As I said, she's perfect for you. Cultured, educated, refined, respectful, and cute as a button. Reminds me a lot of myself thirty years ago, in fact."

I guess this was supposed to be a selling point.

"I've given her your contact information and I'm going to give you hers," Mother continued. "She's waiting for your call. But before you contact her, you need to make sure you take care of that *other* situation first."

Even though I knew the answer, I asked, "Meaning?"

"You need to end it with Claire," Mother quickly answered. "For good this time. You need to move on with your life, dear. You're in your thirties; it's time for you to get serious and settle down. You've sowed enough of your...*wild oats* and had your fun and all that. It's time to grow up."

She made it sound like marriage was some kind of purgatory. Like all fun stopped once you got married. Though judging by Forrest and Giselle, that could very well be the case.

"I see," I finally replied, absently eyeing the cars moving up and down the street.

"So make sure you take care of that, if you haven't already," Mother continued. "Aurora deserves your complete attention, so I don't want you to be preoccupied."

"Right..."

"Let me know when you're in the clear. I'll expect to hear from you soon, dear. No need in dragging this out, especially since you clearly agreed with me and everything I said about you and Claire the other day."

"Actually, Mother-"

"Oh, I have to go let the decorator in; I decided to re-do my bedroom. Talk to you later, dear."

She hung up. I just looked at the phone in my hand before sighing and letting my head fall back, suddenly mentally exhausted. I wasn't thrilled about anything Mother said, regarding trying to set me up or ordering me to officially end things with Claire. I didn't need her to run my love life. It was up to me to determine who my future wife was and up to me to decide if I wanted to leave Claire alone.

Not that it mattered, anyway, as far as that last one, since Claire wasn't talking to me. It was probably already over, as far as she was concerned. This didn't seem like a tantrum or a temporary silent treatment. She'd blocked my calls, she wouldn't answer her door when I went to her house, and the flowers I sent ended up in the trash, confirmed by the picture she posted on her Instagram twenty minutes after they were delivered.

I wasn't thrilled about things ending like this. The thought of Claire getting to this level of 'fed up' with me caused an ache in my gut that I couldn't dismiss.

But maybe this was a sign that Claire and I just weren't meant to be together. We were trying to force something that clearly wasn't there. I loved her, but like she pointed out, that wasn't everything. Maybe Mother saw something that I wasn't able to see. Maybe Mother had done me a favor, albeit in an unpleasant way. She did what I wasn't able to do.

If I was honest with myself, I had been questioning my decision to get back with Claire recently. I just wasn't entirely sure that it was the right decision, at least at this time. When I had gone to Claire's and asked her to take me back, I meant everything I said in the moment. And I was all in, at first. But over time, I felt myself drifting away again. I couldn't even explain it to myself, but that could only mean I hadn't made the right decision. If I had, I'd be sure about it, right?

The idea of meeting this Aurora woman started sounding better and better the more I thought about it. It would certainly be less of a headache for me, since Mother already approved of her. Maybe this was just what I needed.

Claire

• • • •

HOW STUPID WAS I?

Every time I thought about how Montrel sat there mute while his mama disrespected me, not opening his sorry mouth to defend me even once, it just boiled my blood all over again. *This* was the man I wanted to be with so badly? Why did I keep doing this to myself?

Yeah, he called me trying to apologize. But not once in those voicemails or texts did he say he was sorry for not coming to my defense; he just said he was sorry that 'the whole scene happened.' I knew he hadn't really even wanted me there in the first place, and was probably rationalizing it some kind of way to make it my fault. To avoid that, I went ahead and blocked him.

I really didn't need this.

What I needed was to put this man out of my life, and for real this time. When I thought about it, there were more cons than pros when it came to Montrel. He wasn't all the way in like I needed him to be; like I *deserved* for him to be. That wasn't a relationship that could last. Hell, he wouldn't even talk about our future together. That should've told me everything I needed to know right there, but I was too busy making excuses for him to admit it.

After trying for the fifth time to finish the reports I was working on, I moved them to the side and put my head in my hands on my desk at Monroe Hills High School. I wanted to get over this man already. Why wasn't there a button I could press to erase him and everything about him out of my system?

My cell phone vibrated but I ignored it. I didn't have time to read any more of Montrel's half-assed apologies, that he was now sending to my Instagram DMs. I had barely done a thing since I'd gotten to work but agonize over my (again) failed relationship with Montrel and kick myself for how dumb I was for taking him back in the first place. And eat doughnuts.

"Ms. Hutchinson?"

I looked up to see Miranda, one the seniors I counseled, poking her head into my office. I'd been so out of it that I'd totally forgotten we had an appointment scheduled. The last thing I felt like doing was counseling these teenagers in my state of mind, but I needed to get myself together before I was out of a job as well as a man.

"Yes, Miranda, come on in," I said, hurriedly adjusting some things on my desk. "Lost track of time for a second, there."

"That's usually my dad's excuse when he's late," Miranda huffed, dropping onto the small couch I had crammed into the corner of my office. I thought it would make students more comfortable than sitting in a hard chair in front of my desk. "We were supposed to go get my prom dress this past weekend and he never showed up."

"Did he call, at least?" I asked, pulling her file out of my drawer.

"Eventually. But Mama wouldn't let me talk to him. They just started fussing like they always do."

"Did you try talking to your mother about how that makes you feel when she does that?"

"She won't listen. And anyway, I'm used to all that; it's not anything new. I'm about to get my own cell phone so I can talk to him on my own. I wanted to talk to you about something else."

"Okay. What's that?"

"Well," Miranda pushed her long braids over her shoulder. "I'm going to college out of state and my boyfriend is staying here. I'm worried that he's going to meet somebody else."

"Oh..." I'd much rather talk about her parents than this. "And you want to stay together after you two graduate?"

"Yeah! We love each other. But he couldn't afford to go to the same college I'm going to. And he said that we can just Facetime and text and talk on the phone every day, but I'm not stupid enough to think we can keep that up the whole four years we're in school. He could meet somebody in one of his classes or something and decide it's easier to just be with her."

"True. So why not just end things now, then? Or agree to date other people until you graduate from college?"

"I don't really like the thought of him with anybody else."

"Well, Miranda, the truth is, you're both really young with a whole bunch of life ahead of you. College is an amazing time of your life that you should be enjoying instead of worrying about what your boyfriend is doing day in and day out. And if he's hundreds of miles away from you, that's exactly what you're gonna be doing."

"Long distance relationships can work, though."

"Sure, they can. But unless you both are on the same page, things can fall apart. It's hard for *adults* to maintain long distance relationships, let alone teenagers. I'm not saying you two *can't* do it, but I *am* suggesting that you consider whether or not it's worth it."

She played with her silver bracelet. "We *have* to make it work, Ms. Hutchinson."

"Why do you say it like that?" I peered at her. "Miranda, is there something else going on here? Are you pregnant?"

"No!" she immediately replied. "No, I am *not* pregnant. We haven't even gone *there* yet."

"That's good to know."

"But that is another thing I'm worried about, though," Miranda confessed. "I know he wants to. And I kinda want to, but haven't been really ready yet. And if I don't do it with him before we graduate, he'll probably find somebody else to do it with."

"If you think he'll do that, then why would you want to be with him at all?"

"He says he'd never cheat on me. But I know how a lot of boys are; I hear how they talk to their friends and stuff. Ray seems to be more mature than that but who knows what he says to his boys when he knows I can't hear him."

"Sounds to me like you're having some doubts, Miranda. And your virginity isn't something you can get back once it's gone."

"I know. But..."

"But..."

"I don't want to be like my parents," Miranda finally blurted. "Do you know how many times they broke up before they finally got divorced? Now all they do is argue and bitch about-"

"Miranda."

"Sorry. But that's what they do. They just blame each other for everything and try to put me in the middle. And they were high school sweethearts, too."

"So...you want to prove you can have a successful relationship out of high school unlike them?"

"Maybe it's stupid. And I know it probably doesn't make a lot of sense. But they spent so many years going back and forth with each other, breaking up and getting back together more times than I can count, that now they're to the point where they don't even like each other. How sad is that?"

I felt my face flush as I scribbled a note on my notepad. "Yes, that's really sad to hear, how a couple can get to that point after being so in love."

"And I overheard my mama on the phone one day telling my aunt how she wishes she had left Daddy alone years ago. She said something about regretting not getting with some other guy she had met back in the day. Part of me wishes she could find him now and stop being so mad at the world."

"I get that this is a difficult thing for you to be in the middle of. But you shouldn't try to force a relationship with your boyfriend to try to one-up your parents. One way you can *not* be like them is to know when to move on."

She looked down at her hands. "I guess."

"Look, just enjoy your time with Ray while you're both still here. Go to the prom. Do all the fun senior stuff that's gonna be going on. Don't put so much pressure on things. Your parents' issues are *theirs*; don't make them yours. Focus on living your life and doing what's best for *you*. And if that involves you and Ray staying together through college, then great. But if not, it's not the end of the world; who's to say you can't get back together later?"

"That's true."

"You're so lucky, Miranda. You're starting off with a clean slate. You can make your own choices about how your life is going to go. Use what happened with your parents as a learning experience, not as a challenge. You don't have anything to prove, as far as that."

She peered at me, processing my words. "I never thought about it like that. You make a lot of sense, Ms. Hutchinson. This stuff has been bugging me so much lately that I haven't even been able to have fun with Ray these last few weeks. Now I kinda wish I could get that time back. And once I *do* leave for school, I don't want to be worrying so much about what Ray is doing that I can't focus in college and enjoy my time there."

"Exactly."

"Wow, I actually feel better about all this now," Miranda revealed, finally smiling. "Thanks so much for breaking it down for me like that."

"Glad I could help."

"I bet Ray will be glad to hear this; we've been going back and forth about this stuff for days."

"I can imagine. You just have to learn to go with your gut sometimes. Do what's best for you."

"What's best for me. Right. That's what I need to do." She stood, slinging her backpack over her shoulder. "I'm gonna talk to Ray. Thanks for the advice, Ms. Hutchinson."

"Anytime, Miranda."

She left my office and I sat back in my chair, processing our conversation. How was that for a sign? Miranda's situation seemed a little too familiar, with her parents going back and forth for years only to end up unhappy. If I was looking for any more signs to leave Montrel alone, there it was. I didn't want to look up years later and wish I'd moved on with my life. And god forbid we had any children and ended up putting them through what Miranda was going through.

I rounded out my notes from my talk with Miranda and turned to my computer to check some emails. My phone vibrated again and I reached over and grabbed it, prepared to delete whatever message Montrel had sent this time when I saw it was actually Warner calling. I gasped and put the phone down, a little surprised that he was still calling after I'd been ignoring him for so long. I wanted to answer his call but had no idea what I'd say. It was still too embarrassing to admit what really happened. But the larger part of me wanted to talk to him so I told myself to suck it up.

The call had gone to voicemail by then so I called him back. I nervously drummed my fingers on the desk, still not totally sure what I was going to say.

"I was wondering if I was ever going to hear from you again."

"Yeah...I'm sorry about that. Hey, Warner."

"What's been going on, Claire? I've been trying to call and you just fell off the face of the earth, seems like. I'm at least glad to hear you're all right."

"I'm fine. Just...stupid."

"Don't say that. Maybe you *did* something stupid but *you're* not stupid."

"That's sweet of you to say. Warner, I don't wanna beat around the bush or insult you by trying to be vague. I was avoiding you because I had gotten back with my ex and was too embarrassed to tell you, especially since you knew about the stuff I'd been through with him before. I know it makes me look weak."

"I see."

"I understand if you don't want to deal with me anymore after hearing this. If it makes any difference, though, we broke up again."

"What happened?"

"He helped me realize what a mistake I had made, going there with him again. We don't want the same things and I was wasting my time."

"So why didn't you call me?"

"Didn't wanna look like an idiot. Or insult you by ghosting you and then slinking back when my decision blew up in my face."

"Well, Claire, I'd be a lot more upset if we were in an exclusive relationship, but we were just dating and getting to know each other," Warner reminded me. "I can understand it being uncomfortable but I wish you would have just been honest with me about getting back with your ex. I might not have been happy to hear it but I would have understood. You can't help who you love."

"But I don't *want* to love him," I protested. "I want to move on."

"So does that mean you'd be willing to hang out with me again? No pressure."

I grinned. "Really?"

"Yeah. I like you, Claire. I'm not trying to push you or rush you or anything, and if you don't think you're ready, I get it-"

"No, I'm ready," I quickly assured. "I like you, too. Truth be told, I shouldn't have stopped hanging out with you in the first place. And this isn't about me trying to use you as a rebound to get my mind off of Montrel. I really do want to spend time with you and see where things can go."

"I'm glad to hear that."

"I just hope you can be patient with me."

"Of course. We just need to be straight up with each other about what we're feeling so we stay on the same page."

"Absolutely."

"Look, I need to get back to work but I'll call you tonight, if that's okay."

"Looking forward to it."

"Good." He was smiling; I could tell. "Talk to you later, Claire."

"Bye, Warner."

I hung up the phone, feeling better than I had in days.

Thirteen – Montrel

• • • •

I SAT ACROSS THE TABLE from Aurora at the fancy seafood restaurant Mother had suggested, wondering what we'd talk about next. Not that our conversation up until that point had been exactly mind-blowing.

"Would you like to try some of my scallops?" she asked me. Her voice was unusually soft.

"Oh, no thanks. I'm good."

"Are you allergic?"

I looked up at her in mild surprise. "No, not allergic…just don't want any scallops."

"That's too bad."

She was acting like the scallops would give me magical powers or something. I resisted the urge to check my watch again.

I wanted to leave. This date was a waste of time. Aurora was nice enough, but we weren't a match. We didn't have anything in common, from what I could tell. I had to wonder what in the hell Mother saw in this woman to make her think I'd ever want her to be my wife one day.

For one, I guess she was cute, but I wouldn't have given her a second look if I saw her out and about. Two, her voice was so annoyingly soft that it made me want to scream. And three, she just wasn't very interesting. I was actually *bored*.

But I knew Mother would be checking in with Aurora after this and would be on my ass if she got an unfavorable report.

"So..." I hedged, racking my brain for something to talk about. "You, ahh...what do you like to do?"

"Do?"

"Yeah. Like in your free time."

"I've always thought that was a strange expression, *free time*. We don't call the time we're busy *charged time*, do we?"

I stared at her, hoping she was joking. "What?"

"It's just one of those things I think about. Like why God made some berries and mushrooms poisonous."

So she was a ditz, too. Wonderful. "Yeah. Anyway, do you have any hobbies?"

"Not really. Though I do enjoy watching butterfly videos."

"Butterfly videos?"

"Yes. And vacuuming. I really enjoy vacuuming."

Oh my god. I was never listening to Mother again when it came to women, I don't care how mad at me she got.

I started eating faster so we could get this date over with. There was no need in wasting any more time on this. It wasn't happening.

"Why are you eating so fast?" she asked me.

I started to be honest but figured there was no reason to be mean. Hopefully I'd never see her again after that night. "It's getting cold."

"It's a salad."

"Warm, then. I just want to get on with the evening, that's all."

Her eyes brightened slightly and I wondered if she was as anxious to get this date over with as I was. Maybe I wasn't her type, either. Though I thought the likelihood of that was slim.

We thankfully finished eating in relative silence. I paid the bill, then escorted her home, since Mother had insisted that I pick her up. I made myself get out and walk her to her door, silently marveling at her French provincial brick house and manicured lawn. I tried to remember what it was Mother said Aurora did for a living but couldn't. Something with numbers.

"Would you like to come in?" she asked after she had the door unlocked.

"Oh, uh...I should probably get going. It's getting late and I'm sure you have things to do."

"I'd really like to talk to you about something, if you have a few minutes," she persisted, placing a hand on my arm. "Please?"

I sighed but nodded in consent, following her into the house. I guess I could tolerate her for another few minutes, though I wondered what in the world she could possibly have to talk to me about.

"Have a seat; I'll be right back," she offered, gesturing towards the powder blue couch in the living room. She continued towards her bedroom without waiting for a response. I made myself sit down, even though I was tempted to just leave and make up an excuse later.

While I waited, I glanced around her living room. She had lots of Black art on the walls, and her light blue, cream, and brown color scheme was admittedly relaxing. I checked my watch and sat back on the couch, telling myself I'd give her ten minutes, tops, before I made up an excuse to leave.

When Aurora finally came back out, I did a legit double-take. The conservative black dress she'd worn to dinner had been replaced by a hot pink bra and panty set under a sheer robe.

She wordlessly strode over and straddled me on the couch, taking my face in her hands and kissing me. I was so thrown off by the sudden turn of events that it took me a minute to stop her, but I eventually did. Gently grabbing her arms and pushing her back, I looked at her questioningly.

"Um...what's going on?"

"What do you think?"

"I'm flattered, Aurora, but we can't do this."

"Why not?"

"Because we barely know each other. And I need to go."

"You don't find me attractive?"

My eyes swept her body, barely registering anything. "Sure, yeah. But still. I don't think this is a good idea."

Without waiting for a response, I gently moved her off of my lap and stood. She just looked up at me with an expression I couldn't quite read. I couldn't tell if she was hurt or angry or what, not that it mattered either way.

"Have a good evening, Aurora," I mumbled, turning to leave. She didn't say a word as I walked out, thankfully, and I hightailed it to my car, not believing she had just tried that.

What a waste of an evening. I hadn't had this bad a time on a date since that time in high school when the girl spent the whole date agonizing over her nail color not coordinating with her dress. Seriously.

I had no idea what I was going to tell Mother. She would surely be furious, especially if Aurora called her and gave her a report of how I brushed her off, if they weren't on the phone already. I should've just stood firm on my initial decision that I didn't want to go on this date and let Mother be mad about it. But I'd foolishly let the situation with Claire sway me.

Speaking of Claire, that was one good thing about our relationship; Mother didn't like her. I didn't have to worry about any pressure to perform a certain way or reach any certain point in our relationship; I could just be free to enjoy it. And I did. Claire and I might have had our differences but I didn't have to worry about being bored with her. We had a lot of fun together, and I almost never refused her when she seduced me. If she had come out and straddled me in her underwear, wrapping those pretty legs of hers around me, we'd probably already be on our second condom already.

See, this was what I hated about being fixed up; whenever it didn't go well (and it usually didn't) I started thinking about the past when I had the good stuff. And for the past couple of years, that'd been Claire. We hadn't spoken since that disastrous coffee date with my mother and while I wasn't thrilled that she was still giving me the cold shoulder, I figured it was only a matter of time before we patched things up. She'd cool off enough at some point to at least talk to me. At least, I hoped.

In the meantime I had to figure out a way to keep Mama off my back about Aurora because if I had my way about it, I would *not* be seeing her again.

I needed to release some tension again. Part of me hated that I'd shut down Aurora's seduction attempt, but that would've just given her encouragement and that's the last thing I wanted. My first choice would've been Claire, of course, but I didn't have the patience for all the convincing I'd have to do to even get her to open the door, let alone her legs. There was only one other surefire orgasm in my phone, and I'd have to swallow my pride to get it.

"Well, look who it is," Venus taunted when she answered. I could almost hear her smirk. "What the hell you want?"

Resisting the urge to correct her grammar, I tried to sound casual when I replied, "I was wondering if you had any plans this evening."

"Why?"

"Because I'd like to see you."

"Oh you do? I thought I wasn't good enough for you no more."

"I never said that. Don't tell me you're still upset about that last conversation we had."

"I ain't upset at all. Especially since I told you you'd come crawling back when you got horny enough."

My lips curled under, hating that she was right. "Look, Venus, let's cut to the chase. You and I; this is what we do. We have sex. We use each other. We were never going to be anything more than that and we both know it. So there's no need for you to get in your feelings; just let me know what time I can come over there so I can give you what we both want, then I'll leave and we can both go about our business until the next time."

She was quiet for a few moments before she started to laugh. "You are such a joke. You really think that much of yourself, huh? Yeah, we were just cut buddies but that doesn't mean you can just treat me any kind of way. So I'm good. You can take your invitation and put it up your ass along with the stick that's already up there."

A flash of heat washed over me, and not the kind I was looking for. Venus was actually trying to turn *me* down? What was this, tit for tat?

"Venus," I hedged, managing to keep my voice calm, "Will you stop this, please? You know we're good together so all of this drama is really unnecessary."

"Nah, it's necessary. But it's also...what do y'all *cultured* folks call it? Moot? I have a man now so I'm not trying to be fooling with you, anyway."

"Yeah, right," I immediately scoffed. "You have a man now, all of a sudden? What, you're trying to teach me a lesson because of what I said last time? Fine, I'm sorry; is that what you wanna hear?"

"You and that half-assed apology that you don't even mean can go jump in the Atlantic. Nobody has to lie to your stuck-up ass, Montrel; I'm with somebody now that puts it on me *way* better than you ever did. And he wants me for more than just my bedroom skills. So after today, don't bother calling me no more."

"Venus-"

"And if you're thinking about coming over here anyway, I wouldn't. You know what I keep in my nightstand and my man stays strapped, too. And his temper is way worse than mine."

I heard the dial tone, and I looked down at the phone in shock. That didn't go at all like I expected.

Even though Venus and I were nothing more than sex buddies, it kind of stung that she was apparently moving on from me like this. I thought we had an understanding. But she had to go and change everything up and I was left with no good options when I needed to relieve my tension.

I was still thinking about all this when I walked through my front door. But my mind cleared when I turned on my light and saw Forrest laid out on my couch.

"What the hell??"

Forrest jumped, waking out of his sleep. He sat up and rubbed his eyes, frowning at me like I was the one who had broken into *his* place.

"What are you screaming for?"

"What do you think? I wasn't expecting someone to have broken into my house!"

"You gave me a key, you dumb ass," Forrest reminded me, swinging his feet to the floor. "Nobody broke in."

"What are you doing here, Forrest?"

"Giselle kicked me out."

"Why?"

"Because *somebody* gave her the idea that I only married her 'cause she's mixed and could make pretty babies."

"Who would tell her that?"

He glared at me. "You tell me."

"Are you trying to blame *me* for this?"

"Are you trying to tell me you didn't say anything to her about that?"

"Not...on purpose..."

"That's what I thought. So be lucky I'm just crashing on your couch and not kicking your ass."

"I'm sorry," I sighed, placing my keys on their designated hook and trudging over near the couch. "I didn't mean to tell her that but she had called me crying after the latest fight you two had, and she was wondering if there was something you were holding back, and...it just slipped out."

Forrest stood, glowering at me. I took a step back. "Man..."

"You should be thanking me, Forrest. She thought you were having an affair."

"Oh, so you think this is better? Her thinking that I don't really love her but only want her for her light skin and curly hair?"

"Hey, I set her straight. Or tried to...she was too busy freaking out to really listen to me."

"Montrel..."

"I'm sorry, all right? But this doesn't have to be that big a deal; so that was the main reason you got with her at first-"

"I told you I didn't mean that shit, Montrel!"

"Well! I said it just slipped out! I'm sure once she calms down she'll be willing to listen to reason and you can explain this to her. The two of you might even laugh about it one day."

He looked at me like he wanted to rip my head off and I took another step or two back. I knew he didn't spend all that time in the gym taking selfies. He'd kick my ass if I let him catch me.

"I'm too tired to deal with you right now," he finally grumbled, rubbing a hand over his wavy hair. "Going back and forth with Giselle all the time has been wearing me out so I needed a break from her, anyway. Thanks for offering to put me up for as long as I need."

I just smiled weakly, knowing there wasn't anything I could say right then. He wasn't leaving.

"Yeah, great," I muttered, shrugging out of my blazer and hanging it over my arm. "You're more than welcome."

"I better be."

I sighed as he dropped back onto the couch. Well, at least I had something to take my mind off the awful date with Aurora.

• • • •

AFTER THREE DAYS OF Forrest taking over my guest room, he still wasn't willing to talk about him and Giselle. He didn't say it but I could tell the whole situation with his wife was really bothering him. They'd been having problems for a while and I was sure my little slip of the tongue didn't help any. I felt a little guilty about it but as far as I was concerned, they needed to get everything out on the table, anyway. So in the end, I probably did them a favor.

"Why is it so damn hot in here?" he barked, stomping into the living room where I was trying to meditate.

"It's not hot in here, man," I droned, not even opening my eyes. "It's an even seventy-four degrees."

"It's hot," he snapped, practically pounding on my thermostat. "I don't need to sweat through my clothes on top of everything else."

"Maybe if you took off the *sweatsuit*..."

"I can wear what I want."

"And I can have the temperature wherever I want in my own house."

"You're just trying to piss me off, I see," Forrest grumbled, going over to my window and yanking the curtains closed so hard I thought he was going to tear the rod from the wall.

"You break it you buy it," I warned him, eyes still closed.

"Fuck you."

I ignored that. He didn't say anything for a few minutes and I thought (hoped) that he went back to the guest room. But then my peace was broken by a large blast of who I only knew by previous mention as someone named Young Jeezy.

"Damn it, Forrest!" I yelled, turning to him. Now I was pissed, too. "Turn that shit down!"

He ignored me. Well, not really, 'cause he turned the music up louder.

I pushed myself off the floor and went over to snatch the phone out of his hand. He gave me the evil eye as I turned the music off.

"Look, man," I said, tossing his phone to the couch. "I get that you're messed up about Giselle. And I'm trying to be patient-"

"You *should* be damn patient. Considering it's your fault I'm going through this shit."

"I admit I spoke out of turn but let's get real, here; the two of you were having issues before I ever said anything to her. Hell, y'all were butting heads before you even started trying to get pregnant. Just face it; you and Giselle have serious problems."

He waved me off and tried to turn away, but I stepped in front of him.

"Man, you can stay mad at me all you want but at some point you're gonna have to face all this," I told him. "If you want your marriage with Giselle to work, you have take ownership of your part in everything. And you can't do that as long as you're stomping around tearing my house up."

His chest heaved as he (hopefully) pondered my words. He still wouldn't look at me. But at least he wasn't cussing me out or breaking something.

"I'm here for you, man," I reminded him, lightly bumping my fist against his shoulder. "But you're gonna have to do something with all that anger besides take it out on me."

Grunting, he turned and stormed out of the room. I just shook my head and tried to get back in my previous mindset so I could resume my mediation, taking a long inhale of the eucalyptus mint aroma my scented oil diffuser was sending around the room and turning up the ocean wave sounds flowing through the speakers. It was something I had started years before to keep my mind right, especially when I started having issues about my dad being gone. It kicked into high gear when I got to marrying age and Mother started dropping hints damn near every other day.

I had finally calmed down enough and put the interaction with Forrest out of my mind when my doorbell rang. Since I wasn't expecting any guests nor did I want any, I fully intended on just ignoring it, but my unwanted guest was persistent.

"Got*dammit*!"

"Who's at the door??" Forrest yelled from down the hall.

I didn't even bother answering him. I just jumped off the floor and got ready to get rid of whoever it was trying to wear out my doorbell.

The last person I was expecting to see was Aurora.

I blinked, wondering if I was still mediating or something. "Aurora?"

She lifted her hand. "Hi."

"What are you doing here? How did you know where I live?"

"Your mother told me."

My lips curled under as I tried to refrain from cursing out loud. I was going to have to have yet another talk with Mother about boundaries.

"She shouldn't have done that," I said flatly, not in the mood to be cordial. "I don't appreciate people just showing up at my house uninvited. And if I wanted you to know where I lived, I'd have told you myself."

"Are you upset? You seem kinda upset."

Genius. "Yes, I'm upset."

"I didn't mean to upset you. I told Ms. Annie how good a time I had on our date the other night and she suggested I make my move; do something aggressive to show you my intentions."

"Of course she did. And I'd appreciate that more if we were on the same page but unfortunately, we're not. I didn't exactly have an amazing time the other night. And please don't take offense, but don't come by here again unless I invite you."

She looked a little hurt but I was too annoyed to care. "So...you want me to leave?"

It was like I was talking to a plant. "Yes, please."

She just kept standing there staring at me with what I guess was supposed to be a pitiful expression designed to make me relent, but it didn't even faze me. I just started easing the door closed, giving her time to turn and go back to her car before I straight closed it in her face. Thankfully, she finally got the message and left.

"Who was that?" Forrest asked when I closed the door, making me jump.

"Somebody Mother tried to set me up with. How long have you been standing there?"

"The whole time. She's cute."

I shrugged. "Whatever."

"You were kinda rude."

I glared at him. "Oh really? You're gonna admonish somebody about being rude when you commandeered my guest room like you owned it and cussed me out more than once in my own house?"

"All totally deserved. Why don't you wanna date her? What's her name?"

"Why does it matter? It's not gonna happen." When he continued to peer at me, I sighed and muttered, "Her name is Aurora."

"Aurora what?"

"I have no idea what her last name is."

"You wouldn't mess with her at all if you didn't know basic information like what her last name was and be both know it."

"Fine, dammit. It's Chadwick."

"Y'all went out?"

"Yeah. But it won't be happening again."

"I don't see what the problem is. You might as well. It's not like you have any other prospects."

"What kind of reason is that to date somebody? I'd rather lower my standards and go on a dating site than let *her* be my only option."

"Why?"

"Because she's as dull as a plastic bag, that's why. That might be what's floating around in her head, matter of fact. I am not interested."

"Maybe you just need to spend some more time with her."

"I don't need any relationship advice, thank you."

"Seems like you do."

"Truth be told, those couple of hours I spent with Aurora the other night made me appreciate my time with Claire," I admitted hesitantly, having a feeling what he'd say. "Claire is way more exciting and interesting than Aurora."

"Is that a fact?" Forrest asked, looking annoyingly smug. He crossed his arms over his chest and smirked. Very nice that he was in a much better mood now that we weren't talking about him. "Missing what you messed up, huh?"

"I didn't mess anything up. Claire's the one that stopped talking to me over something my Mother said."

"I'm not even getting into all that with you again, man," Forrest waved me off. "You're still acting dumb about that, I see. But whatever. It's not like you can do anything about it, anyway."

I paused in my act of rolling up the yoga mat I'd been using for my interrupted mediation, deciding to not even bother trying to resume it again. "Why can't I?"

"Because she's back with that other dude."

The mat fell from my hands and Forrest didn't even try to hold in his laugh. Sometimes I really didn't like him. "How do you know that?"

He pulled out his phone and after opening Instagram, he showed me Claire's page. There were only a couple of pictures of Claire and this other guy together, but in her Stories, there were several of the two of them doing things like sharing a pizza, comparing movie snacks before they entered the theater, and feeding the ducks at the park. I remembered when she suggested we do that; I was never that into animals so I declined, suggesting she go with Chichi and her kids. But apparently this man she was dating had no problem with it.

I wondered if this was the same man that she had gone on a date with after the last time we broke up, despite what Forrest had just said. I tried to tell myself that I didn't care what Claire did, but I still felt that familiar pang hit my chest. She sure was moving on fast after our relationship; part of me wondered if she'd just been looking for an excuse to end things with me so she could go back to him. I thought she said she loved me; yet she's already putting her new man on social media and broadcasting them together to everybody?

She didn't see me doing that. Whenever I messed around with Venus or whoever else, I had enough courtesy to keep it to myself. That's why I wouldn't answer any of her questions about who I dated (or more accurately, slept with) when we weren't together. Out of courtesy. I wasn't trying to throw it in her face like she was doing with this guy.

The more I looked at her Stories and pictures over and over, the more upset I got. It wasn't until Forrest snatched his phone out of my hand that I snapped out of it.

"You mad?" he taunted, then actually cackled as he strolled out of the room.

I just glared after him before grabbing my own phone and pulling up Instagram.

Fourteen – Claire

• • • •

IF I WAS MAD AT MYSELF for anything, it was for putting the brakes on what I'd been building with Warner. We would've been so much farther along if I hadn't made that stupid, waste-of-time pit stop with Montrel.

Warner was so easy to be with. He made me feel incredibly comfortable and blush-y. There was no pettiness, no selfishness, no everything-being-about-one-person. He cared about what *I* wanted; actually considered it when we made plans together. Compromise existed with him. And I really believed that his feelings for me were genuine. That's a nice feeling for a girl to have.

Sometimes he'd call or text me in the middle of the day and invite me out, and I'd get all excited and look forward to it like an athlete waiting on the first game of the season. We didn't even have to have any elaborate plans; sometimes it was just him cooking for me at his house or holding hands while we took a slow walk around the neighborhood. I was more than happy with that kind of thing.

One night in particular, we had planned to go see a play in town; Warner had told me about it after reading a bunch of good reviews online and I thought it would be fun to see together. I'd spent an hour getting ready; doing my hair, getting my makeup right, choosing just the right seemingly-effortless sexy-casual outfit, and going back and forth about whether I'd kiss him on the cheek or on the lips when he arrived (yes, this was actually a decision for me). He showed up on time, as he usually did, and I offered to get him something to drink before we left. Since he was always one to offer to help, he went to get the ice, and that's when he noticed I had sour bomb pops in the freezer.

Suddenly, the play was forgotten and we spent the evening on my front steps, eating popsicles and taking turns telling stories from our college days. It was one of the most fun evenings I'd had with a man in years. I learned more about him in that one evening than I did after six months with Montrel.

Speaking of Montrel, I was aware that I wasn't totally over him. As much as I would've liked for it to be, that wasn't how real feelings worked. But I was finally getting it through my head that Montrel wasn't good for me, and I was moving on. Dating Warner so soon after ending things with Montrel might not have seemed smart, but to me, it was necessary. If I didn't have something or someone to keep my mind occupied, I'd just start to question and second-guess my decision to break up with Montrel, just like Chichi said. I didn't need that. I wanted to be done. And for real this time.

And Warner was making it so easy because he was almost the total opposite of Montrel.

"So how are you feeling?" he asked me one night when we were hanging out. I was curled up on his couch as we watched soccer, something neither of us had ever watched before but realized it wasn't half bad. The wine probably helped with that, though. "You still think this is a good idea?"

"The soccer? It's no Celtics game but I like it."

"I was talking about you and me," he corrected with a smile. "If you think we're moving too fast."

"Oh," I sat up a little straighter, adjusting the blanket he had draped over my legs earlier. "I absolutely think this is a good idea. I've been loving my time with you."

"You sure? I'm not trying to be paranoid, but I know how it can be when you break up with somebody; you sometimes do stuff you wouldn't normally do if you had a clear head. If you still have feelings for Montrel, I get it; I'd just like to know so...you know...I'm not in the dark about anything."

I looked at him thoughtfully.

"I just don't want any surprises," he continued in explanation. "I've been there before, where I dated someone who turned out to not be over her ex and she up and went back to him without a word to me."

"You mean like I did with Montrel?" I verified softly, hating to bring it up.

"Yeah...only you didn't run off and get married to him in Vegas like she did with *her* ex."

"Ouch."

"Being blindsided like that isn't any fun. And I get that the heart wants what it wants. But if you're having *any* doubts about me or us or what we're doing, please, just tell me. I don't think I can take that again."

I used one hand to grab his while I sat down the wineglass I was holding in my other. He looked so incredibly sincere, there was no way I would ever want to hurt him. And it just reminded me why I liked him so much.

"I'm not gonna lie and say Montrel is totally out of my system," I admitted, looking into his boyishly cute face. I swear, his skin was like dulce de leche. "I *was* in love with him, as you know. But I also realize he's not the man for me. And I've wasted enough time with him. I want to see where this can go with you."

"That's what I want, too," he replied, squeezing my hand. "I really like you, Claire, a lot. You...I look forward to whatever time I get to spend with you."

I was all blush-y again. Grinning, I leaned towards him, my knees almost resting on his as we faced each other. "Same here. I'm developing real feelings for you, Warner. I'm not gonna do you like your ex did. I wouldn't."

He reached out and lightly brushed my hair behind my ear with his finger, sending a little chill down my spine. "Promise?"

I looked right into his eyes. "Promise. I know that pain; I wouldn't do that to anybody else. Believe me, I wouldn't want you to have any regrets when it comes to me, either."

"Well, I *do* have one."

My smile faded a little. Well, this was news. "You do?"

"That I didn't meet you first."

Damn this man and his natural ability to make me melt. Smiling so hard my cheeks were aching, I ducked my head. "Oh, Warner..."

He gently lifted my chin and leaned in to kiss me. I welcomed the kiss, willingly opening my mouth to him and going into his arms. It wasn't our first kiss but it was definitely the most intense so far, and I knew that this one meant something. We had only been dating a few weeks but I was feeling something real for Warner. It wasn't love just yet but it was definitely headed in that direction.

We spent the rest of that evening making out on his couch. He was such a good kisser it was almost unfair. He took his time, treating kissing like the art it was and not just as a hurdle towards sex. The way he stroked my tongue with his, interspersed languid smooches with deep kisses, grabbed my face and the back of my neck (which I *loved*) and ran his hands over my body without creeping into inappropriateness, it all turned me into hot liquid. I don't even know how much time had passed and I didn't care; it felt like we were there wrapped up in each other for hours and I loved every second of it.

Thankfully he didn't try to take it any further than that, because I wasn't quite ready to go to the next level with him yet. But what we were doing was more than enough. The insecurities I usually had about my skinny body or somewhat thin hair didn't exist when Warner had me wrapped up like that. He made me feel so desired...like one of those voluptuous Instagram models that everybody knows probably has fake everything but it doesn't matter because they're *that* sexy.

Warner made me feel *that* sexy. It was a first.

Another way Warner was nothing like Montrel was that Chichi and my parents all liked him. Mother had of course introduced us, and Dad took to him immediately when I brought Warner over to their house with me one day. They bonded over chess, of all things, and Mama and I entertained ourselves with a movie while they played game after game.

I was nervous about introducing Warner to Chichi because, well, she could be a little abrasive if she didn't know you that well or didn't like your vibe. Warner was wonderful but Chichi had her own set of criteria that didn't always make sense to me. She grew standoffish with one guy I used to date when she found out he was a vegetarian. And she wouldn't even hang out with another guy I dated when he revealed he didn't believe in voting (honestly, though, that one was a turn-off for me, too).

But as soon as Warner and I showed up at the park where Chichi and Gerard were with the triplets, it was like they'd been best friends for years. Warner ran around with the boys and played all the games with them they wanted, which scored instant points with Chichi because that meant she didn't have to do it.

"Girl, he's cute!" she marveled conspiringly as we sat at one the picnic tables, watching the males play basketball on a nearby court. "Even more so in person. But you sure like these wiry men, don't you?"

"He is not wiry; he's just long and lean. Believe me, I've seen him with his shirt off. He's *not* skinny."

"You mean like you are?"

"Shut up! But yes."

"Well, hey, if you like it, I love it," Chichi assured, holding up her hands. "Anybody can gain weight but an asshole will usually stay an asshole."

"According to the anatomy books."

"You know what I'm talking about."

"I know *who* you're talking about. And I'm not trying to think about him. My focus is on Warner."

"Y'all made it official yet?"

"We're waiting to have sex. Don't wanna rush into that. But we make out a lot."

"How very tenth grade of you. But I was actually talking about if y'all had decided to be exclusive yet."

"Oh," I blushed, smiling as Chichi shook her head at me. "Not yet. He knows all about Montrel and what happened with him, and he's been *so* understanding; I don't want to take advantage of him or his feelings by rushing into a relationship until I'm totally sure I'm over my last one. He deserves that."

"He does and you do, too," Chichi emphasized. "You deserve to be done with Montrel's ass and I wish I had some kind of magic wand or mind-altering device to wipe him out of your memory completely. But since I don't, all I can hope is that you're staying away from him so you can't be wooed into taking him back again."

"Chichi, come on, give me a little credit-"

"You might as well stop saying that. When it comes to your decisions about Montrel, you haven't earned any credit."

I sighed, knowing she had a point. "Fine. I know I fell for his charms last time but I'm not gonna do that again. All I have to do is think about how he didn't defend me to his mother and it reminds me why I left him alone."

"He's done way more crap than that, but whatever keeps you off his lap, I'll take it." She watched Warner help Devlin with his jump shot and smiled. "Warner seems like a good one, girl. Please don't blow it."

Just then, Warner looked over and smiled at me, giving me a wink. I blushed hard and didn't try to hide it. Chichi just grinned.

I winked back at Warner, giving him a flirty wave. "I have *no* intention of blowing this one."

And I didn't. The more time I spent with Warner, the more it made me realize what I'd been missing all along. I wasn't letting that go.

. . . .

LATER THAT EVENING, Warner had to go handle some stuff with the security company he ran and Gerard took the boys home, so Chichi had a rare opportunity of a child-free evening. She came over to my place and we were going to just have a girl's night, gabbing and eating and watching whatever Chichi wanted to watch.

"I'm telling you, I'm not trying to hear anything about that Disney Plus stuff tonight," she warned me, strolling barefoot from my kitchen with two bottles of tequila. "I wanna see something with some cussing and sex in it, since I almost never get to watch that kind of stuff at home."

"Fine, I'll let you control the remote. But I don't know what you're doing with all that tequila. You *do* still have to go home after this."

"I know this. But I haven't had any in too long."

"It'll be just wine for me. I'm not trying to mess with that."

"Damn, when did you get to be such a lightweight? We used to drink way harder stuff than this back in the day."

"Which is exactly how I know I don't want it now," I concluded, playfully nudging her aside as I reached for my iPad on the end table. "You wanna order a pizza?"

"Ugh, no, I eat enough of that at home with those boys and Gerard. They'd eat that shit every day, if I let 'em. Let's get Chinese."

"Works for me." I was just about to look for somewhere to place the order when my phone rang. "Shoot, I left my phone in my purse..."

Chichi peered at my iPad. "Can't calls come through on there?"

"I turned that feature off."

"Hmph. If that's Warner saying he finished his work earlier than he thought and wants to come over so y'all can *make out* some more, tell him too bad. You're hanging with your girl tonight."

I laughed and sucked my teeth as I retrieved my phone from my purse. "Yeah, yeah. It's not Warner, anyway; it's Giselle." I answered the call. "Hey, girl."

"Hey, Claire," Giselle sniffed. "You busy?"

"No, not really...you okay?"

"I'm not. Forrest and I split up."

"What??" I gasped. Chichi stopped scrolling through Netflix and looked at me curiously. "What happened? You're getting a divorce?"

"No, no; at least, not yet. I just told him to get out and stay somewhere else 'cause I couldn't stand the sight of him after I found out the truth."

"Oh no...please don't tell me he cheated."

"I actually might have been less insulted if that's all it was. I found out the main reason he married me is because I'm biracial and could give him 'pretty-haired babies.'"

My jaw dropped. "Are you serious? He actually told you that??"

"*He* didn't but Montrel did."

My face automatically tightened. Why did his name always have to come up? "Oh."

"I'm sorry to keep calling you with all my drama," Giselle said. "I know you probably get tired of hearing about me and Forrest's crap."

"Stop apologizing. That's what friends are for."

"I appreciate it. A friend is what I need right now."

"Aww...hey, why don't you come over? You shouldn't be alone right now. Chichi and I are gonna have a girl's night. You can join us."

"Really? You sure?"

"Absolutely. We can pig out and watch sex movies and bitch about men."

"Sex movies?"

"It'll be either sex or violence. I'm letting Chichi control the remote for the evening."

"Oh, okay. Enough said." Giselle sniffed again. "Well, if you're sure it won't be an imposition, I'd love to come by. The more I sit around here, the more I'll agonize over what's going on between me and Forrest."

"No imposition at all. Come on over."

"Can I bring anything?"

"Nope. We already have liquor and I'm about to order some Chinese."

"That sounds so great. Okay, I'm gonna throw on something presentable and be over there in a little bit."

"Okay, see you then." I ended the call with a slight shake of my head.

"What was that about?" Chichi asked as she continued her scrolling.

"Giselle and Forrest are going through it again," I replied with a sigh, placing a hand on my hip. "I'll let her tell you the details when she gets here, if she wants to."

"Well, that's too bad. But I hope she's not gonna cry the whole time she's here."

"Chichi!"

"Girl, stop. You and I both know Giselle can be a little weepy. Remember the time she started crying when I broke that nail?"

"It was bleeding. And I acknowledge she can be a little emotional. But I think it's justified this time, given what she's dealing with in her marriage."

"That's all right. I get it. It's not like me and Gerard never went through anything that had me shedding a few tears. We'll get her good and drunk and have her watch something explicit. That'll make her feel better."

"Will it?" I asked, amused. "What do you want from the Chinese place?"

"You know what I like. Just make sure you get plenty of eggrolls. And you know Giselle loves shrimp lo mein and those little doughnuts. Get her her own order so she won't be trying to eat mine."

"Oh goodness..."

"Well, when you have three boys with bottomless stomachs who are always eating up everything, you tend to get a little selfish sometimes. I just want something sweet of my own without having to share any."

"All right, all right."

Giselle showed up a little while later. She wasn't crying but it was clear she had been. Her curly hair was in an off-center knot at the top of her head, her skin looked pale, and she was dressed more casually than I had ever seen her. Giselle was someone that liked to look cute going to the grocery store so it was a little surprising to see her in shorts and a hoodie.

"Hey, girl," I greeted her, giving her a hug which she clung to a few moments longer than expected. "How you holding up?"

"I'm kind of a mess." She looked down at her outfit. "Clearly."

"You don't look bad. We're just hanging out. Though I admit I haven't seen you in a hoodie before."

"It's cropped…"

"Come on in here, girl," Chichi ordered, coming over to usher Giselle into the living room. "You want something to drink?"

"As long as it has a lot of alcohol in it."

We all started diving into the alcohol and gorging on Chinese food while we watched a really bad horror movie. I was wondering if Giselle was going to start spilling the beans about what was going on with her and Forrest, but if she wasn't ready to talk about it, I certainly wasn't going to push her.

"This is *not* a sex movie," Giselle pointed out, flopping against the back of the couch and stuffing half of her eggroll into her mouth.

"No, but I can find one, believe me," Chichi insisted, grabbing the remote. "I just didn't want that to, you know...trigger anything for you."

"No need to worry about that. I can't get any more upset than I already am." Giselle took a long sip of tequila. "And anyway, sex was never one of the problems between me and Forrest."

My eyebrows shot up in surprise. "Really?"

"Yeah. It's just when we wanted it to start *resulting* in something and it *didn't*, that's when our crap started."

"Maybe y'all are trying too hard," Chichi suggested. "You should just enjoy your marriage and let the chips fall where they're gonna fall. Sometimes pregnancy can happen when you're not trying to *make* it happen. Me and Gerard certainly weren't trying to make three boys. Especially not at the same damn time."

"Well, the way it's looking, we won't be making anything," Giselle stated glumly. "And it hurts to think that Forrest blames me for it."

"He said that?" I asked.

"He didn't have to. I can tell. Every time I get my period he looks at me like I'm the villain."

"I'm sure he's just stressed about it like you are. Sometimes that kind of stress can cause you to lash out unfairly."

"Even so, I don't think I can blame stress on him only wanting me for my mixed heritage and curly hair."

"Giselle, girl, I can't imagine he really said that."

"Montrel told me flat-out he said it."

I rolled my eyes. "Not the most reliable source."

"I know you two are on the outs, Claire, and I'm sorry about that. But you know he and Forrest are best friends. He would be the main person Forrest would tell something like that to." Giselle sniffed and wiped her eyes. "Though, to be fair, Montrel *did* clarify that Forrest said he didn't really mean that."

"Well, there you go!"

"But why would he even say it in the first place??"

"Girl, men don't make any sense!" Chichi scoffed. "Trying to make sense out of the shit they say and do is a waste of time. Forrest might have said that stupid shit when he was pissed or drunk or anything. Sometimes people say hurtful stuff 'cause they're hurting and they want you to hurt, too. Doesn't mean they mean it. It could've just been something he said to try to make himself feel better after another failed pregnancy attempt."

"I guess that's possible," Giselle admitted. She grabbed another eggroll but just tapped it against her plate. "Though I wish he would've just talked to *me* instead of Montrel."

"Giselle, come on. I'm sure I don't have to tell you that sometimes you need somebody to vent to and unload on other than your spouse. And sometimes you say stuff that you would *never* say to your man or your woman. That's not a bad thing and it doesn't mean you're keeping secrets or you don't love or trust them; everybody just needs their own outlet, that's all."

Giselle looked at Chichi thoughtfully as she pondered her words. Hell, I was listening too, and making note of that for my own future relationships. Chichi and Gerard had been happily married for eleven years; she must know what she was talking about.

Chichi drained the rest of the tequila in her glass. "Hell, Claire, you remember the time I was pissed at Gerard about leaving a mess in the kitchen, and I called you going off about everything I could think of?"

"Yeah, I do," I nodded. "You were on one that day."

"Half the shit I said I didn't mean...saying I hated Gerard's mama and cursing his extra-ass sperm and fussing about how he likes his steak rare when I like mine well-done. It was just frustration that I needed to get out of my system by saying whatever I wanted to say. And I said it to my homegirl and not my man because it wasn't real stuff; it was just venting."

Giselle sighed, sitting back on the couch. "I can understand that. I've certainly said things to friends when I was upset that I wouldn't have said otherwise. I can see what you mean about everyone needing an outlet."

"And tonight is *my* outlet, since I don't have to deal with my children or my husband, so pass me some more of that tequila," Chichi continued, kicking her legs and reaching for the bottle. "I'm not drunk enough."

"Remember, you still have to go home tonight," I reminded her amusingly. "Though I hope you don't think you're driving."

"That's why I rode with you from the park. I had every intention of drinking tonight so I planned on calling a rideshare, anyway."

We all continued to eat and drink and talk while we watched whatever movie it was that Chichi had us watching (that had more than enough sex in it, let me tell you). I was having a great evening despite the somewhat heavy subject matter and mentions of Montrel. Hearing his name didn't send me plunging into nostalgia like it used to, so I was feeling really encouraged. Maybe I was finally getting over the asshole.

There was a knock at the door. The three of us looked at each other curiously before looking towards the knocking, which was rather persistent.

"Is Warner coming over here?" Chichi asked me. "He texted or something and you told him it was okay to come through?"

"No...he knows we're having a girl's night and he's working, anyway."

"So who's at the door?"

"I don't know, Chichi. I don't have x-ray vision."

"Well, go see. Oooh, maybe it's some more Chinese food! Or apples!"

"I think you were wrong about not being drunk enough."

"Apples come in so many pretty colors," Giselle mused, sliding her bare feet back and forth across the carpet. "Red, yellow, greeeen..."

Rolling my eyes, I stood and headed towards the door, tripping a little bit over my own feet. How many glasses of wine did I have?

"I think we've *all* had enough to drink for tonight," I told them before checking the peephole. "Oh, damn..."

"Who is it?" Giselle asked.

Telling myself to count to ten and take a few deep breaths, I looked through the peephole again, just in case the wine had me hallucinating the first time. But no such luck.

"Let's just say some boys are crashing our girl's night."

"What?"

I raked my fingers through my hair and looked down at my clothes before I caught myself. What was I doing?

Chichi and Giselle got up and came over to join me at the door, flanking me on either side.

"You need backup?" Chichi asked, slurring slightly.

"I actually might," I replied, linking arms with them. Then it registered to me that I couldn't open the door like that.

"Giselle, can you..." I jerked my head towards the doorknob.

"Oh yeah." Giselle opened the door and actually jumped when she saw who was standing there.

Forrest. And Montrel.

Fifteen – Claire

• • • •

"WHAT ARE YOU DOING here?"

I didn't know who Chichi had directed that to and I'm willing to bet she didn't, either. It didn't really matter.

"I came to see you," Forrest answered, looking right at Giselle. "You're wearing a hoodie?"

"It's cropped." Giselle crossed her arms in a huff, though she didn't look totally upset that Forrest was there. "How did you know where I was?"

"We have the tracker thing on each other's phones, remember?"

"Ugh. I forgot about that."

"Y'all track each other's phones? Hmph, me and Gerard sure aren't doing that shit," Chichi muttered.

"Can we talk?" Forrest asked Giselle.

"I don't know. I'm not really in the state of mind to have this conversation."

"You don't know what I'm gonna say, though."

"Words?"

While they were going back and forth, Montrel was looking at me. I was aware of it, but I made sure to keep my eyes elsewhere. I wasn't about to let him get to me. Why didn't his ass just stay in the car? Or let Forrest come by himself? He knew how to get to my house without Montrel's help.

While Montrel was looking at me, Chichi was giving him the evil eye and subtly giving him the finger. Montrel's eyes flitted to her and I could see the shock on his face at her gesture, and I tried to hold my laugh in. Giselle and Forrest were still talking about whether they should talk or not, and I got tired of standing up, so I made my way back over to the couch. Montrel started to follow me but Chichi stepped in front of him, daring him to try to get past her.

"Hey, Claire," he called out instead, looking at me over Chichi's shoulder.

"Montrel." I didn't even look at him as I smoothly lowered myself onto the couch.

"How are you, sweetheart?"

"She ain't your sweetheart," Chichi immediately snapped.

"She's right about that," I agreed. I crossed my legs away from him. "And I'm fine."

"You look good."

"You're wasting your time, Montrel."

"What?"

"Catch a damn hint; she doesn't wanna talk to you," Chichi informed him. "You need to leave her alone. You should know how to do that, right? You've had a hell of a lot of practice."

Montrel sighed, finally looking at Chichi. "Can you give me a break?"

"Why should I do that?"

"I'm just trying to talk to Claire, that's it. I don't want to argue with you."

"You can't argue with me from the car. Why don't you go back there? I don't even know what the hell you came over here for."

"I came to support Forrest."

"Forrest doesn't need your help. Him and Giselle ain't even thinking about us."

I hadn't even noticed that Giselle and Forrest had migrated to the kitchen. I could see them but couldn't quite tell if they were fussing or just talking. They didn't exactly look happy with each other but they didn't look pissed, either.

"Chichi, I don't want to cause any trouble-"

"You shouldn't have brought your ass in here, then," Chichi cut him off, placing a hand on her hip and shifting her weight. I saw her take that very same stance when she admonished her boys more times than I could count. "You've been nothing but trouble for Claire and she doesn't need any more."

"You don't know everything that's happened."

"I know enough."

Chichi and Montrel continued to go back and forth. Giselle and Forrest were still going at it in the kitchen. I tried to ignore them all and focus on the television, but I could hardly even hear it over all the commotion.

Thankfully I had an excuse to leave the room 'cause I had to pee. I stood and hurried towards the hallway, not even bothering to look at Montrel even though I knew he was watching me. But Chichi would tackle him before she let him follow me. I loved her.

Once I was in the confines of my bathroom, I let out a long shaky breath. Seeing Montrel wasn't something I was ready for yet, and it got to me a little bit. I wasn't quite to the point where I could be around him and be unaffected. It annoyed me that I still had any feelings for him at all, considering everything he took me through. I knew it would come in time, but I was impatient.

I took my time in the bathroom, hoping to high heaven that Montrel and Forrest would have left by the time I got out. But I could still hear Giselle and Forrest bantering as soon as I opened the door.

Even more to my chagrin, Montrel was standing there in the hallway, waiting for me.

"Damn it!" I muttered, actually starting to go back into the bathroom but stopping myself. I wasn't going to run. This was *my* house. And I hadn't done anything wrong.

"How did you get back here?" I demanded, sure to keep my distance.

"Chichi's husband called her so she stepped outside," Montrel explained. "Figured that was my chance."

"Your chance for what? What the hell do you *want*, Montrel?"

"I just wanna talk to you, sweetheart."

"Please don't call me that."

"You never had a problem with it before."

"Yeah, well, that was then."

"I don't want to argue, Claire."

"I don't either. I don't wanna see you at all."

"Come on, you know you don't mean that."

"The hell I don't. And I'm about tired of you telling me what I don't mean."

"Look, just because you're dating someone doesn't mean I deserve all this animosity."

Ohhh, so that's what this was about. He saw my stuff on social media with Warner and he realized I hadn't been sitting around pining for him. He never did think I would move on from him after any of the times we broke up. His cocky ass thought I'd always be there waiting whenever he decided he was in the mood for me again.

"You deserve whatever animosity I dish out," I informed him, crossing my arms. "But you know you could avoid all this by just leaving me alone. Then you won't have to hear it."

"Come on, sweetheart-"

"See how your ass doesn't listen to me? I've asked you not to call me that."

"Okay, okay; I'm sorry." He took a step towards me and I took a step back. "I don't want it to be like this between us."

"Oh well."

"How come you didn't tell me you were dating someone already?"

"It's none of your business. Just like it was never any of *my* business when I'd ask you about women you were with after me."

"I still don't see why we had to break up in the first place. Just because we had a disagreement-"

"It wasn't a *disagreement*. You sat there and let your mama downtalk me and basically say I was nothing without uttering one word in my defense. Then you let me leave without even trying to follow me. That told me everything I needed to know right there."

"Just because I didn't say anything right in that moment doesn't mean I agreed with her."

"*I* couldn't tell. You're such a little puppy dog when it comes to her and I'm over it. I'm with someone who has the balls to have my back when anybody disrespects me. Not that his mother would ever do that in the first place."

His expression faltered slightly. "You've met his mother already?"

"I sure have."

I really only spoke to her once over FaceTime, but that was close enough.

"So you two are moving rather quickly, then," Montrel surmised, clearing his throat. "Things are...getting serious?"

"They're serious enough. I'm certainly serious about getting to know him better and seeing where this can go. And I think it can go far."

He looked away. No he wasn't trying to look hurt.

"You're just saying that to mess with me," he accused in a low voice.

"You're giving yourself *way* too much credit. You and I are over; I don't need to say anything to mess with you. It's just the truth."

"Hmm. Well...you're not the only one who's been on dates with other people."

"Uh-huh."

"I just don't put it on social media to broadcast it to everyone. But I've been seeing someone else, myself."

I wished I didn't feel anything when he said that but I did. Thankfully, he didn't know that. "Good for you."

"It's going really well."

"Let me guess; your mama set you two up."

He hesitated slightly. "That's irrelevant."

"Whatever, Montrel. If you're dating somebody else and it's going so well, why are you over here in my face trying to talk and be all up in *my* business?"

"I still care about you." He moved towards me again. "I'll *always* care about you, Claire."

His eyes were on mine and I noticed he was getting closer to me. I became aware of his cologne, his light blue sweater and dark jeans, his manicured hands. I wanted to back up again but my feet wouldn't move. For a second, I got lost in his eyes again...

"What the hell are you doing??"

Thank *god* for nosey friends.

Chichi stormed towards us, wedging herself between Montrel and me. She glared at him as she put both hands on her hips like some kind of cock-blocking superhero.

"You think you slick, sneaking back here when I wasn't looking," she snapped at him, nudging him back farther with her big boobs. "I guess you think I won't go off or move your ass outta here my*self*!"

"There's no need for all that," Montrel conceded, holding his hands up. "I'll, um, I'll leave."

He gave me a lingering look as he turned and left the hallway. Most of me was relieved Chichi showed up when she did. There was still a teeny-tiny part that had wanted to see what Montrel was about to do, though. And I hated that.

Chichi turned to me, the frown still on her face. "You were gonna let him kiss you!"

My jaw dropped. "No, I wasn't!"

"Claire, I saw you. You weren't doing a damn thing to stop him from making his move. If I hadn't caught y'all, you'd probably be slobbing each other down right now."

"Chichi, I..." I figured there was no reason to lie about it. She was my best friend; I could tell her the real deal, even if it was embarrassing. "I'll admit that I felt something just now."

She pursed her lips, looking at me intently.

"I wished like hell I didn't, but I did," I continued, lowering my voice. "I'm still mad at him and I know he's not the man for me, but my feelings...some of them are still lingering. It's easy when I'm not around him but apparently, being near him still affects me. I didn't realize it until he was in my face and...I clearly didn't handle it well."

Chichi glared at me for a few moments before her eyes softened in understanding. Thankfully. "I can understand that," she finally admitted. "This love thing is crazy sometimes. And you were in love with the man, regardless of what I think of him."

"Hey, he's not exactly at the top of my 'favorite people' list, either. But I'm trying to get over him, Chichi, I swear. I *want* to get over him."

"I believe you. And I hope you do. 'Cause I might have been here to stop him this time but I'm sure there'll be another time when I won't be, and you're gonna have to be strong enough to resist him on your own. And unfortunately, you don't have a good track record with that."

"I'm aware. But hopefully by the time that happens again, if it does, I'll be stronger than I was today."

"I hope you are, girl. 'Cause you've been running in place with Montrel for too long now. He clearly only really wants you when he doesn't have you."

"True. I know that's true."

Chichi called herself an Uber a little while later to go home, and Giselle was already laid out on my couch when I finally went back to the living room. I didn't have the energy to clean up the mess in there, but I didn't want to wake up to an army of ants so I quickly gathered the dirty dishes from our dinner and threw them in the dishwasher before trudging back to my room and flopping across the bed.

I was kicking myself for letting Montrel get to me, even a little bit. Nothing happened but it still felt like a setback. The fact that I didn't stop him or even make any *attempts* to stop him when he was coming towards me like that probably gave him some encouragement, and that's the last thing I wanted.

Man, was I stupid. Every time I took a few steps forward I tripped over my own feet and landed several more back. I was more than willing to blame it on the alcohol; maybe all the wine had slowed my reaction time. If I'd been sober, that wouldn't have happened.

I was still internally admonishing and justifying when Warner called. Should I tell him about that scene with Montrel?

"Hey," I answered the phone, rolling onto my back.

"Hey, baby." He had started calling me that a few dates ago and I freaking loved it. "How was the girl's night? Or is it still going?"

"Oh, no, it's over. Chichi went home and my other friend Giselle drunk herself to sleep."

"Did you enjoy it?"

"For the most part."

"For the most part?"

I debated again whether or not to tell him about what happened with Montrel before deciding to come out with it. I'd certainly want to know if his ex-girlfriend was making the moves on him.

"Well, we had some unexpected visitors," I told him, brushing some hair out of my face. "Montrel came by."

"He just showed up for no reason?"

"No, he's friends with Giselle's husband, who came over to talk to her. But it was obvious he wasn't just here to support his boy."

"He tried something with you?"

"He started to," I admitted, praying he didn't ask what I did to stop it. "But Chichi stopped him. But this was only after he tried to make me jealous by telling me he's dating somebody."

"Wow."

"Yeah, he saw the pictures of us on social media and was trying to dig for information, and when I wouldn't tell him anything, he suddenly was in a relationship, himself."

"Sounds like seeing you with someone else hit a nerve for him."

"Oh well. It's his own fault we're not together."

"How did you feel when he told you he was with somebody else?"

"I didn't care." Only a semi-lie.

"Really?"

"Yes, Warner. I told you, I'm done with Montrel. My attention is on you and what we're building together."

"*Are* we together?" he asked me. "Are we...official?"

I bit my lip. "I hope so. Do you want to be? Or do you think it's too soon?"

"It's not too soon for *me*. Especially since I already know I'm falling for you."

I gasped, sitting up. "Are you serious?"

"I'm dead serious. Maybe it's a little soon to be admitting *that* but it's what I'm feeling. I'm *so* into you, Claire. I don't want anybody else. I just want it to be you and me."

I felt warm all over as I processed Warner's words. This wasn't what I was expecting to hear but after he said it, I realized it was what I *wanted* to hear. Warner was who I wanted. And the fact that he was willing to be all in with me meant a hell of a lot.

"Did that freak you out?" Warner asked after I hadn't said anything for a few moments. "I'm sorry if we're not there yet but-"

"No, don't apologize," I stopped him. "Please don't apologize. I loved hearing that. It caught me off guard but I absolutely loved hearing it."

"Really?" I could hear the smile in his voice.

"Really. And please believe, I'm into you, too."

"I'm glad to hear that."

We continued to talk well into the night, and the longer we stayed on the phone, the better I felt about taking things with Warner to another level. He just made me feel so appreciated. I really felt like I had a friend as well as a partner, and that wasn't something I could say about any other man

I'd been with. I certainly couldn't say that about Montrel. It was a nice change of pace, and I didn't want to lose it.

After Warner and I finally got off the phone, I just laid on my back, deep in thought. Maybe I had a slip in composure with Montrel earlier but I decided that didn't mean anything. Warner was who I wanted to be with. There wasn't a doubt in my mind, especially after hearing how deep his feelings were. It was nice to be with someone who was sure I was who he wanted and who wasn't going to change things up once he got comfortable.

Rolling off my bed, I went around my room and gathered anything Montrel had ever given me, stuffing it into the same box he had sent my stuff back to me in. The still-unused pedicure kit, the bathrobe, dried flowers, pictures, clothes, whatever; anything that came from Montrel went in there. When I looked at the pictures, he wasn't even smiling in any of them; I don't think I had noticed that before. I was grinning my ass off, but he was just standing there like he was ready to get it over with. How had I never seen that?

It didn't matter anymore. I tossed the pictures into the box and closed it, making a mental note to send it back to him the next day. I didn't need that stuff anymore.

Sixteen – Montrel

• • • •

I'D BEEN TRYING TO avoid it, but I knew this conversation was coming eventually. Not even the tennis bracelet I'd brought could stop it.

"I cannot believe you, Montrel," Mother scolded. "How dare you be rude to Aurora like that!"

Sighing, I rubbed my eyes wearily. I'd only been at Mother's five minutes and she was already on my ass about Aurora. I knew she had probably told on me after I rejected her unannounced visit to my house.

"Mother, I appreciate the concern, but Aurora and I just didn't hit it off, that's it," I told her. "She's nice and all, but I'm not interested."

"And why not? What's wrong with her?"

I hesitated, not knowing how to say that Aurora was about as interesting as a cardboard box. "We're just not compatible."

"That's ridiculous. You've only had one date with her. That's not enough time to make that kind of determination."

"I disagree. Respectfully."

"Did you even try, Montrel?" Mother asked, crossing her legs and resting an arm over her knee, peering at me intently. "Can you say you gave sincere effort towards getting to know Aurora, or did you already have your mind made up when the date started?"

"Well, Mother, if I'm honest, I only went out with her in the first place because you were so adamant about it. Not because I particularly wanted to go."

"And that's what I don't understand. How could you be so against going out with such a wonderful young woman? It's not like you're seeing anyone else."

"Just because I'm not seeing anyone else doesn't mean I'll settle for anything. Didn't you always teach me to have standards?"

"Well, you weren't remembering those lessons when you dated Claire," Mother snapped. "*She* didn't meet the standards I've set for you, or the ones I expect you to have for yourself. Yet you keep going back to *her*."

"Maybe there's a reason for that," I mused, rubbing my freshly manicured nails. "Maybe she's the one."

"You can't possibly be serious. You're clearly saying that to get back at me for something."

"Why is that so impossible to believe? Claire might not come from money or have some high-profile job but she's a good woman. She's been nothing but good to me and I love her more than I can say. And frankly, I'm a little tired of hearing you always put her down to me."

Rearing back in surprise, Mother's delicate brow arched practically up to her hairline. I didn't usually speak to her like that. "You certainly are defensive."

"I'm sure you would be, too, if I constantly degraded someone you cared about."

"I don't say such things to be cruel. I'm simply speaking the truth. I'm sure Claire is a fine woman...for someone else. But you deserve better, dear."

"Whoever I deserve should be *my* decision, Mother. And regardless of what you think about Claire, I love her. I haven't been able to get her off my mind since we broke up-"

"You mean since you broke up *again*? Seriously, darling, the fact that your relationship with her can never last more than a few months at a time should tell you something. If you two were really meant to be, you wouldn't keep ending things with her. You're constantly telling me you love her...yet you keep leaving her." She looked at me pointedly. "Now why is that?"

She might have gotten me with that one. There wasn't even any point in saying that Claire was the one who ended things this last time; every time before that, it had been me. I'd get restless, start feeling stifled, and then I'd feel the need to break free, even though it didn't take long before I was missing her again. I didn't know what my issue was, but I knew I was feeling that yearn for her again. Seeing her the other night when I went to her house with Forrest just reminded me how much I wanted her back. It wasn't sitting well with me at all that she was dating someone else; regardless of what went down between us, Claire was mine. Period.

And if Chichi hadn't butted in, I'm willing to bet Claire would have let me kiss her. At least for a minute. I knew if I got the chance, uninterrupted, I could remind her of how good we were together.

"I don't know how to answer that, Mother," I finally admitted. "It doesn't make sense. But Claire is the only woman I've been able to see myself with down the line, even if I haven't always been ready for her at the moment."

"I see. And she's the *only* woman on this planet you can see yourself marrying? *Nobody* else is a match for you?"

"Nobody I've met thus far. And *certainly* not Aurora."

"I think you're being too hasty, making that determination. Not all feelings are instantaneous; sometimes they take time to develop. But you have to be open to it. Aurora is willing to meet you where you are; she won't rush or push things. You can go slow and build with her."

I was willing to bet that Aurora didn't tell Mother about how she tried to seduce me on our first date. And it was a little pushy to show up at my house unannounced, especially when I wasn't the one who told her where I lived. None of that was *going slow*.

"Mother, why can't you just leave my love life to me?" I asked, sighing and sitting back on the couch. I looked at my untouched latte and Claire's face flashed through my mind. "I'm perfectly capable of choosing my own woman."

"All evidence to the contrary, dear. If that were true, you wouldn't be over here moping about Claire every other month. Maybe you *do* love her; I don't want to seem insensitive by discounting that. But clearly, there's something holding you back from fully committing yourself to her. You should examine why that is. When I met your father, there wasn't a doubt in my mind that he was who I wanted to be with. And once I had him, there was no letting him go. We stayed together until the day he died."

I pondered her words, hating to admit there was some validity to them. At the rate we were going, Claire and I would never get down the aisle. I wasn't as pressed about getting married as Mother was on my behalf, but I wanted to. And I knew Claire wanted to marry me, considering all the conversations she tried to have with me about it. It never occurred to me how much I shied away from those conversations; why did I do that, if we apparently wanted the same things? What if we got engaged and then I freaked out and left her again? If I proposed to Claire tomorrow, even if she wanted to accept, she'd likely be skeptical about my sincerity. And I couldn't blame her.

I was feeling confused, and I didn't like that. As sure as I had been just moments before that I wanted Claire back, now my assurance was starting to fade.

"Maybe this is something I should think about some more," I muttered, not wanting to admit that part of me agreed with her. "I'm not entirely sure about anything right now."

"Which is exactly why you shouldn't be so quick to dismiss Aurora," Mother emphasized, moving closer to me on the couch and rubbing my arm in a rare show of affection. "You clearly already had your mind made up when you went on the date; of course it didn't go well under those circumstances. You have to open your mind and give her an honest chance. She deserves that."

Maybe she did, maybe she didn't.

"How much time are you going to waste with a woman who clearly isn't for you? Aurora really likes you, dear. And even though she was rather hurt by your treatment of her, I managed to explain to her that you weren't in your right state of mind and she's willing to give you another chance."

Oh, goody.

"So you're going to give her a call, right?" Mother persisted. "And do so with an open mind?"

I wasn't thrilled about it but I figured, what the hell. First impressions can be wrong. Maybe Aurora was so amazingly dull because she was nervous. I really *didn't* get a chance to get to know her. Hopefully once she loosened up some (assuming she was capable of that), we could get somewhere.

"Sure, Mother," I relented. "I'll call her."

I left Mother's a while after that. Partly because I wanted to stop talking about my love life with her, but also because I needed to get over to the nursing home. I liked to visit there at least once a week, as well as volunteer at the food bank and the children's hospital. Despite Forrest always messing with me because I chose not to work, that didn't mean that I just sat on my ass all day. Yeah, I pampered myself with spa days and whatnot but I wasn't *totally* spoiled. I liked to spend some time giving back. My father had taught me that. Claire had even gone with me a few times.

"It's good to see you, Montrel," Mandy, the front desk attendant said to me when I walked in. "I was wondering if you were coming in today."

"You know I hardly miss my time here. Just running a little late, is all."

"Well, I'm glad you made it. Ms. Debra has been waiting on you."

"How's she feeling today?"

"Better than when you were here last week. She's in one of her feisty moods."

"That's always fun," I chuckled, signing the check-in book and taking my Guest badge to pin on my jacket. "I'll see you later."

I'd been coming to the nursing home for a few years, mostly just to keep the residents company. Some of them didn't have anyone to come visit them, and appreciated someone reading to them or playing a game of cards or just sitting and watching television with them. I enjoyed it but it could be tough when I got attached to one of the residents and they died, which had happened a couple of times since I started going there. It made me feel better to think that I had helped make their last days more pleasant, though.

Ms. Debra was someone I had taken to a year or so earlier, after she pinched my ass when I passed by her wheelchair in the hallway one day. It probably should have offended me but I actually laughed when she did it. After that, she was the main person I came to see. I found myself confiding in her about things I didn't feel I could confide in Mother or even Forrest about. She was a feisty little thing who had never fully recovered from a broken hip, and was strangely proud of the fact that she used to have red hair.

"There's my man!" she exclaimed when I entered her room, clapping her hands. Her nails were always painted a deep red. "Come here and give me a hug!"

Smiling, I put the gift boxes I'd brought on her bed before I leaned down and hugged her tightly, planting a kiss on her forehead as I stood up. "You doing all right today?"

"Oh, I'm just fine. Wish I could get out of this blasted wheelchair and go home, but they won't let me do that."

"You...can't walk, Ms. Debra."

"Ugh. Damn these weak bones. Who knew never drinking milk would come back to bite me in the ass?"

I chuckled.

"If my Arnie was here, he'd take care of me," Ms. Debra mused sadly, referring to her late husband. I looked at her, concerned, but just like that, she snapped out of it. "But whatever. At least I don't have to do any more housework."

"That's a good way to look at it."

"Sit down," she ordered, motioning towards the padded chair near her wheelchair before glancing at the boxes. "What's that?"

"Brought you some dressing gowns. They're pure silk; you'll love 'em."

"Fancy. And I love you for it but you know I don't like you spending that kind of money on me. Especially when I'm just slumming around here."

"Doesn't matter; you still deserve nice things. And if I can't spend my money on people I care about, well, that's just no fun, is it?"

She smiled at me, her cheeks reddening behind her full face of makeup that she still insisted on wearing. "Thank you so much, my darling. I appreciate it. So what's been going on with you this week?"

"Not too much," I replied, removing my blazer and taking a seat. "I'm just coming from visiting my Mother."

"Again? Wow, you sure do go over there a lot."

My jaw dropped slightly in surprise. "I don't go *that* much."

"More than once a week?"

"Once or twice. She likes my company."

"Right. She must not have anything else going on for herself."

I let Ms. Debra get away with saying stuff like that.

"She has her own interests. She has friends she vacations with, she goes wine-tasting, she likes to draw..."

"Oh, wow, I think I actually dozed off for a minute. What a life. She still on the crusade to get you down the aisle?"

"Of course."

"What's the rush? You're still young and virile. You've got plenty of time to marry and have kids, if that's what you want."

"Yeah, I want it someday. I actually don't know *why* Mother is so anxious for me to get married; can't say I've ever asked her that."

"You just do whatever she wants you to do."

"I wouldn't say *that*..."

"*I* would, based on what you've told me. When it comes to her, you have zero backbone. You don't know how to tell her no."

"I can't disrespect my mother."

"Who said anything about disrespect? You're a grown man, aren't you? I'm sure you can respectfully tell your mama that who you date and marry and anything else is *your* decision, not hers."

"I tried. But she has a way of getting me to see her side of things. And I admittedly sometimes just go along with her to keep the peace."

"And you're happy with that?"

"I don't love it. But ever since Dad died, I've tried not to do anything to bring her more strife. I guess I don't realize that at times it's to my own detriment."

"You've gotta live your own life, my darling. You can still be there for your mama without letting her dictate what you do. Otherwise you're gonna be sixty years old, still being her puppet. But hey, you've gotta realize you're tired of all this on your own."

That was one thing about Ms. Debra; she'd tell me off and then smooth it over. I somehow received her tough love better than I did from Forrest or anyone else.

"You're right," I admitted. "I let her talk me into calling Aurora and setting up another date. And I had decided I was done with her."

"See there?"

"But maybe she was right when she said I didn't give Aurora a fair chance. I hadn't wanted to go out with her so that probably affected my attitude. It wouldn't be the worst thing in the world to try again, I guess."

"I thought you wanted Claire back."

I turned my eyes towards the television, which was playing some soap opera on mute. "She's dating someone else now."

"You done messed up, huh? Drove her away one too many times. I liked Claire; she's a sweetheart. Needs to eat about twelve steaks, but she's darling."

I couldn't help but chuckle. "Believe me, she eats plenty. She's just one of those people who can't gain weight easily."

"I never had that problem. I've always been all hips and ass. Even more so now that I'm in this wheelchair and can't exercise, and now I've got this belly, too. Have you seen the size of my boobs?"

"Ms. Debra!"

"Look at how red your face is! I love doing that. You young people are so much fun to mess with!"

"I don't know why you like doing that to me," I shook my head, not able to resist smiling.

"Hey, if I've gotta be stuck in this wheelchair, I should be able to say what I want. But back to what we were talking about. You have to figure out what it is you really want, my darling. You seem to make these impulsive decisions without thinking them through. You're not doing yourself or these women any favors by being wishy-washy. You just come off as the bad guy, and you're not really a bad guy."

"I'd like to think I'm not."

"Then stop acting like it. Being someone that jerks people around and toys with their feelings is nothing to be proud of. And wasting someone's time is damn near unforgivable to me. You say you love Claire?"

"Yes, ma'am."

"Then have enough respect for her to leave her alone until you're a hundred percent sure you're ready for her. Especially now that she's seeing someone else; if she's happy, let her be happy. You've certainly caused her enough of the opposite."

"I never wanted to do that," I defended. I ran my hands down my face before letting them drop onto my lap with a sigh. "But I get why you say that. My actions don't really back up my words, as far as how I feel about her."

"Maybe you don't love her as much as you think you do," Ms. Debra offered. "And with this other woman whose name I'm not even gonna try to pronounce, don't be stringing her along, either. If you don't like her, be honest about it. There's no need to be cruel; just direct. But don't waste her time like you did Claire's."

That kind of stung. It wasn't like I set out intending to waste anybody's time. Every time I went back to Claire, it was with the purest of intentions. At least, I thought it was. Things just always changed along the way.

Maybe I just didn't know what the hell I was doing when it came to relationships.

I left the nursing home a while later with a lot on my mind. I wanted to talk to Claire and really lay it all out; see where her head was. I had to know if she was serious about this guy she was dating or if he was a rebound fling to get over me, and if she had *any* desire whatsoever to try things with me one more time. And if she did, I wasn't going to mess it up again.

Instead of reaching out to her in the car, I decided to wait until I got home so I could give her my full attention. Mother and Ms. Debra's words scrolled through my mind as I tried to figure out what I was going to say. It had to be something to relay my sincerity, since Claire would no doubt think I was full of shit.

What I wasn't expecting, though, was to see a box waiting for me from Claire containing every gift I'd ever given her. Even small things, like ticket stubs or little notes I'd written to her on scraps of paper; she liked to save that kind of stuff, even if it wasn't something particularly romantic. And here it was, all stuffed into this box. It was like a blow to the chest that she just had to get any reminders of me out of her house. I wondered if this was how she felt when I sent her stuff back to her months ago, and remembered Forrest's many warnings about one day getting a taste of my own medicine. It certainly wasn't a good feeling.

Maybe Claire really was over me this time. Maybe I'd finally pushed her too far. She'd never returned anything I'd given her before; the fact that she was erasing all traces of our relationship from her life was very telling. She was moving on from me, for real.

I sank onto my couch as that realization set in. Emotion swirled inside me at the thought of Claire being out of my life for good. Sure, we might see each other occasionally because of our mutual friendships with Forrest and Giselle, but who's to say she wouldn't just avoid me altogether if she knew I was going to be around? Or worse, bring her new man in my face? I didn't think I could handle seeing Claire with someone else in person; it was bad enough seeing it on social media. I didn't want to see her with anyone but me, but like she'd said, a person could only take so much.

I started to call her but stopped, remembering she had blocked me. What would I even say, anyway? She had made herself clear; she was done with me and had moved on. And everything I'd ever given her was in a box on my coffee table. Maybe I should do what Ms. Debra advised and respect that. I'd caused her enough headache and heartache, whether or not I meant to.

Putting my phone down, I stood up and left the room, needing to be anywhere other than in front of that box right then.

• • • •

I HAD PROMISED MOTHER that I'd call Aurora, but it took me another couple of days to actually do it. I was still reeling from my decision to let Claire go, and wasn't in a particular hurry to try anything with someone else, namely someone I wasn't terribly interested in.

But then I decided that maybe this was just what I needed; someone to get my mind off of Claire. I'd been moping around my house for two days, not wanting to be bothered with anything or anyone, repeatedly kicking myself for losing the woman I loved. It didn't help that the one time I broke down and DM'd Claire with some carefully concocted excuse, she didn't even read it. Part of me still believed that I could get her to come around if I was just given time to, but I could hear Forrest's voice in my head telling me that was manipulation.

Really, I didn't have to *just* hear it in my head since he was still crashing in my guest room. He and Giselle were still on the outs, and when he wasn't working, he was holed up in there. And you already know he gave me a hard time when he saw the box from Claire.

"So she's finally done with your ass, huh?"

I cut my eyes at him. "Don't start, Forrest."

"I'm just saying. I told you this was gonna happen but you weren't trying to hear it."

"I'm not trying to hear *this* now, either. I'm really messed up over this, man."

"What? I thought you always said that you could get Claire back any time you were ready to."

"Yeah, well, I think that ship has sailed. She's moved on and I have to respect that."

"You're sounding disturbingly mature. Since when do you care about anybody's wants but your own?"

"Damn, what kind of man do you think I am?"

"A selfish, spoiled, entitled-"

"That was a rhetorical question. And people can change. Claire doesn't deserve what I've been doing to her and I know that, so..." I shrugged my shoulders. "I just have to wish her well and move on, too."

"Hmmm," Forrest looked at me thoughtfully, crossing his arms over his chest. "Somebody must have gotten to you. You didn't wise up this much on your own in two days of trudging around this house. You got some counseling or something from somebody."

Forrest knew I volunteered at the nursing home but he didn't know the depth of the conversations I had with Ms. Debra. That was something I kept close to the vest. I can't say why; I just considered my time with Ms. Debra special and in a category of its own.

"Regardless, I'm not gonna bother Claire," I declared, skirting his assessment. "I'm going to try again with Aurora, actually."

"That woman that came by here? I thought you said you didn't like her."

"I went in not *wanting* to like her. I can admit I didn't really give her a fair shot, since I went on the date under duress. But she's nice, pretty...has some things going for her. I'm willing to try it again."

"And I bet your mama stayed on your back until you agreed to try it again, huh?"

"You really don't think much of my mother, do you?"

"I don't like how whipped you are when it comes to her. But you allow it, so..."

"I am not *whipped*. I just take her feelings into consideration, though admittedly more than I should, at times. And true enough, she influenced me to see Aurora again but if I was *really* against it, I could have refused. It'll be good for me to see where things can go with someone else."

"Why, so you can one-up Claire?"

"No. It's not about that. It isn't about Claire."

"Not even a little bit? There isn't the *teeniest* part of you that wants to show her up?"

"Man, what am I, fifteen? I don't need to do that. I'm not going to act like I'm unaffected by Claire being in another relationship but it is what it is. She's doing her thing so I need to do mine."

"Why not just take some time to be *by yourself*?" Forrest suggested. "You're always jumping from one woman to another; it's like you don't know how to be alone or something. Maybe you need to spend some time solo and get your mind right; really take the time to figure out what it is you need and want in a relationship."

I didn't want to do that. I didn't like being by myself.

"I think I'm good with that," I replied, getting some kombucha from the refrigerator. "That's why I've been taking my time calling Aurora; I didn't want to jump the gun too soon after admitting I'd lost Claire. I want to have a clear head when I finally do entertain Aurora again."

"All right, then," Forrest shrugged, grabbing some juice and turning to leave the room. "I guess you think you know what you're doing."

"Hopefully."

Another couple of days passed before I finally called Aurora and asked her out. She seemed happy to hear from me, which I chose to take as encouraging. Plus, I needed the distraction. The very next day after my conversation with Forrest, I was at the spa for my monthly pampering. While I mindlessly scrolled through my phone in the waiting room, I happened to glance out the front window and see a black SUV pull up in the parking lot. A tall Black guy exited the driver's side, rounding the front of the truck and opening the passenger door, holding his hand out for his riding mate. I almost dropped my phone when I saw it was Claire.

I actually rubbed my eyes, not believing what I was seeing. I'd never known Claire to come to the spa. But there she was. And my stomach dropped when the guy took her hand and led her to the front door, holding it open for her. They never even turned my way as they headed for the front desk.

"Hey, good afternoon," the guy greeted the front desk employee Liza (who hadn't had many words for me, since I never called her). "I'm Warner Branson; I made a reservation for a full spa day for my girlfriend, Claire Hutchinson."

I felt like I'd been punched in the chest.

Seeing this guy in person, seeing him touch on Claire, hearing him call her *his girlfriend*, seeing how Claire gave him that lovesick-looking grin when he did...it hurt beyond belief. I winced as I continued eyeing them, though I couldn't tear my eyes away.

Of all the spas in the city...did she come to that spa because she thought I might be there? Was she trying to rub her relationship in my face? She knew I went every month, though I admittedly never told her exactly which spa I frequented....partly because I didn't want her trying to tag along. That was *my* time, and I hadn't wanted it intruded upon, even by her.

But apparently, her man had made the reservation, so it was a coincidence that she ended up at my spa...at the exact time I was there. It was like a cosmic bitch slap to the face, reminding me of what I'd messed up. As if I needed another reminder.

Unable to stomach any more, I bolted to my feet, scurrying off to the bathroom as I heard Warner tell Claire he'd be back to pick her up in a couple of hours. But not quick enough to miss the kiss he laid on her after he did.

Needless to say, that whole scene stayed stuck on my mind, despite my efforts to expunge it. I wasn't even able to sleep that night, tortured with the repeated image of Claire with her new man, holding hands and grinning and kissing. The very next day, I called Aurora and asked her out with renewed determination to move on just as Claire had.

Aurora invited me over to her place, offering to cook for me. I would have preferred doing something a little less intimate, but figured it wouldn't be that bad. Maybe it would keep my mind from wandering. Nothing like a home-cooked meal, after all. I wasn't much of a cook, myself. And Mother always either had things catered or hired a chef; the closest she came to cooking was boiling water for her tea.

"Thank you for coming by, Montrel," Aurora said once we were seated at her dining room table a couple of nights later. I still had to really concentrate to hear her. "And I appreciate the flowers."

"No problem. The food smells delicious. What's on the menu?"

"Seafood pot pies. And I made a trifle for dessert. Is that okay?"

"Yeah, that sounds great. You must be quite the cook."

"I used to always like to be in the kitchen with my mother when I was a girl. I believe knowing how to cook is one of the most important skills you can have."

"I suppose..."

"That and color-coordinating."

I almost rolled my eyes but stopped myself. "Sure."

"I'll go bring the food in."

She headed into the kitchen and I watched her walk away, noting her ass in the white fitted dress she was wearing. I never paid much attention to her shape before but I could admit she had a nice one. Her body along with her smooth tawny skin and thick shoulder-length brown hair made for an attractive package. If only her conversation was as intriguing as her physical attributes.

The food was really good; she certainly knew what she was doing in the kitchen. Unfortunately, though, she was only marginally more interesting than she was on our first date. I didn't know if she was nervous or if this was just how she was, but I didn't know if this could work.

Then I got a mental image of Claire and that other guy, and it reignited my desire to try a little harder. At least I wasn't bored this time.

"So tell me something crazy you did in college," I suggested after we had finished eating and moved to the living room. We both had glasses of champagne. "We all have at least one story."

"Hmm," she mused, taking a sip of her champagne. "I admit I was a bookworm in college. But there *was* this one time I danced on top of a bar."

My eyebrows shot up in surprise. I wasn't expecting that. "You did?"

"Yes. Some girls from my dorm had dragged me out during Homecoming weekend and encouraged me to drink. I wasn't much into alcohol at that point and just asked for iced tea, and had no idea that the Long Island Iced Teas they ordered for me were alcoholic. Just one had me acting outside of myself."

"Wow. I can't even imagine you doing something like that."

"It was rather embarrassing. I didn't drink again for years after that. But I suppose it's okay to laugh about it now."

"It could've been worse. I've done way more dumb stuff than that."

"Such as?"

Letting Claire go. I blinked and shook my head, trying to jar that thought from my mind. I didn't need to be thinking about Claire, especially now that I was finally having a somewhat decent time with Aurora.

"I'll be back to get you in a couple of hours, baby. Enjoy your spa day. You deserve it."

"Umm," I tried to bring my attention back to the conversation and push that guy Warner's words to Claire out of my mind, "I went streaking on a dare. It was barely forty degrees outside. And if that wasn't bad enough, I tripped on some gravel and scraped myself all up."

"Oh!" Aurora giggled. She put down her glass. "Like on your legs?"

"Well, there and other more...delicate places."

"You mean like here?"

She was grabbing my dick. Like, seriously. She was so smooth with it that I didn't even see it coming. Her hand started caressing me through my slacks, and the resistance that I told myself I needed to put forth kind of melted away. Hell, it felt good.

When she saw I wasn't going to stop her, she leaned in and kissed me as she continued her caressing. It wasn't the first time we kissed, but when she did it after our first date, I wasn't thinking about anything but getting her off of me. This time, I noticed how soft her lips were. Then I realized how good she smelled; like jasmine. I eased into kissing her back, opening more to her the more the kiss went on.

Before too long, her hand was down my pants as we kissed hungrily and deeply. My hand had crept underneath her dress. All other thoughts vacated my mind as we progressively fondled each other, getting more and more into it. I wasn't thinking about Claire or Mother or anybody else right then; Aurora finally had my complete attention.

Eventually we were naked on her couch, with her on my lap riding me. I didn't even care to suggest getting a towel or sheet to put underneath us first. I just got lost in the moment, enjoying Aurora's luscious body and surprisingly skillful moves.

"Is it good, Montrel?" she whispered, working her hips clockwise, then counterclockwise. The way she kept switching it up was driving me a little crazy, in a good way.

"Yes," I hissed, biting my lip. "Oh yes..."

She pushed her breasts together and I couldn't resist leaning forward and indulging. I hadn't even realized what a nice rack she had but she boasted a beautiful pair of breasts. Part of me wondered if they were real but the bigger part didn't give a damn.

Grunting in pleasure, she threw her head back momentarily before sitting back up to watch me lick her nipples. I wrapped an arm tighter around her, bringing her closer to me.

"Can we do this again?" she asked, switching from a swirl to a bounce. "Can we have sex again after tonight?"

"*Hell* yes."

She grabbed my face in both hands and laid a deep kiss on me. "You promise?"

"Yes, absolutely," I panted, my eyes sliding closed as she started sucking my neck. "I promise everything..."

She started grinding on me faster, and I felt like I was about to scream. Nobody had put it on me like this in years, if ever. I never, ever would have imagined Aurora had skills like this.

But that wasn't even the half of it, because she eased off of me and began giving me a hand job that had me losing my words. Hand jobs usually did nothing for me because most women didn't know how to do them right, but Aurora certainly did. My hands gripped the couch pillows as I gritted my teeth, trying to keep myself from exploding.

"I'm so glad we're a couple now," she moaned, fondling my balls with the other hand. I felt like I was going to melt right into the couch.

"Me too," I moaned without thinking. "Me too, baby..."

Then she slid her mouth over my dick and my hips shot up about six inches. I grabbed a handful of her hair as she sucked the sense out of me, taking me all the way in to the back of her throat. My body was jerking like I'd been tased, which I would have been more embarrassed about if it didn't feel so ridiculously amazing.

"A-aaur-rroor-ahhhhh..." I stuttered, feeling like I was losing my damn mind.

"Yes?" She licked my inner thighs, sending brand new shock waves through my body.

I couldn't even say anything else. I just laid back and let her do what she wanted to me, occasionally lifting my head to look down at her because part of me actually felt like I was dreaming. This was not what I expected to go down when I showed up at her house a couple of hours before.

She gave me one last long suck before hopping back up onto my lap to finish me off, which didn't take long.

"*Shit!*" I screamed, busting what felt like the biggest nut of my life. I had her body wrapped in a death grip with both arms, holding her to me as I shuddered and convulsed for a good minute or two.

Did that really just happen? Did this woman I had to convince myself to see again and even go so far as to take a drink before getting to her house so I could tolerate her mundane conversation just give me *the best sex of my fucking life*?

She moaned as she gave me a few lingering kisses, wrapping her arms around my neck. Usually after I came I needed a few minutes and didn't want to be touched. But I readily kissed Aurora back, sliding my hands along her slick skin. I don't know if it was the pre-date drink or the champagne or what, but I didn't want her to leave me alone.

"Let's go to my bedroom," she whispered against my lips, then darted her tongue out to lick my chin. Even that was sexy as hell to me.

I just nodded as I continued to enjoy her kisses. I would have agreed to just about anything right then. She slowly eased off my lap and took my hand, leading the way. She really did have a nice ass.

I ended up spending the night. And I didn't think about anything or anyone else the whole time. Finally.

Seventeen – Claire

• • • •

THERE WAS A BRIEF MOMENT where I second-guessed my decision to become official with Warner, but it didn't last long. That was just fear of something new, and I realized that. When I thought about it, it made me really excited.

To be real, he was exciting me in more ways than one. I was starting to crave Warner, and our makeout sessions and light petting weren't really cutting it like it used to. I wanted him in my bed, ASAP.

But we had agreed to wait to have sex, wanting to get to know each other better and all that. And it sounded good when we first said it. But the more time I spent around him and the more times he laid those amazing kisses on me, the more I wanted us to do those things with our clothes *off*. Admittedly, though, I was too shy to actually tell him this, so I just continued to be horny in silence.

Things were going great, but there was one thing I wished we could get past, though.

"Baby, are you *sure* you're over Montrel?"

I sighed, looking over at him. We were just leaving the miniature golf course and he asked that out of the blue, as he tended to do more often since I told him about Montrel coming to my house that night. I told myself to be patient even though I was a little tired of getting asked a question I'd already repeatedly answered.

"Yes, Warner. I've told you that." I shook my head. "Many times."

"I hate to keep bugging you about this, but...I don't know; I just have a bad feeling. Like something's going to happen with you two."

"Why would you think that? Nothing is going to happen."

"I can't explain it but I can't seem to shake the thought. I just get the feeling that sooner or later, he's going to try to come at you again."

"I doubt it, but if he does, I'll handle it." I turned to look at him as we reached his Ford Explorer. "You don't have to worry about Montrel. I'm with *you*. This is where I wanna be."

"And this is where I want you to be. I just don't want anything to mess things up between us."

"So how 'bout we just focus on us and keep certain names out of our conversations?" I suggested, sliding my arms around his waist. "I'm not thinking about him and I don't want you to be, either."

"All right; I'm sorry." He leaned down and kissed me, and I pushed my body closer to his. He backed me against his truck, pressing his groin against me as we made out like teenagers in the parking lot. My body was automatically on fire for him.

"Get a room!"

I didn't know who shouted that to us, but Warner and I started giggling against each other's lips.

"I guess we should go, huh?" he muttered, giving my lips another nip.

"Yeah, we should." I bit my lip, both out of arousal and to work up some nerve. "Whichever house we go to, can we end up in bed together?"

He leaned back slightly, looking into my eyes. "For real?"

"Yeah. I'm ready." I pulled him closer to me by the waist, slipping a hand between us to brush his erection. "I want to feel all of this inside me."

"I want that, too, but I don't want us to rush anything, that's all," Warner replied, taking a step back. "I've made the mistake of bringing sex into things too quickly and it never ended well. I don't want that to happen with us. I want us to go the distance, Claire, and do things right."

"Well, if we both want it, how is it wrong? Not to mention, we're a couple; it's not like we're still just dating. I'd think this would be one of the perks of us making it official, getting to enjoy each other in every way we want to."

"I get it, but I'd still prefer to wait a little bit, that's all," Warner insisted. "Sex changes things."

"Yeah, but it doesn't always have to change things for the worst. It sounds like you're just being paranoid again."

"Okay, fine, if I'm being all the way real about it, I want to be absolutely sure you're *totally* with me when we take it there," he admitted, his eyes going hard for a second. "As long as I still have this bad feeling about you and your ex-"

"Okay, well here's a thought...don't have that feeling. Problem solved."

"You think it's that easy? It's not like I'm *trying* to feel like this, baby. But over the years, I've learned to trust my gut."

"Fine, Warner, whatever." I held up a hand, not wanting to hear anymore. I was frustrated and not interested in hiding it. "Let's just go."

"Come on, Claire, don't be mad," he pleaded, holding his hands out. "It's not that I don't want to; I want you more than anything. I just don't want this cloud to be over us when we take it to that level, that's all."

"Yeah, okay." I shook my head and turned away, hating that I'd even brought it up. I couldn't believe he was refusing me.

"Baby-"

"Can you unlock the door so I can get in? It's cold."

I ignored his pleading eyes as he unlocked the truck with his key fob. Yanking the door open before he could and climbing inside, I just sat there in a huff as he rounded the front of the truck and got into the driver's seat, turning my face towards the passenger's window. I could tell he was looking at me but I wasn't trying to pay him any attention.

"You still want to go to my house?" he asked me as he pulled out of the parking lot.

"No, thanks. You can just take me home."

"Claire, really?"

"Yes, really."

He didn't say anything else, thankfully. We just rode in silence.

On some level I could appreciate patience. I'd certainly been with my share of men who wanted to rush to the bedroom without getting to know me first. But Warner had already proven that he was interested in me for more than that, so it was frustrating being rejected for something we both clearly wanted.

I blamed myself for even putting it out there. I should've just continued with the teenage kissing and petting and been happy with it, and let him make the first move to take it deeper. Now I was feeling stupid.

We pulled up in front of my house and I had every intention of just getting out of Warner's truck without a word, but he stopped me as I was removing my seatbelt.

"I don't want to leave things like this," he insisted, looking right at me. "Can we talk?"

"What's to talk about? You made yourself clear. You don't want me."

"That's not what I said. In fact, I clearly stated I *do* want you. I just don't want us to rush into sex, especially while I have these thoughts clouding my brain. How is that a bad thing?"

I didn't know how to explain it to him where it made any sense. Maybe I was getting a little too in my feelings about this but I couldn't help my pride being a tad bruised.

"It's not, I guess," I finally admitted, still not looking at him. "If you want to wait, there's really nothing I can do about it."

"But you're still mad."

"I'm disappointed. But whatever."

"No, not *whatever*. Your feelings matter to me, Claire. I just want to be sure there aren't any misunderstandings about anything. Please don't take this personally because it's only because I respect you and what we have so much, and because I admittedly still have my reservations and you and your ex. I don't want anything to go wrong. I love you and I want this to go the distance."

My head whipped around to him. "You what?"

"I said I love you." He slid his fingers through mine. "A lot."

He got me with that one. My mouth opened but nothing came out.

"I don't need you to say it back to me right now," he assured, kissing my hand. "Whenever you're ready-"

"I love you, too," I blurted hurriedly, turning to him. My heart was beating super fast all of a sudden. I hadn't even planned on going there but in that moment, I just knew I loved him, too. My anger from minutes before was forgotten.

"You sure?"

"Absolutely."

"That makes me happy to hear that, baby. *You* make me happy. And as corny as I may be sounding right now, just know that whatever I say to you is sincere and from the heart. I'd never bullshit you, especially about something like this."

"I believe you." I smiled at him, feeling warm all over. I was going to have to give my mother a big ol' gift basket for introducing me to this man. The last thing I expected was for things to get to this level. Hell, I initially didn't even want to meet him at all, but I could thank Montrel for pushing me into that decision. At least he was good for something.

"So we're in this, right?" He lightly grazed underneath my chin with his finger, gazing at me in a way that made tingles rain down from head to toe. "It's you and me?"

"You and me."

"Oh, I almost forgot...I got something for you." He reached a long arm behind his seat and produced a gift bag, making my grin stretch even wider.

"Warner, you're spoiling me."

"Of course I am. That's what I'm supposed to do. Plus, I love putting that smile on your face."

This man, this man. He was always giving me little gifts for no reason at all, and I appreciated it more than I could say. It was certainly a change from my relationship with you-know-who, who spoiled his mama more than he did me and hardly ever gave me any gifts unless he was in the doghouse or it was a holiday or my birthday.

Except for my *last* birthday, when he gave me the gift of dumping me.

Pushing that thought from my mind, I excitedly dug into the gift bag to find a beautiful gold necklace with a gold 'C' charm, and a gold heart. I loved it and wasted no time putting it on, with Warner reaching over to help me.

"You like it?" he asked, securing the clasp and letting his hand rest on the back of my neck.

"I *love* it! Thank you so much, baby."

He fingered the charms lying on my chest. "You have my heart, Claire. I hope I have yours, too."

"You do," I quickly insisted, tears stinging my eyes. "You absolutely do."

"I'm glad to hear that. Come here."

He brought my face to his and I eagerly accepted his kiss. As much as I had wanted to end the evening with us naked in bed together, this ending was a hell of a lot better. And it was more meaningful. Sex could be with anybody. But falling for someone special was more important.

I invited him inside, and we spent the rest of the evening on the couch, cuddling and talking. I felt like I knew him so much better after that night. I'd never felt this close to Montrel because there was only so much he would share with me. But Warner was like an open book, and it made me trust him so much more. I only hope he trusted me as much.

• • • •

A FEW DAYS LATER, I was still riding high from my night with Warner. That was the night everything got real between us and it had been hard to focus on much of anything else since then. Every time I thought about that first time Warner told me he loved me, it had me grinning so hard my face hurt.

I had to go to my parent's for dinner and to go over some stuff for their upcoming anniversary party. Thirty-five years was a long time to be married to one person, and now I was having daydreams about me and Warner in that spot one day. We hadn't even been dating that long and I was already picturing us on our coral anniversary. Me and my imagination.

"We're just going to have something here at the house," Mama was telling me as I sat in the kitchen while she cooked. "We want to celebrate it but don't want to do anything over the top."

"Why not?" I asked, peeling carrots into a bowl at the kitchen table. "It's a big deal."

"You know me and your father don't like a lot of fuss. Having some friends and family here with us will be more than enough."

"Is Benny coming?"

"Yeah, he said he was going to make sure to come home that weekend. It feels like it's been forever since he's been back here. He's really loving college."

"I bet. Is there anything you need me to do for the party?"

"No, thank you. We're having it catered because I know I'm not going to want to cook for a crowd that day. They'll do all the clean-up and everything. All we have to do is enjoy ourselves."

"Sounds like my kind of party."

"Are you going to be bringing Warner?"

My smile was automatic. "Of course."

"I'm glad the two of you hit it off so well," Mama smiled, coming to get the finished carrots. "And to think you weren't even interested when I first brought him up to you."

"True. And I admit that I initially only called him to take my mind off my ex. But it turned out to be the best thing I could've done. I've never been this happy with anyone as I am with Warner."

"That's wonderful!" Mother beamed, pausing her action of putting the carrots into the roasting pan. "I usually try to stay out of your personal business but I always knew Warner was a nice young man that would be good for you."

"He is."

A few silent moments passed before Mama spoke again. "You know," she hedged cautiously, "I was going back and forth about whether I should mention this to you or not..."

"Mention what?"

She hesitated before wiping her hands on a dish towel and turning to me. "Montrel called me."

I spun around to face her. "He what?"

"He called me a few days ago...asking about you."

"Asking *what* about me?"

"If you were truly happy with Warner...if I thought you might be willing to give him another chance...if I'd *help* him get you to give him another chance...if I thought you and Warner were serious or just a fling...things like that."

I couldn't believe it. The man just couldn't take a hint. "How come you're just now telling me? What did you say to him?"

"You know me better than that, Claire. I didn't tell him anything, other than he needed to talk to you if he wanted to get any answers. He actually sounded a little drunk."

"Wow." I shook my head, not believing Montrel's nerve. He just wouldn't leave well enough alone. What, was he so bent because I was the one who ended things this time? Usually he was the one who broke up with me and I was the one bugging *him* afterwards. Was this an ego thing?

Whatever it was, it wasn't going to work. I was finally happy and I wasn't about to let Montrel mess that up.

I was sure about this, but Chichi had her doubts.

"I think you need to be careful," she warned after I told her about all this later. "Montrel is probably going to pull some more tricks out of his bag before it's all said and done."

"It's already said and done. Montrel and I are over. And I don't care *what* he tries, it's not going to make any difference."

"I hear you, girl, and I know you feel you mean it. I'm just saying, though..."

"What, because I've been so weak for him in the past, you think I haven't learned anything from all that and would fall for his charms again?"

"I would *hope* not, but-"

"Wow, you really don't think that much of me, do you?" I asked, a little insulted. "Is it *that* impossible to believe I've learned from all the bullshit Montrel has put me through and am ready to move on from him?"

"Don't go getting mad at me, Claire, but you and I both know that you've made these kinds of declarations before only to end up back with Montrel again after he sweet-talks you. And I'm just saying to remember that for whenever he tries something again, that's all."

"Who says he will? He said he was dating someone else."

"And you bought that? Even if he is seeing somebody, she's probably just a placeholder until he can get *you* back. It's like he has some kind of sick obsession with getting back with you every time y'all break up."

"I wouldn't go so far as to use the word *obsession*..."

"What would you call it? Him resorting to calling *your mama* to try to grill her for information?"

"I think he just can't stand it that *I* was the one who dumped *him* this time," I declared. "He's used to being the one to pull all the strings."

"Even more to the point, then. He'll try his damndest to get you back to prove he still has the upper hand, then once he has you, he'll ride it out for a while before he punks out like he usually does. Then you'll be over here crying and kicking yourself again. Don't let it happen."

"I'm not, Chichi. There's nothing Montrel can say to make me want to go there with him again. I'm totally happy in my relationship with Warner. Though if I had *one* complaint, it would be that he's still so paranoid about me and Montrel possibly reconciling. It gets a little annoying, really."

"I don't see why. That's a valid concern, Claire, given how many times you've taken him back. Not to mention how you almost let him kiss you when he came to your house a few weeks ago."

Damn. I'd almost forgotten about that. "That wouldn't happen again."

"Uh-huh. If you ask me, you need to block Montrel's number, block him on social media, block him everywhere. Send him the message that you're for real this time and not just playing a really convincing game of hard-to-get."

"You think I should call him and tell him to step off?"

"Is that what I said? 'Cause I could've sworn I said the opposite of that."

"It's not going to be a social call. I'll just tell him to leave me alone and leave it at that."

"You really think it's as easy as that? You've already done that, Claire, and it hasn't done any good. I'm telling you, block him."

"I've already blocked his calls."

"And what about everywhere else? He's still blowing up your DMs on Instagram."

"It's not like I acknowledge the messages anymore."

"Sure. And if he shows up at your house, do not entertain him; threaten to call the cops if he doesn't leave. You have to do something different this time or he's never really gonna take you seriously."

Chichi had a point. I thought Montrel had gotten the message after I sent that box of stuff to him, but now he had taken to contacting my family about me. He'd sent a few DMs, but I never responded to any of it. As much as I'd like to believe he'd just move on with his life like he claimed, clearly that wasn't the case.

After I got off the phone with Chichi, I immediately blocked Montrel on Instagram and Facebook. But when I scrolled to his name in my contact list to erase his number again (because I'd re-added it after I took him back the last time), I couldn't bring myself to do it. I didn't know why, since I sincerely didn't want to talk to him at all.

Putting my phone aside, I rationalized blocking him was enough. But whether I erased his number or not, *nothing* was going to happen with me and Montrel again. I had something more than just my dignity to lose this time; Warner was too special to me and I wasn't going to do anything stupid to send him running.

And really, I wanted to prove him wrong as well as Chichi, since he apparently still believed I wasn't as over Montrel as I claimed to be. I'd show all of 'em.

Eighteen – Montrel

• • • •

I COULD HEAR THE MOANS and bed springs as soon as I walked through the front door. This was why I didn't have houseguests.

Forrest had a lot of nerve, bringing some woman to my house and sexing her in my guest room. Regardless of how upset he was over Giselle, that didn't justify him stepping out on her. And in *my* house. He could've at least gotten a hotel room.

Not caring about their privacy, I knocked hard on the door a few times before trying the doorknob. To my surprise, it was unlocked. I guess they were too caught up in the throes of passion to lock the door behind themselves.

I stormed into the room but stopped short when I saw who was actually in the bed.

"Montrel!" Giselle shrieked upon seeing me, scrambling to cover herself with the sheet.

"What are you doing, man??" Forrest shouted, shielding his wife with his body.

"What am *I* doing? What are *y'all* doing?" I countered. "Getting busy in my house when you have one of your own?"

"Just get out," Forrest barked, yanking my Egyptian cotton sheets around his waist.

"Yeah, okay. But be ready to explain yourself when you come out of here."

Disgusted, I walked out and slammed the door behind me, wondering how long it was going to take for them to gather themselves. *Surely*, they weren't going to just pick up where they left off when I busted them. I got my answer when I heard the door lock and the bedsprings again.

Seriously??

Sometimes I really didn't like people.

It was damn near forty-five minutes before they finally came out. I was reading on the couch when Giselle scurried out the front door without so much as a good-bye. Forrest came strolling out, shirtless and in a pair of sweat pants like he didn't have a care in the world. The bastard was actually whistling.

I eyed him as he flopped himself on the opposite end of the couch from me and picked up the remote. He was actually going to try to act like that whole episode hadn't happened.

"Um, you want to explain what just happened back there?"

"I was having sex with my wife. I don't need to explain that."

"If you were doing that in your own house, you'd be right about that. But since you're in *my* house..."

"What is the big damn deal? I'd think you'd be happy we're making some progress."

"Well seeing as how she left here without you, I don't see how much progress you made. If you two reconciled, why are you still here?"

"We *didn't* reconcile. She came over to talk; we were going back and forth about all the baby stuff and then before I knew it, we were tearing each other's clothes off. It wasn't planned; it just happened."

"Lovely. You're replacing my bed sheets."

"Whatever. I need to go by Target, anyway."

"Target?!" I put my book down. "Forrest, man, don't you think it's about time for you to go back home? You and Giselle can work things out faster if you're in the same house."

"She's not ready for that. I told her I wanted to come home and she said the time apart is good for us. That's why she left out of here like she did; we argued about that after we finished getting busy."

"Well, why don't you get a hotel? Then the two of you can have all the meaningless romps you want."

"No, thanks. I'm comfortable where I am."

I sighed. I was never gonna get this man out of my house.

"I notice you've been spending more time with that Aurora woman," Forrest said to me, placing the remote on the coffee table after settling on some football game. "I thought you said you didn't like her."

"She's all right," I replied, hoping Forrest didn't notice the immediate flush in my cheeks.

"What made you change your mind?"

"Oh...just figured I'd give her another shot, that's all. Might as well."

"Might as well? That doesn't sound like you. You were pretty adamant against seeing her again before. Usually when you write someone off, that's it. Unless her name is Claire, of course." He eyed me, knowing there something I wasn't telling him. "What, your mama hounded you so much that you changed your tune?"

"Yeah," I quickly agreed, glad to blame it on that. "You know how my mother is. Once she's on a mission, it's futile to try and fight it. And Aurora isn't as bad of company as I thought."

Forrest shook his head. "Like I said. Whipped."

I might've been whipped, but it wasn't by Mother like he thought. The truth was, Aurora had turned me out. That night she put it on me the first time had me daydreaming and going through withdrawals like some kind of fiend. And I agreed to see her again a couple of days later because, well, I had to make sure it wasn't a fluke.

It was not.

Aurora might not have been my dream woman but she had more sexual skills than all the women I'd been with combined. I was spending damn near every night with her because I couldn't get enough of it. What she did that first night was just a mere hint of her full abilities. We did positions I'd only seen in books. It was a fun casual thing that she seemed to be enjoying as much as I was. And it was a great distraction from thinking about Claire.

She still crept into my thoughts more than I wanted her to. I tried to tell myself that it was over and I needed to just leave it at that, but thoughts of her always crept back into my mind. Something in me told me that Claire and I weren't done with each other just yet. That's why I took a few bourbon shots and called Michelle, her mother, asking for information. I knew she probably wouldn't tell me anything; she had always been the opposite of my mother, as far as getting involved in her child's relationship. Michelle politely told me that it wasn't her place to tell me anything regarding Claire and Warner (what kind of name was *Warner*, anyway?), and ended the conversation.

Claire still wasn't acknowledging my messages, as infrequent as they were now. I had hoped that if I gave her some space, she'd come around and be more willing to talk things out. Or at least, we could be friends. But she was really sticking to her guns this time. She'd even gone so far as to block me on social media. It was almost like she hated me or something.

I'd have to do something different to get her attention; something big. I didn't know what yet, though.

• • • •

I WAS STILL MULLING over this the next day; it consumed me more as time passed. When I wasn't volunteering or banging Aurora, my mind crept back to Claire and how I could snag some of her attention back.

Mother called, of course happy that Aurora and I were now hitting it off. I shouldn't have been surprised that Aurora had updated her on things, though I hoped she had enough sense not to tell her *everything*.

"Dear, I am so happy to hear about you and Aurora!" Mother exclaimed.

"It's not that big a deal, Mother. We've just been...hanging out and such. No need to read too much into it."

"How could I not? My son is finally in a relationship with a wonderful woman!"

I had been about to grab a shirt out of my closet but my hand stopped halfway to it. "I'm sorry?"

"You and Aurora. She told me you agreed to be exclusive with her."

I did?? When did I do that??

"Oh..."

"Don't be cross with her for telling me about it, dear. Aurora has taken to confiding in me since her own mother passed away a few years ago. She told me she buried her head in the books, studying everything she could find as a distraction. Such a shame. I've learned so much about her these past few weeks. Did you know she's a former gymnast?"

That explained a lot.

"I don't know why *you* didn't tell me about you and Aurora's new relationship yourself, knowing how much I was pulling for you two," Mother continued.

"I...can't really say I have a reason for that, Mother. Just been so caught up in things that it slipped my mind, I guess."

"Understandable. An exciting new love will do that for you. I just know it'll only be a matter of time before you and Aurora are coming to me announcing your engagement."

"Whoa, Mother," I spoke up, still reeling from learning I was apparently committed to Aurora. "You're moving way too fast with that."

"I'm sure I'm right. And I *know* Aurora wants to get married one day. You'd make a wonderful husband to her."

"We're nowhere *near* that point. I clearly need to...spend some more time with Aurora and make sure we both want the same things."

"You should do that. Communication is a vital part of a healthy and thriving relationship."

"Yes, communication is *vital*."

Mother and I talked for another few minutes before she had to go run some errands, and she didn't believe in talking on the phone while driving. I tossed my phone onto the bed and marveled over what I just heard.

Aurora and I were in a relationship? What would make her tell my mother that?

I started to call her and ask what the hell her deal was for lying to my mother like that, but then I got a flashback of the two of us in bed a few nights earlier. She mentioned something about us making it official and I had agreed, thanks to being all discombobulated over what she was doing to me with her tongue and a silicone vibrator. She could've asked me for my car right then and I would've given it to her.

The manipulative little scamp.

I was going to have to clear this up, but I didn't have the energy or the time to deal with it right then. I was due over at the nursing home for Ms. Debra's birthday celebration, and I wasn't going to let this nonsense cloud my mind while I was there. I'd just have to talk to Aurora later.

On my way to the nursing home, I decided to try to call Claire. I knew she had blocked me, but I kept calling in hopes that something would have compelled her to reverse that decision.

I almost couldn't believe it when I heard her voice. Maybe my luck with her was finally turning around.

"I'm going to ask you really nicely one last time to stop calling me," Claire hissed. "We don't have anything to say to each other."

"I beg to differ," I urgently responded, fearing she might hang up and re-block me at any second. "Why don't we just meet up so we can work everything out? All I need is ten minutes of your time."

"No, Montrel. The only reason I even un-blocked you was to call and tell you once and for all to leave me the hell alone. Now you're calling my mama? I'm *so* sick of you and your damn mind games."

"Claire-"

"Hey, baby, you about ready?"

The man's voice was clear. That must've been Warner.

Hearing him made it impossible to pretend he wasn't real. And hearing him address Claire as 'baby' made my blood boil.

"I have to go, Montrel," Claire said hastily. "And I'm blocking you again as soon as I hang up. Bye."

Dial tone.

That wasn't how that was supposed to go. I had it in my head that when Claire and I finally talked, she'd be willing to listen to reason and hear me out on things. But she had shut me down immediately. I couldn't help but wonder if that would have been the case if she'd been alone and not with...*him*.

I knew the sensible thing would be to just let her do her thing. But I needed Claire in my life; us being on the outs just didn't work for me. Now I was even more determined to get her back.

And after remembering something from my conversation with Michelle, she might have unknowingly given me some help towards doing just that.

Nineteen – Claire

• • • •

IT WAS THE EVENING of my parent's anniversary party and I was in my bathroom getting ready. Warner was watching television in the living room while he waited on me. I was looking forward to us going, having a nice evening celebrating my parents' thirty-fifth anniversary, and then coming back home and spending the rest of the night together. Hopefully with a lot of fooling around.

Part of me was still reeling from Montrel's call a couple of days prior. It didn't even matter what it was he had to say; the fact that he had the balls to call and ask for *anything* from me pissed me off.

Why couldn't he just leave me alone??

"Hey, I need to get in here and brush my teeth," Warner said, appearing in the doorway. "I was out there eating the rest of those chocolates from the other night."

"You and that sweet tooth," I chuckled, moving a little to the side as he reached for the spare toothbrush I kept there for him. We'd also reached the clearing-drawers-out-for-each-other point, too, and the night before, we'd exchanged keys to each other's places. I was absolutely giddy over how things had progressed between us.

"Yeah, but you're what I like nibbling on most," he teased, wrapping an arm around me from behind and nuzzling my neck. I giggled, trying to twist out of his arms.

"Stop that, unless you want us to be late," I playfully admonished, reaching back and swatting him on the ass. "And you're gonna mess up my makeup."

"All right, I'll back off for now," he relented, backing up. He eyed me in the mirror. "But what do you think about us picking this back up when we get home?"

"What do you mean?" I asked absently as I started putting on my mascara.

"I mean us finally making love, Claire."

I almost poked myself in the eye. I jammed the mascara wand back into the tube and dropped it onto the counter, turning to him. "What?"

"I want to make love to you tonight," he repeated, taking my hand. "If that's okay with you."

Damn the makeup. I practically jumped into his arms, kissing the hell out of him. He caught me and kicked the door closed before backing me up against it. The way he was grinding against me made me want to forget the anniversary party and make up some excuse to give my parents later. They'd understand.

"Oooh, Warner," I moaned as he kissed his way down my neck and started licking my chest. I bit my lip and held his head in both hands as he nibbled my breasts through my dress, making my legs feel like mush.

"I want you *now*, baby," he told me, standing up to kiss me again. "But we have to leave soon and I don't want our first time to be rushed."

"Umph. I guess we'll have plenty other opportunities for quickies in the future," I replied with a grin. "I already can't wait to get back here later."

"Oh, we're going to my place. I have something special planned for you there."

Damn, I wished we didn't have to go to this party!

We managed to calm ourselves down enough to finish getting ready. Now all I could think about was what Warner had planned for later. I could only hope that he was as good in bed as I imagined.

When we got to my parent's house, there were already several people there; my grandparents, some aunts and uncles, some cousins, friends, and my brother Benny. Faces weren't really registering since my mind was so preoccupied with the upcoming after-party at Warner's. As happy as I was for my parents, I didn't really care who was there nor was I terribly interested in mingling or making small talk. That might have sounded bad but hey, I was incredibly horny.

"Hey sis, your man is a good dude," Benny commended, coming over to me. "He's really hitting it off with everybody."

"Yeah, he's wonderful," I agreed, gazing at Warner as he stood across the room talking to some of my cousins. "I feel like I've hit the jackpot with this one."

"I believe it. If I'm not mistaken, Aunt Phyllis might have low-key offered to be his cougar."

My jaw dropped. "She what?"

Benny gave a dismissive wave. "Don't sweat it. He was so smooth when he shut her down that she seemed to take it as some kind of compliment."

I grinned proudly. "That's my baby."

"You *do* seem like you're glowing," Benny observed, peering at me. He looked more and more like Dad the older he got. "And to keep from having to burn my ears off, I won't ask why."

"Good idea," I chuckled, not even bothering to tell him that the *real* glow would be getting implemented later on that evening.

After we all ate and mingled for a while, everyone congregated in the living room. Mama and Dad moved to the middle of the room, holding hands.

"Everyone, I'd like to propose a toast," Dad announced, getting everyone's attention. "Thank you all so much for coming to celebrate with me and Michelle tonight. It's been a wonderful thirty-five years with this woman by my side, and I look forward to many, many more."

There was a chorus of gushes about how sweet that was and agreements on how they'd surely make it happen. I smiled at my parents, who usually abhorred being the center of attention or big fusses, celebrating their love amongst love ones. It was beautiful to see. And when Warner put his arm around me and gave me a look that made me forget about everybody else in the room for a minute, it made me imagine us in the middle of a room full of loved ones thirty years into the future. And surprisingly, the thought didn't freak me out; it actually felt possible.

"I feel the same way, darling," Mama responded, smiling at Dad. "It's been such a blessing being married to you. You're my best friend. My partner. We have two amazing children together-"

"That's me, y'all!" Benny exclaimed, shooting his arms into the air triumphantly. Everyone laughed as our amused parents shook their heads. Benny always did like turning the attention on himself when he felt he wasn't getting enough. He still hadn't grown out of that, apparently.

"Yes, Benny, we're very proud of you for working so hard towards your Communications degree," Mama replied, lifting her glass to Benny. "And for our daughter, Claire, for helping so many young people in her role as a school counselor. We're so incredibly proud of you, sweetheart."

I beamed at the unexpected compliment. My job wasn't usually something I got a lot of praise for. And my mother didn't put on airs so I knew she wasn't just saying that because there was a crowd in the room.

"And if I may add, I'm sure I can speak for both Randy and myself when I say that we're thrilled for our daughter to be here with such a wonderful young man in Warner Branson," Mama continued, smiling warmly. "We couldn't have wished for a better partner for our daughter."

Warner smiled and raised his glass towards Mama, and I felt a strong surge of pride shoot through me. It was nice to have someone on my arm that got such a shout-out.

And I almost dropped my drink when I saw the last man I was with who never got so much as a mention.

What the *hell* was Montrel doing at my parents' anniversary party?!?

Chichi, who had been on repeated calls to home because two of her boys were sick, hurried over to me as everyone started resuming their relative conversations.

"Warner, excuse me, I need to borrow our girl here for a minute," she said hurriedly, already grabbing my arm and pulling me away.

"Sure." Warner looked at us curiously. "Is...everything okay?"

"Just some girl talk that can't wait. We'll be right back!"

She yanked me into my old bedroom and closed and locked the door.

"Why is Montrel here?" she hissed, standing right in front of me. "And with a *date*?"

"Girl, I don't know! I'm just surprised as you are!"

The accusatory glint in her eye suggested she didn't really buy that. "Really?"

"Yes, really, Chichi! There is no way in hell I would invite Montrel here. I didn't even *tell* him about it!"

"Well, he found out from somebody. I saw him when he snuck in here during your parents' toast. And despite the woman on his arm, he's been eying you like the last pork chop the entire time he's been here."

"Oh my god..." I put my head in my hands, pacing over to my old pink dresser. "I *so* don't need this right now..."

"What are you gonna do?"

"I don't wanna talk to him, Chichi!"

"You want me to put him out?"

"As much as I'd love that, you and I both know he's not likely to leave just because you tell him to. That'll just make you go off and start making his and everyone else's ears bleed, and that's *if* you don't just start throwing hands. I don't want to cause a scene at my parents' party."

"I'll tell Benny, then."

"That's not any better. Benny doesn't know how *not* to make a scene."

"So..." Chichi held up her hands, hunching her shoulders. "Then what?"

"I don't know..." I felt like I was gonna cry both from anger and panic. Montrel crashing my parents' anniversary party was not something I would have ever anticipated in a million years. This could not be happening.

"Well, we need to figure something out. What if Warner recognizes him?"

"No, no, he doesn't know what Montrel looks like. Thank *god*."

"As paranoid as you said he was, you don't think he's ever looked Montrel up?"

The thought never occurred to me. "If he did, I don't know about it."

"You should let Warner know he's here."

"Why, so he can think that I had something to with him showing up? He might not be as paranoid about Montrel as he used to be but I'm not foolish enough to think it's totally gone. This certainly won't help things any."

"You said you didn't invite Montrel, though."

"I didn't. But I don't want to risk this messing up Warner's evening as well as mine. He won't be able to let it go."

"Do you think Montrel will try something here? In front of your folks? Your brother? Your man?"

"I wish I could say no but honestly, I wouldn't put it past him. He already crashed the party in the first place. I'm still trying to figure out how he even found out about this. This was supposed to be a special evening and he's ruining it!"

"Yeah, thirty-five years is a big deal. It's jacked up that he's messing up your folks' vibe like this."

"That's not what I meant. Tonight Warner and I are finally gonna take things to the next level. Why do you think I've been so distracted all night?"

"Hell, I hardly noticed since I've been on the phone every five minutes checking on my babies. Speaking of which, I'm gonna have to cut out soon; Gerard can only handle two sick boys on his own for so long."

"I understand. And I'm sure Mama and Dad will, too. It was sweet of you to come at all, knowing your boys aren't feeling well."

"Hey, you know I love your folks. I was gonna show my face, at least."

"Okay, I better get back out there," I announced, still not knowing how I was going to handle this potentially disastrous situation. "Damn, just when I thought I couldn't despise Montrel more, he pulls this shit."

"I don't envy you, girl," Chichi empathized, following me to the door. "I still think you're giving him too much leeway and you should let me put him out. But I'll respect your wishes. Hopefully it won't turn out that bad. Maybe he left already."

"One can only hope," I muttered, opening the door. "But my luck ain't that good."

Sure enough, Montrel was still there, lurking in the corner with his date hanging on his arm. I could admit; she was cute. But she didn't seem to be aware of his eyes tracking me as soon as I walked back into the living room. Now that I knew he was there, I was hyper-aware of my every movement. And hyper-paranoid that all of this was going to blow up in my face and still be blamed on me somehow.

"Hey, baby."

I jumped as Warner appeared by my side seemingly out of nowhere. "Oh, Warner, you scared me..."

"Sorry. Everything okay?"

"Ugh, yeah. Well, for the most part. Just some stuff that Chichi and I were trying to work out."

"Yeah, I've been meaning to ask you about that. I noticed she's been on the phone a lot tonight. There's nothing going on with her, is it?"

"Oh...well, yeah, two of her boys are under the weather and she's pretty preoccupied. You know how some mothers are with their babies and all."

"Damn, I'm sorry to hear that. Is that why you're looking so worried?"

I needed to go ahead and tell Warner that Montrel was there and I knew it. It was already a miracle that only Chichi had noticed him. My parents were too busy entertaining their guests. Benny didn't really know him that well and he was trying to mack some young lady, anyway. And thanks to Montrel being so funny about coming to my family functions, none of my extended family knew him, either. I guess I should've been thankful for small favors.

"Well, actually-"

Warner's cell phone rang, cutting me off. He glanced at it and grimaced. "Damn, baby, I'm sorry but I've gotta take this. It's one of my employees. Excuse me a minute?"

"No problem; take your time," I quickly replied, placing a hand on his arm and gently nudging him towards the front door. The relief I felt actually left me a little breathless. "I know how important your work is."

"Thanks, baby. I'll try to make it quick."

"No need. Nothing much is happening in here anymore, anyway. Matter of fact, we can leave soon, if you want."

He winked at me, giving me that sexy smirk of his. "Sounds good. Just let me go handle this and we can go."

"Hurry," I pleaded with a smile. Thankfully Warner didn't notice that I had just totally contradicted myself from a second ago.

I wished there was a way to get Montrel out of the house without my parents noticing or causing Warner to ask who he was, but I suspected there wasn't. I reconsidered Chichi's suggestion to have Benny get rid of him, but he would have asked why and caused more commotion than I wanted or needed. And I already knew better than to expect Chichi to be discreet if I changed my mind about her offer to get rid of him, and she was on yet another phone call checking on her boys, anyway. So there was really only one thing I could think of to do.

Run.

I started to go back to my old bedroom, but I just hovered in that direction until I saw Montrel lean down to hear something his date was saying to him , then I changed direction and darted through the kitchen to the backyard. I figured it wasn't highly likely he would manage to break away from that date of his and find me.

But I guess it just wasn't meant for me to get out of this night drama-free because he did just that.

"Hey, sweetheart."

"Montrel, what the hell are you doing here?" I demanded, not wasting time with preamble. "I can't believe you showed up at my parents' anniversary party trying to start some drama."

"I'm not trying to start anything. You see I've laid low since I got here."

"How did you even know about this? *I* sure as hell didn't tell you."

"I know. Your mother told me."

"Excuse me? Mama invited you here?"

He looked away. "Not exactly...she just mentioned it when I had called her to ask about you. It was inadvertent and she probably doesn't even remember saying it-"

"So you took advantage of that and decided to invite yourself to their house for their anniversary party? That's low even for you, Montrel."

"Well, I had to get your attention somehow," he retorted with uncharacteristic desperation, stepping around so he was in front of me. "You wouldn't talk to me on the phone, answer the door-"

"There's a reason for that, Montrel. I told you we were done. And as you can clearly see, I'm here with someone. As are *you*. This is *completely* inappropriate!"

"I'm sorry, Claire, but I had to get a chance to see you face to face." He reached out and grabbed my arms, tightening his grip when I tried to move away. "I meant it when I said I missed you."

"You're out of your mind if you think I'm going there with you again. And let me go!"

"Doesn't it tell you how serious I am that I would show up here of all places, knowing you'd be here with some other man and knowing your parents don't care for me? And don't even get me started on Chichi. She flashed something at me that I'm almost sure was some kind of gang sign."

"And yet you're still out here disrespecting me, my man, your date-"

"I don't care about them," he declared, pulling me closer. He looked at my lips then into my eyes, his chest heaving slightly and his eyes pleading. "I just want *you*."

"Montrel, please," I hissed, not afraid to resort to begging. "Please, please let me go and leave now. And get it in your head that I've moved on and I'm happy. Why would you want to ruin that for me?"

"Because I love you too much to sit and watch you be with someone else without doing everything I can to get you back," he replied. "We belong together, sweetheart. I'm not letting you go again."

Before I could respond, he yanked me to him and kissed me, quickly wrapping me up in his arms. I tried to wriggle out of his grasp, but when his tongue met my lips, my mouth opened to receive it all on its own. I was actually kissing him back, feeling those old familiar feelings rush over my body again, forgetting about my family and my man who could come out there and catch us at any second. I actually moaned as I let Montrel pull me closer, feeling his hands sliding down to my-

"Claire!"

I gasped, jumping away from Montrel. Chichi stood on the steps to the back porch, staring at us incredulously with her jaw hanging practically to her boobs.

"Chichi...I..."

Montrel looked at Chichi then at me. "Claire-"

"I've gotta go," I mumbled, darting past Chichi into the house. Now that my head was clear again, I couldn't believe what the hell I just did. Had I really just let Montrel kiss me in my parents' backyard? What if it had been Warner instead of Chichi that had come out there looking for me?

Warner. How the hell was I going to tell him about this? Not only that Montrel was there at the party and I didn't give him a heads-up about it, but that he kissed me. And that I *let* him kiss me. I had finally gotten him to stop being so paranoid about Montrel, and now this happened. What was I thinking??

The party was as good as over for me. I had to get out of there.

Warner came back into the house right after I grabbed my purse and hurriedly kissed my parents, telling them that I had to leave. I tried to keep a straight face but I was afraid he would immediately be able to tell what a foolish slut I was.

"I *cannot* believe this," he grunted, looking frustrated.

Oh no...did he already know what happened?

"I'm sorry that took so long," he continued, raising his phone. "There was an emergency on one of the locations we're in charge of. I thought my manager could handle it but it's looking like I'm going to have to go see about it myself."

Thank you LORD!

"I'm so sorry, baby," he expressed remorsefully, taking my hand. "I know we had our special night planned but unfortunately this is one of the things about being the boss."

"I totally understand," I quickly insisted, pulling him towards the door. "There'll be other nights. Let's just go."

I figured Chichi was keeping Montrel cornered in the backyard since he hadn't come back in yet, and his date was making designs in her ranch dressing with her baby carrots. I didn't even have time to mock that.

"I promise I'll make this up to you," Warner assured me as we headed to my house. "I was really looking forward to our night together."

"Me too. But hey, duty calls," I replied, hoping my voice didn't sound as shaky as I thought it did. I still wasn't able to fully look at him and thankfully he'd been too preoccupied with his work issue to notice.

"I'll call you if it's not too late when I'm done with all this," Warner told me when we pulled up to my house. "Are you sure you're not mad?"

"I'm positive, sweetie," I assured him, my hand already on the door handle. "Don't even worry about it. I'll just put on one of my hundred pair of comfy pajamas and turn in early. I'm kinda tired, anyway."

"Okay. I'll just call you tomorrow, then," Warner replied, leaning over for a kiss. "Get some rest, baby."

"I will. Send me a text to let me know you made it home."

"I sure will."

I got out of his truck and hurried to my front door on shaky legs. It was a miracle that I didn't drop my keys as I opened the door and turned to wave to Warner before he drove off. Thank goodness he didn't walk me to my door like he usually did.

Once inside, I leaned my back against the door, exhaling loudly. I sank down to the ground, my head in my hands. This was bad.

I was so sure I could handle being around Montrel. Not that I was *expecting* to be around Montrel, and certainly not at my parents' house. Why did he insist on making my life so difficult?

Hell. Why did I make my *own* life so difficult? It wasn't like I could deny having a hand in this, too. I should have told Warner that Montrel was there as soon as I noticed him. I should have let Chichi put Montrel out when she offered to. I should have run from the backyard as soon as Montrel followed me out there or screamed as soon as he touched me. Or at the very least, kneed him in the crotch when he put his lips on mine instead of kissing him back like a spineless backslider.

I was laying face-down on my couch when there was a hard knock on my door, making me jump. Should have known it was only a matter of time before Chichi showed up at my door to chastise me for my idiocy. She was going to use every cuss word in the book on me for this one.

"Shouldn't you be home with your sick babies by now?" I asked as I pulled the door open.

But it wasn't Chichi pounding on my door. It was Montrel.

I immediately tried to close the door in his face but he stopped me. "Claire, please."

"You've already caused me enough trouble, Montrel," I snapped, trying like hell to push the door closed. This was yet another time I hated being so damn skinny. "Just go away and leave me alone!"

"Just give me a minute, sweetheart-"

"And stop calling me that!"

"This is clearly something we need to work out."

"There is nothing to work out, Montrel. I've already messed up once with you tonight and I'm not about to do it again by letting you into my house. Now go!"

Montrel sighed, finally letting go of the door. He stood there looking at me as if that pleading look was going to sway me. Once upon a time, it would have.

"What happened earlier was a mistake," I told him, easing behind the door. "I'm with someone, you're with someone...where *is* your date, by the way?"

"I sent her home."

"You shouldn't have done that. I feel bad, Montrel. Maybe you don't have a conscience but I do, and I'm sick to my stomach about how I've hurt Warner. You see, *I* actually care about people other than myself."

"I care about *you*, Claire," Montrel insisted, stepping closer. I stepped further behind the door. "Why else would I be doing all of this?"

"Because I dumped you and you don't know how to deal with it. Because you always want what you can't have. Yet we've been doing this dance for two years and you didn't appreciate me when you had me. You pay me more attention when we're not together than when we are and you might want to ask yourself why that is. But whatever the reason is is *your* problem, not mine. Now leave." My eyes pleaded with him because I was running out of energy for this. "Please. If you care about me at all, go home. And let me move on."

Montrel started to say something, but thankfully closed his mouth and turned to walk away. I closed the door in relief, thankful that he finally respected my wishes. For once.

I was trudging back to my bedroom when the front door suddenly opened. I whirled around to find Montrel coming right at me, looking more determined than I had ever seen him. Since when did I forget to lock the door?

He grabbed my face in both hands and kissed me with more urgency than he ever had. I really did try to push him off of me, but he wasn't having it. He just held me tighter.

"Please, sweetheart," he begged between kisses, a hand sliding to the back of my neck. "I miss you so much...please don't push me away..."

"Get off me!"

"You still love me, Claire. You *know* you do! And I damn sure love you! I'm *so* sorry for everything..."

The more he kissed me, the more my resistance weakened. Again. I didn't know what the hell it was about this man. I tried to conjure up Warner's face but that only worked for a second; before too long, I was melting into him.

"I love you, Claire," Montrel muttered, kissing down to my neck then back to my lips. "I love you so much. Let's make this happen again. Be my wife; have my babies. I need you. *Please*, sweetheart..."

I didn't respond. Not with words, anyway. I just let him have his way, kissing and touching me in ways that was *supposed* to be reserved for Warner. But by then, that thought worked less than it had minutes before. I was too far gone.

And in deep trouble.

Twenty – Claire

• • • •

I WAS AVOIDING EVERYBODY.

I had royally fucked up, and I didn't need anybody to tell me that. As *soon* as Montrel left my house, I realized just what I'd done, and had been sick about it ever since.

I've never been a cheater. That's something that had been done to me numerous times and I never wanted to do that to anyone else, especially someone as awesome as Warner. He had done nothing but respect and love me during our relationship and this was how I repaid him; letting my ex bang me on my living room floor not an hour after Warner dropped me off. On the very night we had planned to consummate *our* relationship. Every time I thought about it, it made me want to throw up.

Montrel pleaded with me to talk things out when I was pushing him out the door after our stupid romp, but what was there to talk about? It's not like I wanted us to get back together, as had been the case the last umpteenth times I had given in to him after we broke up. I still wanted Warner and only Warner. But Montrel had some kind of way with me that I couldn't explain; he knew what buttons to push to make me forget all of my common sense. I had cheated on my man, Montrel had cheated on his woman, and there wasn't even a good reason. It wasn't about some deep, all-consuming love that I couldn't let go of. I was just stupid.

Especially since Warner could have walked in on us at any time, considering I'd given him a key to my place. He could've seen me laid out wearing nothing but the heart necklace he gave me, with my ex between my legs. It was like I just *looked* for ways to sabotage myself.

And now I had to tell Warner. There was no way I *couldn't* tell him. Knowing all the concerns he had about me and Montrel...I honestly didn't think this would happen but now that it had, I owed it to Warner to be honest. That didn't mean I wasn't dreading it or fearing what would happen afterwards. What if he couldn't forgive me? What if he left me over this?

It was a couple of days after the anniversary party that I finally went to see Chichi. Warner had been (thankfully) pretty busy with work and hadn't really noticed that I'd withdrawn from him again; we hadn't talked over the phone but had exchanged some texts. I could handle texting; it was talking to him or seeing him that I wasn't ready for.

"Go ahead and let me have it," I droned to Chichi, bracing myself. "Just tell me I'm a brainless spineless slut who has all the sense of a dung beetle. I deserve it."

"I'm not gonna do that, Claire," Chichi replied, surprisingly calm. "You're feeling bad enough and I know that."

"'Bad' doesn't even begin to describe how I'm feeling. There isn't an appropriate word to describe how I'm feeling. I just keep wishing I could go back in time and make better decisions."

"If only."

"Chichi, I feel so *stupid*!" I exclaimed, putting my head in my hand. "I had sex with Montrel and ruined a perfectly good relationship-"

"Wait, what? You two had sex??"

I sighed. I forgot she didn't know about that part. She had only caught us kissing.

"Yeah...Warner dropped me off so he could go handle some work thing and Montrel showed up not too long after that. I tried to send him away but he came back and..." Tears came to my eyes yet again. I was too ashamed to say it out loud. "I gave in to him."

"Oh, damn..."

"I regretted it as *soon* as it was over. I can't even say I was drunk or pissed at Warner or anything like that. There's nothing and nobody I can blame this on but myself. And I just..." I wiped the tears streaming down my face as it continued to hit me what I had done. "I can't believe I did this."

"So...what, you and Montrel are back together now?"

"No! I don't want Montrel, Chichi. He was saying he wants me back and apologizing for everything but my feelings for him haven't changed at all. I just want Warner."

"Then why did you..."

"I don't know. I really don't know." I sniffed. "Montrel just...caught me at a weak moment, I guess. And that was supposed to be the night Warner and I were going to consummate our relationship finally. I'd been horny all night, looking forward to that. And I go and fuck my ex instead."

Chichi sighed.

"At least if I was still in love with Montrel, I'd at least have something of a reason. But I finally realized that I wasn't a little while back, and I'm sure of it. If anything, sleeping with him again only made me want even less to do with him. When I looked at him after we were done, it came crashing down on me just how wrong he is for me. How wrong he *always* was. Especially considering he kept saying 'you're mine' over and over while we were doing it; like he just knew he could have his way with me whenever. And I can't even blame him for that, with how dumb I've been over him these past two years."

"Yeah..."

"Now I resent him for how he dogged me *and* for how he kept pursuing me after he did. I *begged* him to leave me alone..."

"You don't think he's actually sincere this time?"

"No. He wanted me 'cause he couldn't stand to see me with someone else. I'm like a toy he hardly plays with but still doesn't like to share. But even if he *is* sincere, it wouldn't matter. Getting back with Montrel would be like some kind of consolation. I just want Warner."

"And he doesn't know about this yet?"

"No. We haven't talked much since he's been so busy, but I know I have to tell him. There's no way I can look him in his face and keep this secret."

"Why not...keep it to yourself? *Don't* tell him."

I sat up, shocked. "What?"

"Hear me out," Chichi hedged, sitting up straighter. "You messed up but at least you realize how huge of a mistake it was. You're not confused or conflicted like you would have been a few months ago, wondering if this was some kind of sign that you and Montrel were meant to be together. It gave you clarity, which might've been what you needed. Now you're a hundred percent sure that Warner is who you want to be with."

"I was sure of that before I did this, Chichi."

"Are you sure? Ever since you met Montrel, he's been your weak spot. And even if you were sincerely happy with Warner – and I believe you were – that doesn't mean that you had *real* closure with Montrel, or totally purged those feelings. You've never gotten enough distance to do that; everything was always so raw and emotional because you hadn't given yourself time to really heal. Fucking him might not have been the best way to get Montrel out of your system, but now you have, and you know for sure that the two of you are done. That's a good thing."

"Chichi, I can't spin this into being anything *good*. I can't absolve myself like that. I don't deserve to feel better about this."

"It's not necessarily about you feeling better; it's just digging to the root of things. Look, you know I don't get down with cheating and I'm not saying it wasn't wrong. But girl...Montrel has already taken you through *so* much. Don't let him ruin the relationship you've always wanted and finally have with a man who adores you. Only you, me, and Montrel know about this, and I'm willing to bet Montrel isn't going to spill the beans. Just chalk it up as a lesson learned and go on with your life."

"Even if I wanted to go along with that, I couldn't. Every time Warner would tell me he loves me or give me one of those foot rubs I love or do or say something sweet, it would kill me. Do you know he actually bought me a new couch, just because he knew how much I wanted one? That's the kind of man he is. I couldn't lie in his arms and tell him how much I love him knowing I'd done this behind his back."

"Well, would you rather lose Warner altogether? Just consider having to deal with what you did as your penance. Don't hurt Warner if you don't have to."

"You and I both know this kind of thing only stays hidden for so long. It'll come out eventually, some kind of way. And he'd never forgive me for keeping it from him, especially after what his ex did to him. He deserves my honesty and even if he..." I took a minute to gather myself, since I was getting choked up. "Even if he can't forgive me, I have to tell him. He's been too good to me for me not to."

"Claire, girl...are you *sure*? You know I'm usually all about honesty but this time, I'm thinking about *you*. What if Warner leaves you over this?"

The thought had already occurred to me a million times over the past couple of days, and each time it caused a new wave of shame and tears. I absolutely didn't want to lose Warner. But I had too much respect for him to keep him in the dark about this.

"I'd deserve it," I finally answered. I fingered the gold heart charm hanging around my neck; Warner's heart. The tears welled up again. "I was stupid enough to make this mistake; I need to be woman enough to own up to it and take whatever comes from it."

"All right," Chichi conceded with a sigh. "I hope he can find it in his heart to forgive you."

"Me, too."

"And for the record, I'm proud of you for this," Chichi added, reaching over to rub my arm. "For owning up to what you did. I know you've been beating yourself up over this and not everybody would be able to tell their man they got down with their ex."

"I appreciate it," I mumbled, managing a small smile that didn't last long. "I have no idea how I'm gonna make myself say the words to Warner but I will."

"Let's try to think positively...maybe it won't turn out that bad. Maybe he'll just be pissed at you for a while but come to appreciate your honesty and you two can move on from it."

"You really believe that?"

"Most men probably wouldn't but who knows. Stranger things have happened. But either way, I'm here for you; just call me if you need me."

"Thanks, girl." I took a deep breath. "I appreciate that."

I left Chichi's house, went home, and decided to go ahead and bite the bullet; there wasn't any use in putting off telling Warner. The longer I waited, the worse it would be. Except when I called him, it went to voicemail. He sent me a text soon after letting me know he'd call me back later. And that he loved and missed me.

Dropping my phone beside me, I buried my face in my hands and cried yet again.

• • • •

WHILE I WAITED FOR Warner to call me back, I decided to get out of the house. A day had passed and I was going crazy just moping around. There were some errands I needed to run that I'd been putting off, so I threw on something presentable-enough and headed out. I didn't care about looking cute. I didn't deserve to look cute.

It would only figure that would be the precise time I ran into Montrel's mother.

"Perfect," I muttered, glancing down at my baggy sweats. I was surprised to see the prissy Annie Burns shopping for her own groceries at Trader Joe's; I thought that was the kind of thing she hired someone else to do, or have delivered. The only thing I'd ever seen her do the entire time I'd known her was get dressed up to sit on her couch and drink coffee, listening to that tired classical music.

"Claire?"

Well, there went the hope of her not seeing me. I contemplated ignoring her; it's not like I cared about getting on her good side anymore. I was surprised she was even speaking at all, considering she never liked me. This would be the perfect time for her to shun me but now she wants to be polite.

I made myself turn and force a smile at her. "Mrs. Burns."

"I didn't imagine I'd see you here," she droned, eying my outfit. I could see the distaste. She didn't try to hide it.

"I'm not sure why. I *do* buy groceries."

"Yes, but I figured you'd do so somewhere like...Walmart. Or Piggly Wiggly."

Before I clocked this heffah, I needed to get away from her. I was already having visions of tossing a nearby jar of organic marinara sauce all over her silk jumpsuit. "Have a nice day, Mrs. Burns."

I turned to walk off but she apparently wasn't done with me.

"I hope you're not planning on trying to reconcile with my son again," she called out. "He's finally moved on from you."

Counting to ten, I slowly turned back towards her. "So?"

"*So*, he's practically engaged to Aurora Chadwick, who is much more suited for him. If you try to worm your way back into his bed, you'd just be making a fool of yourself."

She'd never get the marinara sauce out of that suit. I was sure of it.

"Mrs. Burns, with all due respect – which isn't much – you really need to get your facts straight. You clearly don't know your son as well as you think you do."

"And what is that supposed to mean?"

"You don't know what you're talking about; that's what it means. I can't put it any more plainly than that. But regardless, I do not want Montrel back."

"Hmph," she scoffed, looking at me like she pitied me or something. "Sure you don't. You know a good thing when you see one. Why else would you keep going back to him after he kept dumping you? He's wealthy, handsome, educated-"

"You know, this fixation you have with Montrel's love life is a little disturbing. But I guess it makes sense, since you clearly don't have anything going on for yourself. All you do is sit on your ass in the house your dead husband left you and worry about what Montrel is doing. Why don't you get a life? How long has it been since you've wormed *your* way into somebody's bed?"

Her face went about as red as that marinara sauce. "How *dare* you!!"

"What, you think you can keep disrespecting me and I'm just going to keep taking it? I've always been respectful and polite to you but you don't extend me the same courtesy, which would just be the *decent* thing to do, regardless of whether or not you think I'm right for your son. Guess it just proves that having money doesn't mean you have manners or class. Which is wild considering from what *I* heard, you didn't come from money your damn self; it was your husband that was loaded."

I could literally see the color drain from her face. Guess she didn't think I knew about that.

"You were working at a damn dry cleaners when y'all met," I continued, absolutely gleeful at how shook she looked all of a sudden. Why hadn't I thought to record this?? "And you clamped onto him and wouldn't let go until he put that ring on your finger. Which he mainly did because you *accidentally* wound up pregnant with Montrel. Yet you walk around like you're a descendent of the royals and not like your parents were fry cooks who sent you to junior college, which you promptly flunked out of. *Oops.*"

"H-how did you...how do you know about all this?? Did you trick Montrel into-"

"Nope, Montrel is just as delusional as you are, thanks to your wannabe bougie ass. He doesn't know any more about the real you than you think you know about him. Believe me, it wasn't that hard to find out. But I kept it to myself because I wasn't interested in rubbing it in your face. But since you wanna mess with me, it's time somebody finally told you about yourself. Maybe you could do a reality show, since you have nothing but free time, apparently; *Perpetrating Divas from the Dirt Road.*"

"You just *wait* until I tell Montrel how you spoke to me!" she exclaimed, actually raising her voice. She was practically screeching. How undignified. "He'll be furious with you!"

"I don't give a flying fuck *what* you tell Montrel or if he gets mad about it or not. Get it through your outdated French-rolled head; I do not want your damn son. He's bad enough, but being with him means having to deal with you and that's more than enough reason to run. Him and Aurora can have each other. I'd even send them a wedding gift, if they end up getting married. Walmart has some good sales."

I turned and walked off, leaving her standing there seething. That felt *so* good, and it was long overdue. Warner was the one who actually got me that information about Annie's background after I'd told him about my issues with her. I'd been holding my tongue with that woman for too long and since Montrel was not a factor anymore, I no longer had to do that. She was going to get back whatever she dished out from then on, though I hoped I wouldn't have to see the bitch again after that.

Thinking about Warner, I felt like it was the right time to finally come clean with him, especially since I was so keyed up. I suddenly didn't want to put it off any longer.

I headed to his house, hoping this was one of the times he was working from home. I breathed a sigh of relief when I saw his truck parked out front, but it also reignited my nerves. This was not a conversation I was looking forward to, but I knew it had to be done. All I could do was admit to my indiscretion and hope he'd be willing to move past it and give me another chance, even if it took some time.

I tried to ignore the little voice in my head saying how huge of a long shot that was.

"Hey, baby," he greeted me after answering the door. He looked happy to see me, which would have made me feel great any other time. "I wasn't expecting to see you today."

"Yeah, I know. I'm sorry to bother you; I know you're working..."

"It's cool. I need to step away for a minute, anyway. And you're the best reason to do that." He pulled me inside and wrapped his arms around me, burying his face in the crook of my neck. I could feel the tears building already.

"Warner..."

"I missed you," he murmured against my skin before lifting his head and giving me a kiss. "I'm so sorry I haven't been that available these past couple days."

"It's okay; I understand. Look, Warner...there's something I need to tell you and I need to do it before I lose my nerve." I eased out of his arms, not feeling like I deserved his embrace. "Can we sit?"

He looked at me with concern. "Okay...what's wrong, baby?"

My hands wrung together as I moved over to the couch. I eyed Warner as he came over to sit next to me, placing a hand on my knee. Chichi's suggestion to keep what I did to myself and just live with it crossed my mind, but just as quickly, I forced it out. Warner deserved the truth from me. I loved him too much to keep something like this from him.

"Warner..." I tucked my hair behind my ears with both hands, taking a deep breath. "I did something that I have to tell you about. And I wish to god I didn't have to but...I do."

"What is it?"

Momentarily squeezing my eyes shut, I just blurted it out. "I slept with Montrel. The other night; after the anniversary party. Really, the whole truth is he was *at* the anniversary party, which I should have told you but I didn't know how to. I *swear* I didn't know he was gonna be there. He followed me outside and kept talking about us getting back together, then he kissed me. Then he came over after you dropped me off and I tried to make him leave but he didn't, and then he made another move on me and I eventually gave in." I was babbling but I had to get everything out while I could. Tears were already streaming down my face but I couldn't make myself look at Warner; I could only imagine what he was thinking of me right then. "It was a *huge* mistake and I should have handled the whole thing better. I'm so sorry, Warner..."

His hand fell from my knee. The tears started to come harder.

Several moments passed with no response, and the fear of what he would eventually say spurred me to keep talking.

"I know there's probably nothing I can say to make any of this any better. I messed up. Please know, though, that I do *not* want Montrel back. It was a stupid, senseless, weak moment that I regret with everything in me, but if it showed me anything, it's that I'm sure he's not the one I want. I want you and only you. My actions might suggest otherwise, but it's the truth. It's the absolute truth."

Still no words from Warner. I dared to look at him and he was just sitting there looking at the ground, his jaw clenched. He was angry; of course he was angry. As soon as he gathered himself, he'd probably curse me 'til my ears bled and kick me out of his house, and I knew I couldn't bear to hear that from him. So I figured I should beat him to the punch.

"I don't deserve your forgiveness and I know it," I continued, wiping my eyes. My hand drifted to the heart charm around my neck. "You've been so good to me and I messed everything up. I'd love it if you said we could try to work through this and move on, but I know better than that. So it's probably best to just end things now." I stood, sniffling and wiping my face with my sleeve. My heart broke as I removed the key to his house from my keychain and placed it next to him. "I get it if you hate me for this. But I still love you, Warner. And I'm so, so sorry."

Without waiting for a response or a reaction, I quickly headed for the door. He didn't say anything or try to stop me, and by the time I got outside, I was full-on ugly crying. I'd ruined the best relationship I'd ever had, and I only had myself to blame.

Twenty-One – Montrel

• • • •

THIS WAS GETTING RIDICULOUS. It had been days and Claire was still avoiding me.

We needed to talk about what happened. I knew she was probably feeling guilty about stepping out on her man, but I'd hoped that by then she would have gotten some perspective and realized that it was all for the best. There was clearly still something between us; we couldn't stay away from each other. She was supposed to be mine. I didn't know why Claire couldn't see that.

I figured I'd give her another day or so before I went over there and forced her to talk to me. In the meantime, I had agreed to mediate for Forrest and Giselle. They were finally ready to hash things out, but knew that they probably wouldn't get anywhere on their own. They'd either end up screaming at each other or senselessly sexing again, which I wouldn't care as much about if they weren't doing it in my house.

"Thanks for doing this, Montrel," Giselle said we all sat around my kitchen table. "I think it's past time we worked all this out."

"Yeah, well," I mumbled as I scooted my chair closer to the table. "I'm not sure how much help I can be but if it'll get Forrest out of my guest room any faster, I'm all for it."

"Shut up, man," Forrest snapped. "Let's get this going."

"Fine. So why don't we start by each of you stating what it is you're *really* mad about. Straight-up honesty; no bullshit. Giselle, you go first."

"Well," she tucked some hair behind her ear. "Forrest seems to blame me because we haven't been able to get pregnant. That hurts. And it wasn't a great feeling to hear the real reason he married me."

Forrest sighed and rolled his eyes. "For the millionth time, I didn't mean that!"

"Then why would you say such a thing? Do you know how insulting that is? What if I said I only married you for your dark skin and big dick?"

"Ugh..." I scoffed.

"That wouldn't bother me," Forrest shrugged. "Because I have enough sense to know that the things that initially attract you to someone don't have to be the only things that keep you attracted. You find out more as you grow together, as I have with you. And anyway, I'm *proud* of my dark skin and big dick."

"Can we not talk about your dick and keep it to your marital issues?" I requested. "Forrest, what is it *you're* really angry about?"

Forrest tapped his finger against the edge of the table. "I'm pissed because we keep failing at making a baby. That's something a man is supposed to be able to do, you know; plant a seed in his wife. And the fact that I can't do that is a little emasculating."

Giselle looked at him in surprise. "Really?"

"Yes. And especially after finding out there's nothing medically wrong with me-"

"What??" Giselle screeched. Forrest must have forgotten he hadn't told her that part yet. "You went and got yourself checked and didn't tell me?"

"I had to find out what was going on. It was driving me crazy. We were doing everything we were supposed to do and getting nowhere..."

"Wow, Forrest," Giselle crossed her arms in a huff and shook her head at him. "Well, that makes me not feel so bad about going to get *my*self checked without telling *you*."

"Oh, really?" Forrest frowned, crossing his own arms. "And how long have you been keeping *that* from me?"

"How long have you been keeping what you did from *me*?"

"I asked you first."

"So?"

"Oh my gosh!" I exclaimed, slamming a hand on the table. "It's like you two just like to fuss for the sake of fussing at each other. What does it matter how long ago either of you did it; the fact of the matter is, it was something that needed to be done, clearly. Why either of you felt the need to keep it a secret from the other is the *real* question. You two are supposed to be in this together yet it seems like you're competing against each other and it doesn't make sense."

Forrest glared at me for a moment before turning his eyes to Giselle, who was already peering at him. They sat there looking at each other, and my mind started wandering back to Claire. Part of me wished there was someone that could mediate between me and her like this.

I was still seeing Aurora as I waited for Claire to get back to me. Hey, we weren't officially back together yet and Aurora's sex wasn't an easy thing to give up. She was still thinking we were in a relationship and I hadn't set her straight on that yet; she might shut down the sex train, and

I didn't want to lose that until I had to. It wasn't about love; my feelings for Aurora were purely sexual. I'd tell her the real deal eventually.

"Hello?" Giselle was waving her hand in my face. "Earth to Montrel."

"Huh? What?" I looked back and forth between her and Forrest.

"You're supposed to be helping us and you're over there daydreaming," Forrest admonished. "Please don't tell me that you're thinking about Claire."

"So what if I am?"

"Haven't you caused her enough trouble? Why don't you just leave her alone?"

"Because she's mine and I want her back. That's why."

"*God*, Montrel," Giselle groaned, running her hands down her face and then looking at me like some kind of petulant child. "This is getting ridiculous. You've been jerking her around for too long. She's with someone else. It was one thing for you to pursue her when there wasn't anyone else in the picture but to do it when you know she has a man is just wrong. And you *know* that!"

"All I *know* is that Claire couldn't possibly have with him what she had with me."

Forrest shook his head. "You switch your shit up every other day. One minute you're all into her, then you're dumping her for some inane reason, then you decide you want her back, then you say you'll respect her relationship with the other dude, then you forget all that and decide to go after her again. Maybe *you* oughta think about why you can't make up your damn mind and don't seem to have a problem hurting someone you claim to love over and over."

That gave me pause. I *did* love Claire. And I never purposely wanted to hurt her, despite what it seemed like. Maybe I had some fears about commitment that I hadn't realized, but I knew I didn't want to spend my life alone. And Claire had been the first woman that I seriously thought about anything long-term with; hell, I'd kinda proposed to her in the heat of the moment at her house after the anniversary party, though she hadn't acknowledged it. And I felt like I meant it. When we were together and she started trying to have those conversations with me, though, it triggered some kind of panic that made me fall back. It was something I'd never stopped to think about before but now that I was, I could acknowledge that it wasn't very fair to Claire.

Wow. It was the first time I *really* thought about why I did what I did, in regards to our relationship. And true enough, she didn't deserve that. Maybe I wasn't as ready to settle down as I thought.

"Montrel?" Giselle called out, looking at me curiously.

I looked at her as if I'd forgotten she was there. "Huh?"

"Something wrong?"

"Nah, I'm just...thinking about some things, that's all." I shook my head, trying to shake it off. This wasn't about me right then; I was supposed to be helping Forrest and Giselle with *their* shit. But I knew I had a lot to think about later. "Sorry; back to you two..."

We all continued to sit there for about another hour, with Forrest and Giselle hashing out their issues and me keeping things from getting too heated. At the end of the day, they were both just frustrated and scared, but they loved each other and weren't going anywhere. Forrest eventually stood and rounded the table, gently grabbing Giselle's hands and pulling her to her feet. They shared a long kiss before wrapping each other up in a long hug, each whispering how sorry they were. I smiled a little at the scene, glad that I was able to help them in some small way.

Forrest finally went home that night, and I grabbed a bottle of scotch and parked it on my couch. It was nice to have my house back, and I started wondering if I was ready to have someone there with me twenty-four-seven like a wife would be. I was sure I loved Claire, and I believed she was better suited for me than anyone else. My mind imagined waking up to her every day, sharing responsibilities, planning a wedding and making babies, not to mention, dealing with Mother through all of it. As much as I loved my Mother and tended to let her convince me to do things I didn't always want to do, I knew that when it came right down to it, I wouldn't put her before my wife. I was sure of that.

If I was going to be with Claire again, I needed to be sure I was ready to stay with her this time.

And since Claire still wasn't contacting me, I had some time to think about all this. Even I was tired of the back and forth by now. It was time to grow up and do what I felt was right for me, regardless of what Mother or anyone else thought about it.

I took a couple of days holed up in my house doing some serious soul searching. I didn't want to ask anyone's advice because I didn't want to be influenced; this was something I needed to work through on my own. My entire relationship with Claire got dissected from the beginning, over-analyzing every breakup and make-up. I even pondered over the relationships prior to Claire, comparing them to her. I couldn't say I'd treated any other woman like I had Claire; usually once I ended things with someone, that was it. But Claire...she was different. Everything in me knew it, which is why I always got so freaked out and ended things instead of recognizing the fear for what it was and working through it.

And I wasn't delusional enough to think that Mother's pressure didn't play a part in things. I knew I'd made mistakes in how I allowed her to treat Claire, and even her overall influence on my love life, in general. If Claire was going to be in my life, I couldn't allow that to happen anymore.

Like Forrest and Ms. Debra told me several times, I needed to man up. Both with my mother and with Claire. I could only imagine what my father would think of my behavior, if he were still alive. This wasn't the kind of man he'd been raising me to be.

The more I thought about it, the more I knew...Claire was it. I just couldn't imagine my life without her in it. She was the one. And I was sure this time.

Once I made my decision, I knew I also needed to talk to Aurora. We clearly needed to get on the same page, since she was still thinking we were something we weren't.

Okay...I was *letting* her think we were something we weren't. I acknowledge that.

Now that I'd made up my mind, I didn't want to waste any more time. I called Aurora and asked if I could visit her to talk. She readily agreed, as I thought she would.

"Would you like something to drink?" she asked after letting me in. "Those pants look great on you, by the way."

"Thanks. And I'm good on the drink. I just thought it was about time we had a conversation about some things."

"All right." Aurora glided over to the couch, crossing her legs. I had to stop myself from looking at them too long or remembering some of the things we'd done on that couch.

"Aurora," I began as I sat on the opposite end of the couch from her, "I want to clear up any misunderstandings you might have about us."

She blinked. "What do you mean?"

"You're under the impression that we're in a relationship and...that's not really the impression *I'm* under," I said carefully, trying not to sound cruel. "I guess I should have cleared all this up before, but I've been having a good time with you, and-"

"Montrel, let me put your mind at ease," Aurora cut in, sounding stronger than I'd ever heard her. Almost like a different person. "Despite the way I've portrayed myself, I'm not an idiot. I've been using you just like you've been using me."

Now it was my turn to blink. "What?"

"There's a trust fund that I won't get until I'm married," she revealed, looking right at me. "But I never wanted to reveal that to a man up front because I knew that would influence their reason to be with me. I met your mother at some fundraiser and she went on and on about you, and she didn't exactly make it a secret that you all were well off. So I figured you'd be perfect since you already have your own money and wouldn't need mine."

I couldn't believe what I was hearing. "So...you were cavorting with my mother to get me to marry you so you could get your trust fund?"

"No, she doesn't know anything about that part; I didn't tell her. Truth be told, Montrel, I don't really care for your mother. I think she's a pretentious poser but she was my in to what I needed, so I turned on the simpleton act and told her whatever she wanted to hear to get her to introduce us and hype me up to you."

My jaw was in my lap. "So...wow."

"Are you offended?"

"I probably *should* be. I'm definitely thrown for a loop."

"I can't imagine you'd be too upset, seeing as how you're still hung up on someone else," Aurora stated, resting her arm on the back of the couch. She was as cool as a cucumber. "When we went to that anniversary party, you were clearly there on a mission."

Damn. "A mission?"

"Seeing as how no one looked particularly glad to see you or really even addressed you, I got the feeling you hadn't been invited. And you couldn't keep your eyes off that skinny woman with the cute bobbed hair. Then I saw you follow her outside. And when she left, you were in such a hurry to bring me home and leave with that flimsy excuse that I knew you were just going to see her."

I had really underestimated Aurora. Big time. Here I thought she was an airhead but she had been playing all of us so she could get what she wanted. On some level, this made me more attracted to her.

"I admit, I don't really know what to say right now," I finally managed to say. "So you're not really interested in me, then?"

"No, I like you. But would you be my first choice if not for my situation? Probably not. I'm certainly not in love with you or anything. You kinda have a stick up your ass most of the time, Montrel. And you're a little too much of a mama's boy for me. But I can handle Ms. Annie. And," she arched a brow, "It's not like you and I don't have our fun together."

She was giving me that look, and I felt a stir in my pants. We *absolutely* had our fun. And when she uncrossed her legs and displayed the fact that she was panty-free under her skirt, I was ready to have some fun with her right then.

Just one more time for the road.

"You're right about that," I couldn't help but agree, biting my lip.

She got on her knees on the couch and started to crawl over to me. "Are you in love with that woman? Claire, is it?"

My eyes were on Aurora's cleavage. Damn, she had some of the most amazing breasts. "Yeah...yeah, I am."

She slowly began unbuttoning my shirt with one hand. "And she feels the same way about you?"

"Honestly, she wants to move on. She was with that tall guy at the party..."

"He was cute," Aurora observed, sliding a finger down my exposed chest. "So I take it you crashing the party and chasing her around didn't yield the desired result?"

She was unbuckling my pants and I had to fight to keep my thoughts straight. I was already harder than a Bedrock newspaper. "It did and it didn't. But I wasn't ready to give up..."

"Hmm. How about we talk about all of that later." She gently sucked my bottom lip. "All right?"

Damn, now she was licking on me. There was no way I could function or keep a clear head when she was licking on me. I knew I shouldn't be doing this; that I had decided that it was Claire that I wanted and continuing to fool around with Aurora wasn't the smart thing to do. But Aurora had a touch that no other woman had, and giving that up wasn't something I wanted to think about right then.

So I didn't. I let Aurora do whatever she wanted to me, putting everything else out of my mind and enjoying it, assuring myself this would be the last time.

Claire

• • • •

I WAS SITTING AT THE kitchen table at my parents' house, staring into a cup of coffee. Mama was sitting across from me, her chin in her hand, peering at me through her glasses.

"This is embarrassing," I mumbled, still looking into the cup. "I'm too old to be this stupid."

"You've been beating yourself up about this for days, haven't you?" Mama surmised.

"How can I not? I lost Warner because of my own dumb actions. I had the best relationship with him and I ruined it for no reason. I could see if I was still *so* in love with Montrel and sleeping with him made me realize that he's who I really want to be with, but it was just the opposite. It made me realize that I *don't* want him and I really want Warner. And now I don't have anybody."

"Sweetheart-"

"Can you...*not* call me that?" I requested, holding up a hand with a slight wince. "Montrel always used that on me when he was trying to sweet-talk me and now it just makes me sick every time I hear it."

"Okay, fine. Claire...what is it that you want, ultimately?"

"I *want* Warner to forgive me so we can move forward. I totally realize cheating is a big deal and I'm not trying to excuse what I did at all, but I was really hoping this was something we could get past."

"Would *you* be able to get past it if the roles were reversed and *he* was the one who had slept with his ex?"

"I'd like to think so. Eventually." I said that, but I knew it would be way easier said than done. Which was why I knew I had to check myself.

"Have you and Warner talked about all this?"

"Not since I confessed everything, if you could even say we talked then. I just kind of spilled everything and ended it before he had a chance to. He really didn't even say anything."

"So you don't really know how he's feeling, then."

"I'd think the fact that he hasn't reached out to me at all since isn't a very good sign."

"Maybe he's processing everything. You hit him with that out of the blue and then ran. You should have stayed and taken whatever came of it."

"I couldn't bear to hear him say it was over," I admitted. "To hear him curse me out or call me a slut or anything like that wasn't something I could take, even if I deserved it."

"You two were in a relationship. You claimed to love each other. He deserved a conversation, not a drive-by. You took the cowardly way out, Claire."

I looked at Mama in mild surprise. It wasn't like her to be so blunt.

But she was right. I was a punk. Yeah I had told him to his face, but I didn't stick around for his reaction, whatever it may have been. Who knew *what* Warner was thinking of me after that. For all I knew, I made things worse.

"I guess I did," I agreed with a sigh, sitting back in my chair. I fingered the charm on the necklace Warner had given me, as I now did often. "Maybe...I don't know. Maybe this is for the best."

"How so?"

"You know how people have those crazy stories about things they went through with their spouse but at the end of it, they ended up together and were happy? That they stuck with it because they knew deep down that that was the person for them? You think Montrel could be that for me?"

Mama frowned. "I thought you *just* said that what happened with Montrel only assured you that he wasn't who you wanted."

"Right, but there has to be a reason why I have such a weakness for him," I countered. "Maybe he's who I'm going to end up with down the line and this is a crazy story we'd tell our grandkids one day. Maybe I'm confused; I clearly don't have good judgment when it comes to men. It's possible that this all happened for a reason."

"It sounds to me like you're trying to talk yourself into a contingency plan in case Warner doesn't forgive you," Mama observed. A little too accurately. "You don't want to have gone through all of this for nothing and Montrel, as flawed as he is, is better than nothing. Right?"

I hunched my shoulders, not wanting to admit out loud that she was pretty much right on the money. "Is that such a terrible thing?"

"When is settling a *good* thing? You ended things with Montrel for a reason. And even if Warner decides not to take you back, that doesn't mean you should go backwards. The right man wouldn't knowingly disrespect you, and Montrel has done that countless times. At some point, you have to want better for yourself, even if that means you end up *by* yourself."

I returned my eyes to my coffee cup. Of course Mama was right. But the idea of being alone didn't appeal to me at all. I wanted someone to share my life with. My heart wanted Warner; he was undoubtedly the better man for me. But if Montrel was the consolation prize, I decided I could live with it.

Twenty-Two – Claire

• • • •

MORE DAYS PASSED WITHOUT hearing from Warner. It had been almost two weeks since I confessed what happened with Montrel, and I hadn't heard a word from him. I didn't know if that meant he was totally done with me or if he was still trying to figure out what to say. I had sent him a couple of texts, but he didn't respond.

In the meantime, I figured it was okay to finally talk to Montrel about all of this. He had been leaving notes on my door, sending gifts, trying to get me to agree to hash everything out, and I hadn't wanted to since I was still waiting to see what Warner was going to do. But I was getting antsy; I needed *something* to happen. So I figured I might as well hear Montrel out, if for no other reason than sheer curiosity to see what he'd come with this time.

"Thank you for finally letting me come over," he said once he was in the house. "I think its past time we talked about all of this."

"You're probably right." I slid my hands around my hips into my back pockets, jerking my head towards the couch. "Have a seat."

Montrel moved towards the couch, a thoughtful expression on his face. Thoughtful and determined. I figured his campaign to get me back was about to come on full force. I sat in my armchair near the couch, thinking it smart to keep some distance for now.

He paused, apparently noticing the couch wasn't the same secondhand one I'd had since we met. He ran a hand over the wine-colored chenille fabric. "This is nice. Finally decided to upgrade, huh?"

I immediately blinked back tears, knowing Warner had bought me that couch. Both it *and* him had been upgrades from what I had before but I was only left with the couch, looks like.

"Uh-huh," I replied simply.

Montrel turned his eyes to me. "Claire, first off, I want to apologize."

"Yeah?"

"Yeah. For any pain I've caused you, during the times we were together or in between. And definitely for what happened after the anniversary party. I shouldn't have come at you like that."

He was sounding contrite and it wasn't feeling like an act. I peered at him strangely. "Are you serious?"

"I'm absolutely serious. Sometimes when we want something badly we justify any means we use to get it. And that's what I did with you; I considered you mine regardless of what you said or what situation you were in. But that was wrong of me; you were with someone else and I should have respected that."

This was throwing me for a major loop. Usually Montrel's apologies were emptier than voluntary detention, and came with some kind of caveat or spin to absolve himself of total blame, but not this time. He was actually taking full responsibility.

"I appreciate you saying that," I finally replied, once I got over my shock. "It means a lot, Montrel."

"I hope you believe me when I say that I sincerely do love you, Claire." He leaned forward, resting his forearms on his knees. "And if I had my way, we'd be together forever. Some things have happened recently that make me sure I'm ready for forever now, and not just the idea of it; that's why I always pulled away when we got close. I enjoyed the concept of a relationship but not the reality of it. But I'm past that."

"Really?" I couldn't resist a small smile. He was sounding more mature and balanced than I'd ever heard him. It was a nice change of pace and it made me look at him in a new light. "So, what, you wouldn't run this time?"

"I absolutely wouldn't. I'm sure of what I want now."

"And what about your mother?"

"She has no say in this. I've given her too much say in the past, and I know that, which is another thing I apologize for. But I have to do what I think is best for me, and what's going to make *me* happy. Hopefully she can learn to live with that."

I had to wonder if Mrs. Burns had told Montrel about our little showdown at Trader Joe's. I figured she probably would have forbidden him from seeing me again after that. But apparently Montrel was finally thinking about himself for once, and not what would appease her.

"That's good to know," I replied, my smile widening. Maybe this wouldn't be as bad of a compromise as I thought. "You don't know how long I've been waiting to hear you realize how necessary that is."

"It's past time I put my foot down with her. I love my mother but I've let her know that my love life is no longer up for discussion with her. And whatever decisions I make are mine and mine alone."

Finally! This was something I'd been trying to get Montrel to realize for pretty much the entire time I'd known him. Maybe he really *was* serious this time.

"I have to say, Montrel," I hedged, stepping over to the couch and sitting near him but still keeping a little distance. "This is shocking me but I'm loving it."

"Good." He grabbed my hands, stroking my fingers with his thumbs. I eyed the movement before lifting my eyes back to his. "I owed you this much, Claire. I finally realized how unfair I've been to you all this time. I don't want to do that anymore."

I took a deep breath, looking into his eyes. "I don't, either."

"Do you think you can forgive me for all of my bullshit? I know I don't deserve it but-"

"Yeah, I think I can," I interjected, gripping his hands a little tighter. "Hearing how sincere you sound right now makes me believe you're really ready to make a change this time. And that's all I've wanted from you, Montrel; to consider my feelings and the effect your actions had on me."

"I get that." He reached out and palmed the side of my face. "I don't deserve you, Claire. Thank you for being willing to give me another chance, to be in your life. I'm not trying to cause you any more trouble; I know you're with Warner and all-"

"Warner actually isn't speaking to me," I corrected, forcing my voice to stay strong. It still caused a pang in my chest when I thought about it. "I told him what happened and that was pretty much it."

"Damn. If I'm honest, only part of me is sorry to hear that." His hand slid down to my shoulder. "Would it be inappropriate to ask for a kiss right now? I'll understand if you don't want to..."

"That would be okay. I guess." I didn't want to sound eager. But part of me felt this was necessary to see if I felt anything for him still.

I tucked my necklace with Warner's golden heart underneath my shirt.

He smiled and leaned in, and I met him halfway. He kissed me gently, taking his time as if he was savoring the moment. I leaned into him a little more, and he lightly gripped my forearm. Just when I was starting to feel a little tingly and open my lips to him a bit more, he pulled back.

He didn't want to move too fast. I appreciated that.

"Thank you, for indulging me with that," he said, rubbing my arm. "I don't think I'll ever really get you out of my system, Claire."

I bit my lip, eying him and taking a deep breath. "I've been thinking the same thing, actually." I took his hand and stood. "Umm, we can go to my room and...get more comfortable. If you want."

He looked up at me, hesitating. I felt his hand squeeze mine. "I would love to, but...I shouldn't. Claire, baby...please sit down for a second."

I frowned curiously as I retook my seat. "What's wrong?"

He kissed my hand and peered at me thoughtfully for a moment before speaking. "I'll *never* love another woman like I love you, Claire. Never. And...I'm glad you're willing to forgive me so we can put the past behind us and get on the road to rebuilding our relationship as friends."

"Friends?"

"Yeah. I hope we always remain close." He retracted his hands, intertwining his fingers and resting them in his lap. "Even after I'm married."

It took a second for me to register what he said. Then it finally hit me. "Y-you're getting married?"

"I am. To Aurora. She and I had a long talk and realized that we were better suited for each other. And once we realized we both wanted the same things, we figured there wasn't any need in wasting time. I proposed and she accepted. The wedding is in a few months."

I sat there frozen in place. Did he...did he really just sit here and announce his *engagement* to me??

"I get that this probably comes as a surprise," Montrel observed, seeing my reaction. "I just wanted you to find out from me, in person. After everything we've been through, I felt it was the right thing to do."

"I..." My throat actually felt hoarse. I looked around the room as if I expected some hidden cameras to come popping out of nowhere. This had to be a joke. Montrel had to be pranking me. "Are you for real with all this? Or are you messing with me?"

"I'm absolutely not messing with you, Claire. I wouldn't do that again. This is all sincere and from the heart. I wish I had come to these realizations when we were together, but we never know what curveballs life is gonna throw at us. But I can at least say our relationship taught me a lot that

I'll definitely be using in my marriage to Aurora. And that's invaluable."

With that, he stood. Straightening his blazer, he gave me a pleasant gaze, seemingly oblivious to the rage that was bubbling to the surface by the second. He leaned down and took my face in his hands, kissing my forehead.

"I'll send you an invitation to the wedding," he had the balls to tell me. "But I totally understand if you don't feel comfortable attending. I really do hope you're able to work things out with Warner; if you do, you're both more than welcome to come."

Then he strode to the door and walked out.

What the *fuck*??

Once again, Montrel had made me look like a dumb ass. Here I was actually contemplating getting back with him – was gonna *sleep* with him - for no other reason than he was a passable second-choice, thinking he was saying all that stuff about loving me and wanting my forgiveness because he wanted me back, and he was engaged to someone else. He only came here to clear his conscience so he could start fresh with another woman. After everything, this was how it ended with Montrel.

I looked down at my hands, which were actually shaking. This had to be a dream or something. It *had* to be. *Any* minute now, I was going to wake up from this. With any luck, I'd wake up still in a happy relationship with Warner with no Montrel backslide.

But after sitting there for another fifteen minutes, I realized this was the reality. Montrel had found a way to make a fool out of me yet again. Even when he was making things right, he was dogging me.

I sat there in my humiliation for I don't know how long until my phone rang. When I saw Warner's name, I snatched the phone up.

"Warner?" I answered, hoping my voice didn't sound as shaky as it felt.

"Hey," he greeted, his voice low. "Is this a bad time?"

"No, your timing is perfect, actually."

"I want us to talk but I hope you can understand why I'd rather not come there to do it. Could you meet me somewhere?"

I pursed my lips. Of course he wouldn't want to be in the space where I cheated on him. Though I had to wonder what that meant for us down the line, because if we managed to work things out, he'd have to come here eventually, I'd imagine. But we could cross that bridge when we got to it.

"Sure, no problem." I cleared my throat, trying to push Montrel's visit out of my mind. Him and that Aurora could have each other. "Where and when?"

We agreed to meet at the park in a half hour. It was the same park that he had gone with me to when we played with Chichi's boys, and I chose to look at that as a good sign. At least he wasn't so angry that he didn't want to go anywhere we'd been together.

I hurriedly fixed myself up, splashing some cold water on my face, changing into something cuter, and quickly running a flat iron through my hair. I was nervous as I headed to the park, hoping that Warner being willing to meet meant that he was willing to reconcile. I thought he was done with me and it was encouraging that he wanted to work things out.

He was waiting at one of the picnic tables when I got there. There were two Starbucks cups next to him. Another good sign, in my head.

He turned and stood when he heard me approaching. I couldn't quite read the look on his face.

"Hey," I greeted.

"Hey. Thanks for coming."

"Of course." I wanted to hug him but wasn't sure he would accept it, so I just rubbed my hands together. "I'm really glad you called."

"I figured it was about time." He seemed to suddenly remember the Starbucks and handed one to me. "I got you a latte."

"Thank you." I smiled as I accepted it, wasting no time taking a nervous sip. "I needed this."

He motioned towards the table, and I sat on the bench. He took a moment to gather himself before sitting down, facing me.

"Claire, I've been going over and over what you told me that day in my head," he began, his brow furrowed slightly. "Hearing that Montrel was at your parents' party and you didn't tell me, and that he kissed you while I was there...you have no idea how angry that made me."

I looked down in my lap.

"Then to hear that he went to your house and you *gave into him*," he continued, using my words. "It makes me think of all those times I asked you if you were over Montrel and all the times you insisted you were. You would actually get frustrated with me for asking so much, but something in my gut told me I had reason to worry. And, apparently, I was right."

My spirits and hope were slipping a little bit. I looked up at him, seeing the hurt expression on his face. It made me feel awful. "Warner, I know there's no excuse, and I won't insult you by trying to make any. I was wrong. I honestly *did* believe that Montrel and I were over; I was all in with you."

"If that were true, Claire, you would have told me that Montrel was at that party as soon as you saw him. None of what he did would have happened because you wouldn't have allowed it, even if it meant you making a scene at your parents'. He clearly felt encouraged enough from that kiss to come and try to get more from you, and you gave it to him. That's not being *all in* with me."

I'd told myself I wasn't going to cry but that was already out the window. "I get it; I should have handled all of that differently. I'm totally in the wrong, and I know that. But I don't want to lose you, Warner. I'm still so in love with you and I want nothing more than for us to try to move forward together."

Never mind that I had been willing to give Montrel yet another chance barely an hour before. That wasn't really what I wanted; Montrel would have been nothing but a fallback. Warner had never stopped being my first choice.

"I want that, too," Warner admitted, a hand clamped on the back of his neck. "I've been going back and forth with myself over the past few days about whether I thought I could put this behind me. Sure, people make mistakes...but this cut me deep, Claire. And I'd probably always be wondering in the back of my mind what you're doing when you're not in my sight. I can't live like that."

My heart sank. Was this really happening?

"Warner," I pleaded, putting down the cup and grabbing his hand. "You have my *word* that I would never do anything like this to you again. Being without you these past couple of weeks has been lesson enough that I don't want to lose you from my life."

"Claire...you dropped that bomb on me and then ran without even giving me a chance to respond. I'm just...it's going to take me a while to get over this. As much as I love you and miss you – and I do, more than I want to admit – it just makes me wonder how you'll handle difficult things that come up down the line. I need someone who's gonna stand with me when things get tough, and be woman enough to stick around and take whatever the consequences are when they mess up. You just threw the grenade and left me to deal with the damage by myself."

"But I acknowledge that I handled that wrong, baby...I wouldn't do that again, either. Warner, I'm willing to do whatever I need to do. I want to prove to you that I've learned my lesson."

"Even if you have, though, I know myself; this is going to stick in my mind. And you *know* what I went through when my ex did what she did and how that jacked me up..."

"I know," I acknowledged, my shoulders slumping even more.

"I just don't see myself getting past the cheating," he declared, sitting up straighter. "Even if I could forgive you, it's the betrayal and the disrespect that I can't get with. I wish like hell I could; that I was a brother who could just say that all I needed was some time and then we could see what happened. But I can't do that."

His hand eased from my grasp and tears fell onto my jeans. I could almost hear my heart breaking.

"So that's it?" I asked softly, not able to look at him. "That's just *it* for you and me?"

"Yeah." His voice was gruff. I could tell he wasn't looking at me, either. "I was hoping that maybe seeing you might make me want to try to work it out. But it only makes me picture you letting him kiss you and do all the things I wanted to do to you myself. And it causes a whole new wave of pain and anger. I just...I can't do it."

We just sat there for a few moments in silence, with me crying like the fool I was. I felt stupid for giving in to Montrel and cheating on Warner, stupid for how I handled telling Warner about it, stupid for even considering going back to Montrel yet again, and stupid for thinking that Warner buying me a latte meant he was taking me back. He was just a nice guy, but that didn't mean he was going to forgive me. And even if he did, he apparently couldn't let himself be with me anymore. I'd permanently be affixed with that scarlet letter in his eyes.

Finally, Warner stood. I looked up into his eyes, silently pleading for another chance that I knew I wasn't going to get. He moved like he was going to lean down and hug me, then stopped himself. He just removed my house key from his key ring and placed it on the table next to my cup. Then he wiped a hand down his face and abruptly turned to walked away, leaving me sitting there alone.

Twenty-Three – Claire

• • • •

THERE WAS SOMETHING to be said for life lessons. And this one was kicking my ass.

I kept hoping that I would get a call or text from Warner saying that he had reconsidered and was willing to work things out. But a week had passed since he left me sitting in the park with a broken heart and two cold lattes and I hadn't heard a word from him. And with each day that passed, it just cemented the reality that I had officially blown it and lost Warner for good.

Chichi and Giselle tried to encourage me. They insisted on coming over, not wanting me to spend another evening crying my eyes out and listening to begging love songs. I appreciated their concern but they were wasting their time; there really wasn't anything they could say to cheer me up.

"Girl, I hate to see you like this," Chichi said, standing over me as I was sprawled out on the couch. "I really wish there was something I could say to make you feel better."

"I wish there was, too," I muttered, my face buried in the pillow.

"Claire," Giselle cooed, kneeling next to me and stroking my hair. "Maybe Warner just needs some time. You never know, after a while, he might have a change of heart and be willing to try again. Or at least be friends at some point. This doesn't necessarily have to be the end for you two."

"I wish I could believe that. But I'm not gonna get my hopes up. To him, I'll probably always be the cheater who got with her ex after repeatedly telling him I wouldn't. And given what he had already been through, I don't see him getting past that."

"Have you heard any more from Montrel?" Chichi asked me.

"No," I grunted, pushing myself up and adjusting my blanket around my waist. I mindlessly played with my raggedy nails. "I haven't heard from him since he told me he was getting married. He's too busy planning his wedding, I'm sure."

"I still can't believe that. After everything he did, he came and rubbed it in your face that he was getting married to somebody he's only known a couple of months, at most. This is the kind of shit that can make you hate men."

"Yeah." I couldn't bring myself to tell them how I had been considering taking Montrel back and that's what I thought he was leading up to when he sprung the whole marriage announcement on me. He'd had me completely fooled and it was just way too embarrassing to admit. "Turns out you were right on the money, Chichi...you said that it would take me getting majorly hurt or humiliated to see the light. And that Montrel would probably end up with somebody else after everything he put me through. You were three for three."

"Girl, believe me, I don't take any pleasure in that. I'd give anything to have been wrong."

"You tried to warn me. Many times. I just wouldn't listen."

"I swear, if Montrel weren't so close with Forrest, I wouldn't have anything else to do with him," Giselle insisted. "I just can't believe he'd do you like this, after everything."

I ran a hand through my messy hair. "I can't blame it all on Montrel. It was my dumb ass that made the mistake and handled everything poorly. I guess I can understand why Warner can't deal with it."

Chichi and Giselle sat on either side of me and enveloped me in a group hug. It just made me start crying again, because I didn't feel I deserved their sympathy, as much as I appreciated it. I didn't know how long it was going to take me to get to where I could think about Warner and how I'd blown it with him without breaking down.

"We're gonna help you get through this," Giselle assured me, rubbing my back. "We're right here with you."

"Absolutely," Chichi confirmed.

"Thanks, y'all." I took the napkin Chichi jammed into my hand and wiped my eyes. "It's just hard to believe that I'm alone again."

"I know this might not be what you wanna hear right now but maybe that's not the worst thing," Chichi offered. "You were on that merry-go-round with Montrel for so long, then you jumped right into things with Warner, then back to Montrel, then *back* to Warner, that maybe you need some time by yourself to decompress and reevaluate some things. Use this time to get you some clarity and heal from everything. Do something to take your mind off things instead of just laying around here."

"Like what?"

"Don't you have hobbies?"

"Besides watching movies, not really. Never really realized that before. Great, now I'm even more embarrassed."

"You could help babysit in a few months," Giselle suggested with a small smile.

"Please, I don't have the energy to run behind Chichi's triplets right now," I dismissed with a wave of my hand. "I love them but I just don't have it in me."

"What about a newborn, then?"

Both my and Chichi's heads snapped to her. "You mean..."

"Yep. Me and Forrest finally did it. We're pregnant!"

Chichi screamed and lunged across me to hug Giselle. I was happy for her, but didn't have the energy to show it. If anything, it reminded me that Giselle was still friends with Montrel and she and Forrest would probably start hanging with him and his new wife at some point. And then Montrel and Aurora would start having babies, and I'd be the odd one out, single and childless. The thought made me want to cry all over again.

"Gerard and I decided to renew our vows," Chichi announced excitedly. "Our first wedding was kind of a throw-together, so we want to do something a little nicer this time. I was so surprised when he suggested it."

"That's wonderful, Chichi! I'm so happy for you!" Giselle gushed, squeezing Chichi's hands. I looked down and saw their gleaming wedding rings, and my eyes squeezed shut. I really felt like I was being tortured.

I couldn't muster up any more words or force any more smiles. I excused myself, hurrying to the bathroom while Chichi and Giselle continued to chatter about the new milestones in their lives. As soon as I closed the bathroom door behind me, I leaned over the sink, my face in both hands.

This was my life right now. I had let Montrel waste my time, just like Chichi said he would. And regardless of what lessons I'd learned from it, I couldn't get that time back. I'd foolishly gone back to him over and over, ruined an ideal relationship with a wonderful man, only for Montrel to go off and marry someone else.

And I had no one to blame but myself.

THE END

Whew! That was something else, wasn't it? I hope you enjoyed reading Claire's roller coaster with Montrel and Warner. She got on *my* nerves. LOL

Will there be a sequel to this? There just might.

Reviews mean so much to us indie authors, and are always appreciated. And if you want to show *extra* love, share that you read *Mr. Time Waster* on social media! ☺

You can find me on Instagram and TikTok at @authorjessicaterry and on Twitter at @itsJessicaTerry. And don't forget to subscribe to my email list at jessicaterry.com.

Also by Jessica Terry

Some Like 'em Thick

It's All Right...Now

Not By a Long Shot

Get Right

Decisions and Consequences

Take One For the Team

When You Share Too Much

Backtalk

Emasculated

Restless

The Beginning of Again

Always and Nevers

She is Me

Split By the Bell

The Karma Call

Forehead Kiss

All Because of Ava

Love Intolerant

<u>The Introvert Series</u>

An Introvert's Christmas

Wooing the Introvert

The Introvert Roast

I, Take Thee Introvert

The Introvert Series Compilation (paperback only)

Discussion Questions

1. Who was more infuriating, Claire or Montrel?
2. Do you think Claire jumped the gun by starting something with Warner when she was still hung up on Montrel?
3. What did you think of Annie, Montrel's mother? Did you feel she was manipulating her son?
4. Do you believe that Montrel sincerely loved Claire as he claimed?
5. Chichi warned Claire what could happen if she kept messing with Montrel, and she turned out to be right. But did you ever think Chichi was being too hard on Claire?
6. Did Aurora play dirty by using the methods she did to hook Montrel?
7. Forrest and Giselle were somewhat goals for Montrel, despite their issues throughout the book. Chichi and Gerard were goals for Claire. Do you think this is why the both of them tended to act-first-think-second when it came to their relationship decisions?
8. Do you think Warner's paranoia played *any* part in Claire's indiscretion?
9. Was Claire weak? Desperate? Both?
10. Claire made a lot of bad (or just stupid) decisions. Do you feel sorry for her for how things ended up, or do you think she got what she deserved?

Did you love *Mr. Time Waster*? Then you should read *Love Intolerant*[1] by Jessica Terry!

[2]

Adele Mozley was used to the friend zone. Men liked hanging with her but when it came time to get romantic, she usually got the polite stiff-arm.

But so what, right? She had a job she liked, a loyal BFF, an amazing son and slightly-curmudgeonly father, and Friday nights with Jamaican takeout and her remote. That's not so bad.

Enter Kingston Ferrell, who is persistent, younger...and so hot it's almost intimidating. And he has eyes only for

1. https://books2read.com/u/bPNk9j

2. https://books2read.com/u/bPNk9j